JESSICA STRANGE

BLACKWING SAGA BOOK 2

STEPHEN DRAKE

Dedicated to Linda and Susan, this work would not have been possible without their help and support.

A heart-felt thank you to my beta-readers:
Katie Kuhn and Corinne Dutton

A special thank you to Paula Shene, K.J. Simmill, and J.C. Stone, authors in their own right, for their friendship, suggestions, help, and taking the time from their busy lives to read my work. Words fail to convey my deep appreciation for them.

"The universe is full of magical things, patiently waiting for our wits to grow sharper."

— EDEN PHILLPOTTS.

CONTENTS

1. The Meeting   1
2. Reunited   12
3. The Best of Times   24
4. An Unexpected Visit   35
5. Unexpected Gunfire   46
6. California, Here I Come!   58
7. Building Tensions   69
8. The Search Begins   80
9. Escape and Evade   91
10. No News is Good News   102
11. Resuming the Search   113
12. The Calm   124
13. The Storm Begins   135
14. The Eye of the Storm   147
15. The Passing of the Storm   159
16. Turning the Page   170
17. Clearing the Air…Somewhat   182
18. Return to Q'estiria   193
19. Trials on Q'estiria   205
20. Cha-Cha-Changes   217
21. Back into a Fold   229
22. No more Q'estirians   240
23. The Last Dance on the Eighth Plane   251

Glossary   263
About the Author   265
Other books by this author   266

1

THE MEETING

J essica Strange, recently a Special Diplomatic liaison, and an ex-Detective in the Tacoma, Pacific Coast-Washington Police Department, was sitting alone in a bar outside the cordoned downtown area.

"It's been a month since the Event..." a television reporter for a national news station was saying, *"and the CDC is no closer to the cause than it was that horrendous day in which millions died in the Pacific Coast States."*

"Why doesn't that surprise me?" Jessica grumbled, but no one in the noisy bar heard her. She finished the shot of Jack Daniels she'd previously poured. The back of her hand rubbed across her mouth to keep herself together. She grabbed the half-empty bottle and poured herself another.

"To add a historical perspective, in the mid-2020s, the western parts of Washington and Oregon were trending to be bastions of extreme liberalism, while the eastern parts of those states were trending towards being more conservative. The conservative sides, feeling that they no longer had a voice, divided the two states, from north to south, down the Cascade Mountain Range's crests. The areas west of the line became commonly known as Pacific Coast-Washington, or PC-Washington, and Pacific Coast-Oregon, or PC-Oregon.

1

"Californians, also being extremely liberal west of the mountains, divided their state evenly from Mount Shasta in the north to just east of Sacramento and down to the mid-point between Chula Vista, California, and Yuma, Arizona, with the same 'PC' designations, a few years later.

"These three states tended to be more politically correct, since the 1990s. Those living on the eastern part of the states, now called the western side, 'PC' for politically correct."

Jessica was only half-listening as she sipped her JD. *A month and no one can tell me anything,* she thought. *I can't get into the PD because they haven't cleared it of all the bodies, damned Feds.* She could feel the tears welling as she thought of Irving Strange, her late husband, and Captain Trooper, her boss, friend, and father figure. She gulped another shot to try to wash the thoughts of them out of her mind.

"You better go easy on that stuff," a male voice said.

When Jessica looked up, she saw a tall, well-dressed, insufferable federal agent wearing sunglasses inside the darkened bar. She knew him only as John Smith.

"Mind if I sit?" Smith asked as he slid the chair out from the table before sitting.

"If you must," Jessica replied with as much surliness as she could muster. "What do *you* want? You called this meeting." She leaned back, draping her right arm over the back of the chair next to the one on which she was sitting.

Smith sat and pulled something from a pocket. "I thought you might want this," he said as he slid a cell phone across the table.

It appeared to be Irving's phone; she recognized the graphics on the case. She tried to turn it on, but it wouldn't.

"The battery's dead. How am I supposed to turn it on if the battery's dead? How am I supposed to confirm it was Irv's?"

"You can take my word for it—"

"If you said the sky was blue, I'd have to go out and check," she interrupted, overly loud. "With me, you lack the required

2

crumb of integrity necessary for believing the simplest of facts coming out of your mouth!"

"Is this guy *bothering* you, Jess?" a booming voice said. A meaty hand slapped Smith's shoulder. Smith looked up at the speaker and shrunk a little from the huge man.

"No, Billy, I can *handle* this Federal gnat, should the need arise, but thanks anyway."

The one called Billy nodded and removed his huge hand from Smith's shoulder. Smith watched the big man return to his place behind the bar as he straightened his clothing.

"*Handle* me? *You're* going to *handle* me. And if I choose not to be *handled* by you, then what?" Smith ranted as he turned to face her, trying to keep his voice low. He felt something hard tap the inside of his knee and then heard the distinctive sound of a cocking revolver. He'd failed to notice her change in position.

"My *little friend*, which used to be yours, will...explain it to you," Jessica grinned mirthlessly.

"You won't shoot," Smith said dismissively, "You're a cop, and you took your oath seriously."

"I don't think you've been keeping up with current events," Jessica said. "There's no police in Tacoma anymore. I wasn't a cop the last time you saw me, remember? Add to all that, I don't like, nor trust, you, so tell me again how I won't...alter your equipment?"

Smith blanched. "I have information for you, so I hope you leave my testicles, and everything else, intact." He swallowed hard.

"Give me your *information*. If I like it, I might spare you the conversion."

Smith studied her face quickly and saw her resolve in the scowl she wore.

"We are trying to select an interim mayor," Smith said after exhaling loudly, "until an election. We're going to need an interim police chief," he said finally, raising his eyebrows at the end.

"Not interested," Jessica said stoically.

"Okay, you know that Tacoma was the only city not totally wiped out, and we still don't know how someone could've accomplished it."

"That's not news."

"Well, whatever happened, it only took out ninety-five percent of the population. Those that survived, locally, are gathering outside the cordon. We're in dire need of police to keep the peace."

"I'm going to be busy hunting the ones that did this," she growled.

"But we need you!"

"So? As I said, I'm busy! Now, get outta here, while I'm still feeling generous!"

Smith got up slowly and glanced under the table to see the barrel of his *Desert Eagle*. "That might be a bit more firepower than you're used to."

"I hopped over the pass and bought a few cases of ammo for it and have been practicing for the last month, so I'm quite used to it. Care to find out?"

Smith looked dubious but decided not to test his theory and left. Jessica poured herself another drink.

Irving awoke in what appeared, to him anyway, to be a dimly lit concrete storage room. On the floor next to him was Captain Trooper. As he looked around, he noticed huge barrels with markings that he recognized as runes. They all said the same thing, "Ale". His brain saw the runes and translated them without thinking about them. He'd recognized them from the documents he'd translated for Blackwing. He saw boxes with more of the runes. "Dried Meat", he read.

"Hey, Cap'n!" he said, trying to rouse the older man.

He shook him gently, and the captain's head lolled to one

4

side. Irving could see the captain's hair and skin had aged dramatically. Half of his head looked as expected, but the other half had aged forty years, or that's how it looked to Irving.

What the hell happened? We were in the cap'n's office, and the PD had an alarm sound, one I've never heard before, and then the T'et Faqin Q'estirian threw something big at us. As I remember, it was big and black —looked like a black hole— and then there was something electric in the air. And now, we're here, wherever here is.

He looked around for a door and failed to find one. He opened a barrel of ale. As he smelled it, he could detect the alcohol. He tasted it and found it similar to the brew that Blackwing served. He cupped his hand and drank, dipping it to his mouth, slurping it loudly.

Not the most sanitary, he thought, *but without a cup, what can you do?*

He opened the top of one of the wooden boxes, and it also seemed to be the same as the bits Blackwing had given him.

I know this is safe. I've had some of Blackwing's, and it didn't kill me.

He went back to try to rouse Captain Trooper. As he did, he heard a noise, like a door being opened. When he turned to look, he saw a diminutive person standing in a doorway staring at him in terror. It ran off, screaming something unintelligible.

"Wait! Don't leave us here!" Irving yelled as the door closed and latched. "Great! Maybe the little guy will bring help."

Irving heard Trooper moan. "Cap'n, you okay?" he asked.

Captain Trooper didn't answer. He just moaned and passed out again.

It wasn't long before Irving heard the door open again. As he stood, he reached into his pocket and pulled out his wizard-step coin. Another *T'et Faqin Q'estirian* entered the chamber. Though this one looked similar to Blackwing, he was younger, more polished, and carried a curving staff in the shape of a snake. In the snake's mouth was a crystal that looked, to Irving, to be onyx.

5

"Hey there, friend! Can you get some help for my cap'n? He's not coming around, and I'm getting concerned."

Irving heard the man say something, but he couldn't understand him. *It must be a different dialect,* he thought. The *Q'estirian* was looking at him warily, and the crystal in his staff seemed to be glowing.

Svengol Broadaxe was nothing special, as dwarves go. Good dwarves raised him to be a good dwarf. As such, he was a firm believer that conjurers battle conjurers. Those with no magic skills had no business fighting "magic-throwers", as he called them.

He'd been working in the vaults for many years. The *Q'estirians* were good to him and his family, and they had meaningful work to do and a pleasant, safe environment to work. His job was to empty the storage vaults of the deceased *Q'estirians*, redistribute consumable items found in them, and pack up anything else to be claimed by any clan members that cared to.

When he reached the door of the next vault to empty, he marveled at the enormous hinges that were spring-loaded to help with opening the heavy door. Some captured beasts had raised havoc with the doors, many years ago, before they were hidden, through magic once the door was closed.

When he unlatched it, the door pulled back into the hallway a bit. The springs allowed him to open or close the entrance to the vault easily. As he swung the door open, he saw the unexpected creatures inside the vault. When he recovered from the initial shock, he quickly shut and locked the door before raising the alarm

"Demons! Demons in the vaults," Broadaxe yelled as he ran down the hallway. "Demons! Bloodthirsty demons are in the vaults!"

The dwarf rounded a corner and skidded to a halt at the

young Samir Thunderclap's feet, the resident *T'et Faqin Q'estirian*, placed here for just this sort of thing.

"What is that you are screaming, Broadaxe?" Thunderclap asked as he scowled at the dwarf.

"Demons, your Lordship! Demons come to invade, come to kill us and feed on our bones!"

"Demons! Phah!" Thunderclap scoffed. "Take me to these... demons! I wish to see for myself! And, so help me, if you are telling tales, I will turn you into a toad!"

Broadaxe turned and started a hop-shuffle style of walking sideways to keep up with the much longer-legged *Q'estirian*. "They are right this way, your Lordship, trapped inside one of the storage vaults of one of your brothers!"

Thunderclap glared at the dwarf, "They better be!"

At the door, Broadaxe made to open it. "You open it and stand aside," Thunderclap ordered. "Whatever you do, stay behind me!"

As the door swung open, Thunderclap was staring at...something. He didn't know what it was.

"Hey, there! What are you doing here?" he asked.

He saw one of them staring at him, and the other was lying on the floor, unmoving. The one staring at him just looked confused and started waving his arms around and babbling something. Thunderclap knew it was probably a language of some sort, but he had never heard anything like it before.

"Are you going to answer me?" Thunderclap boomed. "I demand you tell me who you are and what you are doing here!"

He was answered by more gibberish and accompanied arm-waving. When he entered, he was prepared. His battle-staff was ready, and he was well versed in combat. *If they throw any vile energies, my staff will absorb it and let me turn it back on them,* he thought.

He saw the standing creature gesturing toward the one lying on the floor with both hands and spouting more gibberish.

Thunderclap floated a gold coin from an inside pocket of his duster. Plucking it from the air, he whispered the incantation and tossed it to the standing one. Before the coin could reach its target, the creature disappeared and reappeared behind him. The coin clattered to the floor not far from the unmoving one.

The one lying on the floor rolled, and the back of its hand touched the coin. The coin immediately turned into a band and secured itself around the reclining one's wrist.

Irving, trying to get help for Trooper and seemingly getting nowhere, saw the coin tossed in his direction. With the glint of gold, he thought it was one to secure him, like the ones he'd seen Blackwing use, so he wizard-stepped out of the way before the coin could touch him.

"Hey! He's not hurting anyone!" Irving yelled as Trooper rolled and touched the coin. "We need help here! We aren't dangerous to you!" *If I use my sword, he'll cut me to ribbons*, he thought. *I've never been able to best Blackwing with a sword, or any of the other Q'estirians with whom I trained. Do I surrender? Is that the only way I can get help for Trooper?* Thinking better of the situation, Irving put the wizard-step coin back in his pocket. He had no more than pulled out his hand than he felt something powerful grab his legs just above the knees. Irving hit the floor.

"I have him, your Lordship!" Broadaxe yelled as he felled the much taller creature. He had hit him from behind to aid in the capture.

Thunderclap walked over and placed a gold coin on Irving's hand. Both of Irving's hands became bound by golden manacles.

"That should hold you until we figure out what you are and what you are about," Thunderclap said. He noticed the tone of his voice seemed to calm the creature, and this puzzled him.

8

Once the creatures were secured, Thunderclap looked over the one lying on the floor. He didn't seem to be injured, just unconscious. The other one was standing and looking at his companion with a concerned expression.

Thunderclap murmured the incantation to levitate the unconscious creature, and the other creature walked out of the vault, being led by Thunderclap, leaving Broadaxe to complete his chores.

"Jessica," a familiar *basso profundo* voice said from behind. She didn't need to look to see who it was.

"Blackwing," she whispered. "What are *you* doing here?"

"I've come to see you home and get you to buy some of that Sichuan I'm fond of."

"Did you come here to pull your drunken friend out of the bar?"

"Are you?"

"Am I what?"

"Drunk."

"Not nearly enough to suit me."

"It's difficult...dealing with loss."

She turned to face him. "What would you know about loss?" she asked with as much surliness as she could muster. "I lost my husband! I lost someone as close as a father, all in a single instant. Having a husband was something new for me, you know, and I wasn't ready to give him up."

"You lost a husband, and I lost two friends," Blackwing whispered. "In my life, I've lost friends and family, a lot of friends and family. I'm no stranger to loss, even though I don't understand *your* particular loss.

"We are alive. And I find that I need my friend," Blackwing smiled at her, a compassionate, sad smile. "Maybe we can find some consolation in each other's company."

"Suzanne isn't here?"

Blackwing shook his head, "No, she has other responsibilities to see to at the moment."

Suzanne Hawks, well, the person who was born Suzanne Hawks, presented herself to *S'hyrlus* on the Hamadryad Plane.

"The Lady *S'hyrlus* has called, and I present myself," Suzanne said as she knelt and bowed her head.

"Arise, Suzanne," *S'hyrlus* commanded.

Suzanne did as she was commanded and stood, clasping her hands in front of her.

"Has Blackwing found Phelonius?"

"Not that I am aware of," Suzanne answered. "I know he is actively searching, though."

S'hyrlus nodded. "He will. He has never failed before, and I doubt he will start now. We are aware of the tragedy Phelonius has caused, and we felt it here. Consequently, any assistance we can give, Socrates is welcomed to it."

She rose and started to pace. Suzanne followed.

"Is he prepared to do what is necessary?" *S'hyrlus* asked after some time.

Suzanne shrugged, "No one knows what will be asked of him or how he will respond. He will do as he thinks is fitting, as always."

"That is not what I was asking. I know the high council will order him to terminate Phelonius personally, and I need to know how that will affect him. Will he do as ordered?"

"You know him better than I," Suzanne said. "I know he will do as he determines is fitting, without regard for any orders one way or the other. It is something you would have to ask him directly. How do you know what the council will order?"

"Usually, we are against termination, but not in this case.

10

Officially, the Hamadryades are on the side of the council, in this matter."

Suzanne looked to *S'hyrlus* with a questioning look.

"We have consulted with the council, and we agree that Phelonius has recklessly endangered all the *Planes*. My son needs to know what our stance is on this matter."

"I will let him know your stance," Suzanne said. "I do not know what he will do, but I will inform him. That is all I can do."

2

REUNITED

I rving and Captain Trooper were escorted to a holding cell.
Irving was manacled to the central table and sat on a rough-
hewn bench. Captain Trooper was placed on another bench
away from the door. Being the only one lucid, Irving was being
talked to, sternly, by the *Q'estirian* that had affected their capture.

"Look, like I said, I don't understand you," Irving explained
testily. "We aren't here to cause any trouble. The captain needs
help," he gestured towards his unconscious companion, and the
Q'estirian looked in Trooper's direction. Irving thought he was
starting to get through to him, a little, anyway.

It was then that another *Q'estirian* entered the tiny cell. *Are
these two twins? There certainly aren't many differences in appearance
of these two Q'estirians or too many differences between them and
Blackwing,* Irving thought, *except Blackwing looks old enough to be
their father.*

The *Q'estirian* that had just entered continued giving orders
to him and gesturing. All Irving could do was shake his head.
He didn't understand anything being said.

Samir Thunderclap was trying to get his questions answered when Clo'Cha Hornsdoodle entered.

"Where did these two come from?" Hornsdoodle asked.

"They were in one of the vaults," Thunderclap explained. "The one lying down has yet to regain consciousness, and this one is incapable of the simplest understanding."

"What do you mean, incapable?"

"I have tried every language I know, and I get no look of understanding. It just keeps pointing to the other one, gesturing and blabbering."

"What species are they?" Hornsdoodle asked.

"I have no idea. The pair appear to be something of a cross between several species."

"Do they have any magic capabilities? How safe are they?"

"I do not know, sir. I did not think to scan them for *the Source*."

Hornsdoodle raised his sphere and began looking at the strangers through it. "They have something with traces of *the Source*," Hornsdoodle said, "upper right arm. And there is something else close to the hip."

Thunderclap stepped forward, indicated his upper arm, and gave the creature a questioning look. The creature looked to his upper arm and touched it. It stood and opened its suit and showed the platinum band above the bicep.

Hornsdoodle and Thunderclap looked at the platinum band with amazement. Hornsdoodle brought the sphere closer to the band, which shifted colors and showed a warning.

"Blackwing?" Hornsdoodle questioned as he read the sphere.

"Which one?" Thunderclap asked. "There are a number of them."

"I do not know, but I am reluctant to contact any without more information," Hornsdoodle said.

Having had the platinum band around his arm for a while, Irving had forgotten about it. He was as shocked as the *Q'estirians* when one of them indicated his upper arm and looked at him with that questioning look. When he exposed it, he saw the sphere they were holding change colors, and then he got more questioning looks from both of them.

"Well, it seems you two are curious about this band," he said aloud. He knew they wouldn't understand him, but it made him feel better. "A friend of mine gave it to me—" It was then that, in a flash of inspiration, Irving sat at the table and started drawing a few of the runes he knew on the tabletop with his finger. He didn't know if he could get it across to them that he needed something to write on and with.

The pair talked amongst themselves for a bit, and one produced what looked to be parchment and something resembling a pencil. Irving sat and started to reproduce some of the runes he had seen from the letter of appointment that Blackwing had shown. He did translate it, somewhat, with Blackwing's help. Now, he was trying to remember some of them. As he drew a few, he was starting to remember a few more.

After some time, Hornsdoodle snatched the parchment and pencil away from him.

"What does it say?" Thunderclap asked, trying to see what the creature had drawn over his superior's shoulder.

"It is crude and lacks any finesse or refinement, but it says something about ambassadorial services," Hornsdoodle said.

"Ambassadorial services? Where would this creature possibly have contact with anyone in our ambassadorial service or our writing?" Thunderclap asked skeptically. "I think you might be reading too much into the crude drawings of this creature."

"I am not so sure," Hornsdoodle said skeptically. "It has a

band that indicates *K'obi Sha Shin J'oi Faqin*. It drew runes saying something about ambassadorial services, and it is too much for coincidence." He commanded a tankard of ale from the inside pocket of his duster. Immediately the creature reached out for the tankard and made drinking motions. Hornsdoodle slid the tankard over, and the creature grabbed it up and started drinking.

"Wait until the ale is gone," Thunderclap said. "The creature will be lost on how to get more."

As the creature finished the tankard, it tapped the handle three times, and the tankard refilled.

"That," Hornsdoodle said, "was no accident. It knew what to do."

"Let me check on someone named Blackwing in Ambassadorial Services," Thunderclap said, still shocked by what he saw.

The creature was making motions that Hornsdoodle thought were eating movements. He produced some of the dried meat and slid it across the table. The creature snatched it up right away, and the bits disappeared down its throat.

"Anything?" Hornsdoodle asked over his shoulder.

"Yes, sir."

Thunderclap looked flushed when Hornsdoodle looked at him. "Well, out with it!"

"The only Blackwing in Ambassadorial Services is *Socrates Blackwing. Chief Commander* and *Ambassador to the Eighth Plane...*"

"Is that all?"

"No, he is also great-great-grandson to Cornelius Blackwing—"

"Cornelius Blackwing? As in leader of the high council? That Cornelius Blackwing?"

Thunderclap nodded slowly.

Thaddius Crowfoot and H'Difa Thunderclap were sitting in Thaddius' office.

"We may have a problem," H'Difa said under his breath.

"What kind of problem? You know I hate problems," Thaddius said.

"My grandson, I do not know how far back, works in the vaults."

"How nice for him," Thaddius said without looking up.

"He has apprehended two…creatures in the vaults. One of them carries the *K'obi Sha Shin J'oi Faqin* of Blackwing."

Thaddius stopped and raised just his eyes. "Which Blackwing?" he asked.

"At this point, we are uncertain. Only one of the creatures has demonstrated writing of runes and drinking ale from one of our tankards. Thus showing familiarity with us."

"And the other?" Thaddius asked.

"He remains unconscious and has been since found. He also has the *K'obi Sha Shin J'oi Faqin.*"

"In what form?" Thaddius asked.

"Bands, around their upper arms."

Crowfoot closed his eyes and rubbed between his brows. "Well, that is quite the pile of *P'koosh Z'airka.* Who else knows?"

"No one, yet. I heard about it from my family communications network, and I brought it to your attention as soon as I could."

"What do you suggest?" Crowfoot asked as he continued to rub between his brows.

"I would suggest getting a healer in to see to the unconscious one," Thunderclap said quietly.

"Any other suggestions?" Crowfoot asked.

"I am uncertain how, but we need to discover who they are, where they come from…and how they got here."

"At what point do you want to inform Cornelius?" Crowfoot asked.

"I do not want to inform him unless and until we get some answers," Thunderclap stated.

"That is a dangerous gambit," Crowfoot said quietly. "It could work against us."

"I cannot see how. We did not bring them here, and our security requires that we determine how they got here."

Crowfoot was about to say something and stopped himself.

"You had an idea?" Thunderclap asked.

"I had a thought, but I need more information. Work on getting the information quietly. If anyone prevents you from proceeding, let me know and keep me informed about what you find out."

Blackwing and Jessica walked in the back door of the house that Suzanne had purchased. Currently, it was the ambassadorial residence. Blackwing sat Jessica down while he laid out the Sichuan for everyone. He did have to see to his fellow *Q'estirians*.

"You know, I need to hire a cook of some kind," Blackwing said as he worked.

"You can hire me a bartender while you're at it," Jessica sniped. "If you get a chef or a cook, they'll just try to change how you eat."

"And will a bartender change the way you drink?" Blackwing quipped.

"Pro'ly," Jessica slurred as she put her head down on the table.

"What were you doing there, anyway?"

"I had a meeting...with our ol' buddy Smith. You know, the one that tried to ventilate you at the PD?"

"What did *he* want?" Blackwing asked with surliness.

"He wants to make me chief of police...or something. I think that's what he said."

"Sounds like something you'd enjoy. How you say, 'right up your alley'?"

Jessica made a spitting sound: "Not bloody likely! I told 'em I wasn't in'erested."

"Why aren't you interested?" Blackwing asked as he came in and sat at the table.

"I got some huntin' ta do, firs'." Jessica had managed to get the heavy gun out of her holster and laid it noisily on the table.

Blackwing eyed the pistol and assessed Jessica's state of inebriation. "Well, eat up. It won't be tonight."

"I'm looking forward to it being soon," Jessica said as she dished up some of the food. "I do need another drink," she said before she began eating.

"I think your stomach will appreciate the break from the alcohol," Blackwing said. He did send out messages to let the other *Q'estirians* know they could come into the house and eat.

As they filed through, helping themselves, Suzanne entered. She made up her plate and sat next to Blackwing.

"Hiya, Suze!" Jessica slurred.

"We need to talk," Suzanne said to Blackwing, speaking Q'estirian.

"What di' she shay?" Jessica asked thickly.

"It was something...personal, Jessica. Please eat. You'll feel better for it," Blackwing said in English.

"Yes, Jessica, please eat. It's important that you keep up your strength," Suzanne said sarcastically.

The room became void of conversation. The *Q'estirians* ate and watched Blackwing and Suzanne. None of them understood English and thought all the strange-talk was...strange. Blackwing and Suzanne were watching Jessica as they all ate. Suzanne was half-expecting Jess to pass out and hit the floor, given her level of intoxication. Blackwing was just trying to get his friend to eat enough to offset the alcohol she'd absorbed already.

"I think we need to hire a cook," Blackwing said after an extended silence.

"*Grum K'sha U'ien* or human?" Suzanne asked.

"Either is acceptable to me, but I'm leaning more toward the human. I'd like someone able to cook Sichuan, more than once in a while," Blackwing said.

"Wha' the hell is a grum ka shoe in?" Jessica asked through blurry eyes. She was wavering in her balance and was about to fall over onto the floor.

"She will have quite the head in the morning," Suzanne commented. "Why did you let her drink so much?"

"I didn't *let* her. You know Jess. She does pretty much what she wants. I couldn't stop her," Blackwing said.

"Well, that's not exactly true, is it?" Suzanne asked. "*The Great Warrior* couldn't handle Jessica? There's nothing in your bag of tricks to get her to slow down on the alcohol? Somehow, I think you could if you wanted to."

"If she said that she has a problem and wants to quit, I can help. What I can't do is violate her free will."

"Take her to her room and put her in bed," Blackwing said in Q'estirian. One of the guards that had finished eating got up to comply.

The guard bowed slightly and levitated Jessica to her room, placing her gently on the bed. As he closed the door, the covers flipped over Jessica without apparent external forces causing it.

Once the guards finished, they cleaned up and left Blackwing and Suzanne alone in the living room.

"What was it you wanted to tell me?" Blackwing asked in Q'estirian.

"I am to pass the word that the Hamadryads are backing Phelonius' termination. So, it is the great council and the Hamadryads."

"I was expecting that," Blackwing mused. "He has angered enough people over the years that now they are all screaming for his head."

A guard entered, stood a respectful distance, and waited to be recognized.

"Yes?" Blackwing acknowledged.

"Pardons, sir, but a messenger is waiting to see you and the Lady."

"Send them in."

The guard bowed and backed away. The guard was replaced by the messenger.

"Yes?" Blackwing asked. "You have a message for me?"

"Yes, sir, I have a message from Cornelius Blackwing."

"I wonder what *he* wants," Suzanne whispered.

"Mister Ambassador. Greetings. It is with a glad heart I request your company and that of the Lady Suzanne, immediately in my private chambers at *Sh'tuk Q'estiria Faqin* concerning a private matter."

The messenger bowed and left.

Blackwing stood. "I'll be making a trip to *Sh'tuksa Q'estiria Faqin*," he said to the senior guard. "I'll need three guards to escort myself and the lady, well-rested and well provisioned. It will be as quick a trip as is possible."

The guard bowed.

"Also, I need the remainder of the guards to keep Jessica here and away from the alcohol and her firearm."

The guard bowed again, and Blackwing dismissed him with a wave of his hand. The guard disappeared.

"I wonder what this summons is about," Blackwing commented. "It can't be good news, being summoned this way. Usually, it is 'at your earliest convenience'."

"He did start it 'with a glad heart'," Suzanne said, "so, how bad could it be?"

The trip to *Sh'tuksa Q'estiria Faqin*, the court of the Q'estirian Ruling council, took three days of hard traveling. Once Blackwing and Suzanne presented themselves at Cornelius Blackwing's office, his adjutant told them to wait, and he entered Cornelius' office. A long time passed before he returned.

Finally, the adjutant escorted them into Cornelius' office.

"Socrates!" Cornelius greeted jovially. "And the lovely, as always, Lady Suzanne." Cornelius gave a stiff bow to Suzanne.

"Cornelius," Suzanne said coyly.

"What did you want to see us about that would warrant us presenting ourselves immediately?" Socrates asked flatly.

"Ever the pragmatist, eh, Socrates?" Cornelius cleared his throat. "Alright then, I have something I think belongs to you." Cornelius turned towards his private entrance and clapped his hands together loudly.

As the door opened, two individuals, manacled and unwashed, were led into the plush office.

Socrates looked blankly at the pair and said nothing until the guards were dismissed. After the guards left, he attempted to make a more systematic assessment of the pair.

One of the pair seemed...lopsided. In Socrates' opinion, he was older on one side of his body than the other, but that would be ridiculous. A glance at Suzanne showed that she found the smell offensive.

"Blackwing?" the apparent younger of the pair said...in English. "Is it you?" the individual started to weep. "And Suze!"

Suzanne got to her feet and looked closer, in shock. "Irving? Is that you under all that dirt and hair?" she asked.

"Do these belong to you?" Cornelius asked Socrates in *Q'estirian*.

"Not exactly," Socrates responded. "I think I know who they are, just not how they came to be here."

Cornelius exhaled loudly: "That is a major point for the council. Everyone is panicked, and they demand to know how they managed to get here in the first place."

"Where did you find them?" Socrates asked.

"They were in the vaults, in one vault in particular. The vault belonged to Aenta Nighthawk."

"There was an Aenta Nighthawk assigned by me to protect these two before the catastrophe," Socrates related. "I included his name in my casualty report the day after. How long have they been here?"

Suzanne, who kept an ear out for Cornelius' questions, repeated them to Irving and relayed his responses. "Irving says they were in the captain's office when an alarm sounded, and then a gigantic black something was thrown at them by the Q'estirian guard. The next thing he knew, he was here, sort of. Not here in this office, but here."

"Irving? What is an Irving?" Cornelius asked.

"The younger of the two," Socrates informed.

"We asked them several times who they were and got no response," Cornelius said.

"Did you ask them in English?" Socrates asked.

Cornelius looked blank. "What is this...English...you are asking about? I have never heard of it."

"Just as you did not understand them, they did not understand you. To them, we are speaking gibberish right now. They do not understand Q'estirian."

Cornelius looked shocked. "They don't understand Q'estirian? How can they thrive, or hope to be civilized, without the beautiful mother tongue of the Seven Known Planes?"

Socrates chuckled: "They probably think the same thing about you not knowing English."

"Do you have any means that they may shower?" Suzanne interrupted.

Cornelius looked dumbstruck. "You mean they want to stand out in the falling rain?"

Suzanne smirked. "No, but strangely, that is close to the mark. They want to wash their bodies...in water. Do you have something like that?"

Socrates shook his head. "They will have to wait until we get home...assuming they are free to leave?" he looked to Cornelius questioningly.

"How did they get here?" Cornelius asked. "I need to know if I am not opening the *Seven Known Planes* to invasion by releasing them."

"From what I can understand," Socrates stated, "the guard assigned to them got them away from the trap that Phelonius had set. He had no idea if it would keep them safe, but he tried and succeeded, apparently. They cannot get here on their own."

"How will you get them back to their own plane?" Cornelius asked.

"The obvious way is the same way they got here," Socrates said. "They cannot go through a portal; they have...devices... that prevent the portal's use, so they have to go the same way as they arrived. Suzanne, please explain it to Irving."

Socrates pulled out the black cloth he last used to move the bookstore. "Ready?" he asked the pair. They nodded, and Socrates tossed the fabric, and it covered them. As it did, the pair disappeared.

"Make certain they do not return here," Cornelius said sternly.

"I would suggest certain of our brothers learn English. It should be part of their training, should they need to travel to the *Eighth Plane*."

"I will take it under advisement," Cornelius said.

3

THE BEST OF TIMES

I rving and Captain Trooper were back into the vaults, but this time, they were in Socrates Blackwing's vault. The same vault he had used to move the entire bookstore. Irving knew it. There were still some of the books from Suzanne's store here.

"At least we have some reading material," Irving smirked as he picked up a book and opened it to the first page. "It was the best of times. It was the worst of times."

"Oh, please, Irving. Not that! I can't handle Dickens right now!"

"There are other ones here, Cap'n," Irving responded. "There is one called Displaced...nice cover...never heard of the author, though."

"How long are we going to be in here?" Trooper asked, irritated.

"I don't know," Irving said as he looked at another book. "Blackwing is making his way to our home...on our plane. When he gets there, he'll let us out of here. Did Suzanne say anything to you?"

"Just that Jessica is beside herself. They'd assumed we were dead."

"If it wouldn't have been for that *Q'estirian's* quick thinking, we would've been. Suzanne did say that there have been a lot of changes since we've been gone."

"Did she say how long we been gone?" Trooper asked.

"She said something about several months having passed," Irving said. "I'll be glad to see Jess again, though. I've been missing my wife, not that your company hasn't been scintillating."

Trooper smirked. "I understand. I could use a change of companions myself."

"How long will it take us to get home?" Suzanne asked.

"It'll take as long as it takes," Blackwing responded. "It took us three days to get to *Q'estiria*, so it should take three days to return. You know that, so why did you ask?"

"I was thinking of Irving and Trooper. While we are traveling through the *Faewyld*, they are stuck in a vault somewhere."

"There's no reason they can't travel with us now that we're outside the city limits."

"I think we could learn a lot about what happened to them by talking to them, and I'm certain they'd be less bored. They've been locked away a long time. Besides, this is their first trip to the *Faewyld*, and who knows when they'll ever get here again."

"I do know," Blackwing laughed. "They won't be this way again, not if anyone on the council has anything to say about it. Cornelius said as much as a condition of their release."

"When we stop, let them out so they can walk with us, rather than being locked away," Suzanne said.

"And the guards?" Blackwing asked.

"You're their Chief Commander. You can do pretty much what you want, can't you?"

"That's what most people think. Being in charge, leading others, has a limiting effect. We can ask Irving and Trooper to join us on the trek across the *Faewyld*. They may prefer to stay where they are."

"Why would they want to stay where they are?"

"It's hot out here, and it isn't where they are. Out here, they'd have to walk. Where they are, they don't have to. Out here, they'll be at risk. They're safe where they are."

"Get out of my way!" Jessica ranted at the two *Q'estirians* preventing her from getting close to her gun. *She thought I've spent the last few hours trying to get past these Blackwing wannabes.* She opened a cabinet containing alcoholic beverages as she walked through the kitchen. The cabinet door closed on its own with a loud bang. "What the hell is going on around here?" she yelled.

The ambassadorial guards were stoic and acted like they didn't understand anything she said. *How can that be*, she wondered. *They've all been here long enough to start to learn English.*

Jessica was beginning to have a hard time. It was close to seven days since she last held the Bushmaster or had a 'chat with Jack'. She had punched one of the guards and made contact, but it didn't seem to faze him. When she tried it again, he had deftly moved out of the way. Now, all of the guards would move if she tried to punch them, making her only means of acting out ineffectual.

When she decided to go out and get another bottle, the guards had stopped her. She knew they had. She'd tried to use the wizard-step coin, and it failed. She knew the guards had done something. The only other explanation was that Blackwing had disabled it before he left. *He wouldn't do that*, she thought. *I can't walk into town. It's too far and too many questions when I get there. No car, nothing to carry me the thirty miles to town.* She sat, chin in her palm, thinking of a way out of this predicament. It was then that she heard talking outside the back door.

She opened the door to Blackwing's back as he talked to the guards.

"Is there a reason you always talk to them in some other language than English?" she asked, frustration tingeing her words. "Do you know how rude that is?"

"How is it rude?" Blackwing asked her as he turned to face her.

"How do I know you aren't talking about me? I would like to be included."

"One way is to ask. Was I talking about you? Yes, I was. I was getting a report from the guards of all the things that went on while we were gone."

"And I suppose they told you how violent I was," she accused.

"Actually, they said nothing that would indicate any violence on your part. So, now, I have to ask, what *did* you do?"

Jessica said nothing and shut the door on Blackwing. She stormed back to her place at the table and sat heavily. It was a few seconds later that she heard the door open.

"I don't care to discuss it!" Jessica yelled without turning around.

"What is it you do care to discuss?" asked a voice she'd not heard in a long time.

Her mouth fell open, and she stood to face the door; her tears started to flow from her eyes, making it difficult to discern who spoke.

"I-I...what...how..." was all that came from her mouth.

"Hello, Jess. Did you miss me?" the person speaking was grinning at her. He was suddenly hit and was driven to the floor by her weight as she threw herself at him.

"You know, that shouldn't have worked," Blackwing said as he sat in the living room with a tankard of ale.

"I, for one, am glad it did," Suzanne said, grinning and holding her tankard high in salute.

"Hear, hear!" Marshall Trooper said, grinning, raising his tankard.

Everyone looked to Jessica and Irving, but nothing came from that quarter.

"They're not finished with their 'hellos'," Suzanne said. Everyone, except Irv and Jess, laughed.

"Why do you say that, Socrates?" Suzanne asked.

"Their Identifiers should have raised all kinds of issues with them when they passed through the event horizon of the multi-dimensional passage."

Everyone stared at Blackwing with blank looks.

"What?" Socrates asked as he became uncomfortable with the stares. "Irving, help me out, here."

"What's the matter?" Irving asked while Jessica ran a finger around his ear. "Stop, Jess, just for a second."

"I was saying that I was surprised you two managed to cross the event horizon," Socrates said.

"And why is that?" Irving asked, looking blankly at everyone in the room.

"The Identifiers," Socrates added with some impatience.

"What about them?"

"They shouldn't have allowed you to survive the crossing."

"Okay, I think there are some assumptions and misconceptions at play here," Irving said. "I don't recall any tests being conducted with activated and functioning Identifiers, and your multi-dimensional storage tarp. Socrates and Suzanne don't have Identifiers, nor do any of the *Q'estirian* guards. That leaves me, Jessica, and Cap'n Trooper—"

"I'm no longer a captain," Trooper interrupted, slowly shaking his head. "I'm just a civilian, just another 'average Joe'," he said with a serene smile.

"You've never been an 'average Joe' to us," Jessica said, with a warm smile and a gentle touch on Trooper's arm.

"Be that as it may," Irving shouted, reclaiming the floor, "the rest of us don't *know* that the Identifiers are working. They have functioned during our lifespans, so we aren't aware when they're on or off. They only turn on when needed or inside a predefined sphere of a device requiring one to activate for all we know.

"Has anyone thought to test if the Identifiers are even on after *the Event? The Event* itself, in my opinion, could've been similar to an EMP." Everyone looked at him with a blank expression. "An electromagnetic pulse. For all we know, the Identifiers are off and have been since the first vestiges of the 'explosion'.

"The other assumption is this, is the multi-dimensional... um...passage the same as a passage created by Suzanne. I know I haven't done any comparative analysis to determine if the two are the same. For all I know, they're as different as apples and oranges."

"What do apples and oranges have to do with anything?" Trooper asked.

"To those of us familiar with them, they're different, but what about those who don't know the difference? They're both food and fruit, so, to someone who doesn't know, they could think they are the same, just different colors."

"So, you're saying that you see no reason why our escape didn't leave us vegetables because there were no tests to say otherwise?" Trooper asked.

"I'm saying that there are too many variables to be certain that what we are assuming is actually what is going on. Did it work? Yes. Would I do it again? Not unless I had to. We made it this time, but that doesn't guarantee the next time won't fry our noggins."

"There is this," Jessica said, holding a phone in her palm.

"Whose phone?" Irving asked.

"I was told it was yours," Jessica said, handing it over to Irving.

"It isn't charged, so how can I tell?" Irving asked.

"I was led to believe it was retrieved from the PD," Jessica explained. "If true, then it should have evidence of the released radiations. It could be useful for you to investigate what the hell happened."

Irving sat at the table, sipping some of Jessica's Jack Daniels and scowling.

"What's wrong?" Blackwing asked as he came into the room, sat opposite Irving, and got out his tankard. He sipped.

"I've done all the tests I can do from here. I don't have the equipment I need here, so I couldn't do half the tests I want to."

Irving glanced around before leaning in to talk privately with Socrates. "I've been trying to determine what happened to Cap," he whispered.

"I'm certain he knows something has happened to him, and he knows you...and your curiosity." Blackwing chuckled.

"I know, but it's frustrating! I have more equipment at my lab, but I can't get to it," Irving whispered as he set his glass down after sipping some more of the golden liquid.

"Why can't you get to your lab?" Blackwing asked.

"They have quarantined the entire area, and I can't wizard-step close enough."

"Who has?"

"The Government investigators," Irving answered, his frustration evident in his tone.

"Well, they must know what they're doing—"

Irving laughed heartily, interrupting Blackwing. "Not likely! From what I understand about the incident and your capabilities, *The Event* had something to do with other people's life force. I'm suspecting that is what happened...a life-force bomb of some kind sucked the life-force out of everyone in its blast radius."

"Sounds logical," Blackwing said as he sipped again.

"I suspect that is what happened to Cap'n Trooper. From

what I remember, I was slightly closer to the guard who threw that magical tarp you guys carry. When the blast hit, I was more covered than Trooper was." Irving bowed his head and shook it slightly side-to-side. "That guard could've saved himself instead of us," he said, looking at Blackwing as a tear rolled down his cheek.

"He could have, but that is not our way," Blackwing said stoically. "We run towards the danger, not away from it." Blackwing sipped some of the liquid. "So does your wife."

"Boy, don't I know it!" Irving said, finishing off the drink and standing. "And I'm glad she has those inclinations. So does Trooper. I don't have it as they do, so I do my part by finding the answers they need. Right now, that's being prevented by people who don't even think there is such a thing as a 'life-force', let alone that there might be something that can drain it."

"Speaking of your wife, where is she?" Blackwing asked.

"Suzanne is teaching her Q'estirian. She's certain that you, and your guards, are talking about her behind her back." Irving chuckled a little.

Blackwing nodded while he drank. "Do you know how to find Smith?" he asked finally.

———

Irving was sitting alone in the darkened bar, sipping some Jack Daniels. He looked around at the rest of the clientele and actively looked for Smith.

"I got your message. What is it you wanted?" Smith asked in low tones as he sat across from Irving.

Irving jumped. "Where did you come from? I was looking for you and didn't see you," he explained.

Smith smirked. "You weren't supposed to see me. Where's your wife? I was half-expecting her to be with you."

"So, I won't do?" Blackwing said as he placed his hand on Smith's shoulder.

Smith tried to free himself from Blackwing's iron grip before relaxing to the inevitable.

"My friend wants to get into the Police Department Building," Blackwing said quietly. "How can that be accomplished?"

"You can't," Smith said, maintaining a level voice. "They haven't cleared that particular building yet. It's what's called 'a crime scene'."

"And what if you were to let us in?" Blackwing asked menacingly.

"I can't!" Smith insisted. "I don't have the clearance for something like that. Why do you want to get in there anyway?"

"The 'why' doesn't concern you," Irving warned. "So, they haven't cleared out the bodies yet?"

"Oh, they have, some time ago. They tell me that the PD was ground zero, so they're trying to determine what the hell happened," Smith said.

"What about the surveillance cameras?" Irving asked.

"That place was covered in cameras before *The Event*. That hasn't changed. *The Event* didn't affect services to any building, just the people," Smith explained.

"We're going in," Irving said quietly.

"Well, smile for the cameras when you do," Smith said. "Who's going?"

"All three of us," Blackwing said with a mirthless grin.

Smith looked to Irving and then glanced in the general direction of Blackwing. "Three?" he asked. "You and Irving and..." his head was shaking slightly.

"You're going to accompany us," Blackwing said.

"The hell I am!" Smith insisted. "I said I couldn't let you in. I don't have the clearance."

"Nevertheless, you will accompany us," Blackwing said softly.

Blackwing, Irving, and Smith appeared on the roof of a building not far from the PD.

"There doesn't appear to be anyone on the roof of the PD," Irving reported to Blackwing.

"Is that true?" Blackwing asked Smith.

Smith felt compelled to answer. "They have no use for a physical presence; they have cameras. They'll know who you are before you can enter the building."

"They will?" Irving asked Blackwing, concerned.

"I'm sure. They'll know that Agent John Smith, or whatever alias he's using now, entered the building by way of the roof. They'll have it on...video." Blackwing had a broad smile.

"Wait! What?" Smith asked with shock. "I'm not going into the PD. I'm way too close, right now, as it is!"

"You don't understand," Blackwing said. "You, me, and Irv are going to enter the building. They're going to see on the video that you and you alone, walked around the building. You aren't going to wait here or be released. You *are* going into the PD."

"What floor are we going to?" Blackwing asked as Irving used his phone to control the elevator.

"Tenth floor," Irving answered. "My lab was on the tenth floor. Jess's cubical and Trooper's office was on eleven."

"And you're sure they'll have all the equipment you need?" Blackwing asked.

"I would prefer to be able to come here to run all the tests I need to run, but we can't do that. What about 'Sleeping Beauty'?" Irving glanced to Smith, who was lying quietly on the elevator floor.

"He'll wake up when they investigate. He won't remember anything since the last time he saw Jess. Doesn't the equipment require power?" Blackwing asked.

"Yes, as a matter of fact. Quite a bit of power," Irving said while he worked on the phone he'd purchased for this particular project.

"Where are you going to get that much power?" Blackwing asked.

"That is a wrinkle I haven't fingered out yet," Irving said sheepishly.

"Why not do the tests here?" Blackwing asked as he looked around.

"Because I don't want to focus on watching out for intruders while I work," Irving said as he picked up an electronic notepad and started aiming it in different directions.

"We could wizard-step from here home, if need be," Blackwing said as he watched Irving work. "I'll go set some wards that will alert us to any presence of intruders; then, if we have to, we can be gone before anyone can spot us."

Blackwing returned a few minutes later. "Find anything interesting?" he asked as he entered the lab.

"I did a cursory scan for radiation and found nothing, which is troublesome. I managed to set up a blanketing field to eliminate any sounds that the microphones attached to the cameras might pick up. How big is your interdimensional tarp?" Irving asked without looking at Blackwing.

"It can be unfolded to any size I need, within reason," Blackwing said. "It can be big enough to place a room from the bookstore into storage or small enough to pass your hand through. Why do you ask?"

"I need a square about two-feet on a side," Irving answered. "I need something small to test for disturbances and energies around the edges that may influence the Identifiers."

Blackwing walked over to an empty tabletop and unfolded the tarp a couple of times to make it the size Irving requested. "Will this work?"

"Close enough," Irving said, smiling, glancing over at the table.

4

AN UNEXPECTED VISIT

Agent Smith, which was the name he'd given when asked, slowly began to regain consciousness. He found that he was lying on the floor of an elevator somewhere. However, Smith didn't remember lying down, let alone in an elevator. He didn't even know what building he was in. All he could figure out was he was lying in an elevator with a headache. *Why is my head aching? I don't remember hitting my head.*

As he stood, his head ached more; he could feel the pounding matching his heartbeat. He placed his forearm on the elevator sidewall, to the left of the door, and put his head against his forearm, bending slightly, and closed his eyes to try to wish the pounding away.

"You will not remove the band on your arm," came, unbidden, to his mind. His hand went to his upper bicep and touched the band he found there. *"You will not expose the band to anyone. Losing the band, in any fashion, will end your life. It must remain where it is. The pounding in your head will stop when you put the band out of your mind."* He tried to relax and comply. After a few deep breaths, the pounding in his head began to subside.

A few minutes later, he stood, straightened his clothing,

brushed off debris, actual and imagined, and pressed the button that would open the door.

As the door opened, the wind pulled at his hair and clothing. He thought: *Why am I on a roof? Which roof am I on?* He looked around the roof and noticed the police hovercars. *Why am I on the roof of the PD? Jessica!*

He entered a hovercar and pressed the button to start the six fans located under the vehicle. *You just wait until I see you again, Jessica Strange.* The fan-whine increased, building up speed. *You're going to answer for this.* The car lifted from the roof.

Irving had been working for hours, and then he became aware that he heard no movement from Blackwing, not even his breathing. He looked up with a start to see Blackwing studying him, Blackwing's sphere sitting on a table close to a computer. The globe was flashing through different shades of red.

"What's that doing?" Irving asked.

"I'm...downloading all the data I can from your...computers," Blackwing said offhandedly. "I thought it might be useful, should things change with Jessica's position here, just in case someone tries to alter the documents."

"Have you checked on Smith, lately?" Irving asked.

"He left some time ago."

"What?" Irving yelled. "He'll blow the whistle on us! Where did he go?"

"I have no idea where he went," Blackwing said calmly. "Ah! Blow the whistle: relay information of criminal activity to authorities. He may, as you say, *blow the whistle*, but I doubt it. His ego would prevent him from looking foolish to his superiors. He's the type that would prefer to stay out of the light and will, probably, deal with us in his own time and when it will benefit him."

"You're more trusting than I would be," Irving said, shaking his head slightly and turning back to his work.

"You know you need to learn the *Q'estirian* language," Blackwing said.

"I don't have time right now, and I'm slow when learning languages," Irving said without looking up.

"I don't want you to feel like an outsider in your own home," Blackwing said. "Besides, you could be stuck again in *Q'estiria*. I can't see the future, so, to be on the safe side, maybe you should."

"Aren't you concerned with someone seeing that?" Irving asked, pointing to the sphere on the table.

Blackwing chuckled. "I didn't just set up wards. I created a... bubble, of sorts, that anyone monitoring would see your lab with no one in it. The bubble will keep out those who would interrupt your work."

Irving chuckled. "And I set up a loop on the cameras to show that no one was here. Great minds think alike, I guess. I'm almost done here."

Irving moved over to his desktop computer and started typing and clicking on things. Blackwing was trying to make sense of it all, but Irving was doing things too fast to follow.

"Done," Irving announced a few minutes later. "Now, let's go home."

Blackwing placed his hand on Irving's shoulder, and they both disappeared.

It seemed to *S'hyrlus* that the time was close at hand to visit the second *Q'estirian* Lord for which she was consort, Cornelius Blackwing. *I have not personally seen the old Rhu'Inai Z'oot for a long time. Not since Socrates came to Neh'Krim's household.*

She wondered: *How many have I named?* Being consort gave her the privilege of naming the younglings that came to her care. *I did not name Cornelius, but I influenced his father's consort, Phelonius Blackwing, Socrates Blackwing, of course, and influenced a lot more, including Malthuvius Nighthawk, with a large number lost in the war with the Ha'Jakta Ha'Dreen B'kota.*

When her thoughts turned to her age, she quickly rose and, leaving the shade of the *Great Oak*, made her way to her house to change her clothing. She wondered: *What season is it in Q'estiria? I know the seasons do not change drastically, but I must wear something appropriate, and something to grab their attention.*

Cornelius Blackwing was looking forward to his accustomed mid-afternoon tankard of ale. He left word that he wanted to be undisturbed until further notice. He exhaled loudly as he secured the door for privacy.

"You have not changed," *S'hyrlus* said as the door closed.

Cornelius jumped as he spun around. "How did you get in here?" he roared.

"The same way you did," *S'hyrlus* grinned, "through the door. Why so, apprehensive?"

Cornelius exhaled noisily. "Everyone is, lately. We are still looking for Malthuvius and Phelonius. Both are still secreted somewhere. As you know, both are dangerous."

"I know," *S'hyrlus* whispered.

There was an awkward silence building as both looked at each other.

Suddenly, *S'hyrlus* slapped her thigh and stood. "I've come to take you on an adventure."

"An adventure? What kind of adventure?" Cornelius asked warily, eyes narrowing.

"I have decided that we should visit my son on the *Eighth Plane* before either of us become too much older," *S'hyrlus* grinned.

"I cannot go on any...adventure! I am much too busy here. I have duties—"

"That is *P'koosh Z'airka!*" *S'hyrlus* interrupted good-naturedly. "It was not so long ago that you would have jumped at the chance of leaving this...this tomb. What restrains you now?"

"It is dangerous for anyone to wander—"

"More excuses?" *S'hyrlus* asked innocently. "Where is the warrior? Where is Cornelius Blackwing, Chief Commander of the *Q'estirian* hosts? I want to travel with *that* individual, not some whiny politician hiding behind heavy walls of books about nothing. Be *Ha'Jakta Ha'Dreen*, once more; be the *Commander of Dragons*, just once more."

Cornelius sat heavily in his luxurious chair behind his large, ornate desk and glared at *S'hyrlus*. "You sorely tempt me, *S'hyrlus*," he said as his tankard drifted to his hand. He drank.

"Do you have another tankard?" *S'hyrlus* asked as she wandered around the posh room.

"In all the years I have known you, you have never partaken, but..." Another tankard floated towards her, and she took it and sipped.

"I have decided that there are many things I have refrained from doing, in all my years. I used to indulge more than you would believe. I feel the need to do so again, maybe not to the extremes of the past, though.

"So, will you escort me, or will you remain and become part of this room, become part of this collection, a room of ancient relics and forgotten glories."

Cornelius' fingers twitched, the rings clinking on the side of his tankard. *S'hyrlus* knew it to be a nervous habit that meant he was thinking.

"You presume to pass judgment on those populating the *Eighth Plane* without ever going there yourself," *S'hyrlus* prodded, "that seems rather arrogant to me." She sat once more, a leg over the arm of the finely upholstered chair and drank while looking at him over the rim of her tankard.

"How many guards did you have in mind for this little jaunt of yours?" Cornelius asked finally.

"No guards, just you and me," she answered with a grin. "Besides, you have grown rather rotund in your old age. It would do you good to get some exercise," she teased.

"I do not understand it," Cornelius said as they stopped for water. They were several miles from the city. "This duster used to fit me a lot better." He moved his shoulders around with the tight-fitting garment.

"Maybe it shrunk," *S'hyrlus* teased.

"Maybe it did. Have you been to the *Eighth Plane* before?" Cornelius asked.

"More times than you can possibly imagine," *S'hyrlus* said.

"Just to reiterate, I think this is ill-advised," Cornelius looked around expectantly.

"There is something I want you to deliberate on while we travel," *S'hyrlus* said as she drank her water. "I want you to sift through all of your knowledge about dragons and tell me what happens to the old ones, the most ancient of their kind. Where do they go? What happens to them? Feel free to speculate if you do not know."

"I have a rather large tome on them in my office," Cornelius offered, "if you are curious."

"We are not *in* your office. This is the *Faewyld*," *S'hyrlus* snapped, "in case you had not noticed."

It had taken many hours of walking before Cornelius and *S'hyrlus* stopped for the night. They sat, ate, and drank water, at her insistence, around their fire.

"What fruit has come from your ruminations?" *S'hyrlus* asked.

Cornelius sat quietly, ordering his thoughts. "I know what everyone knows, dragons, from the time they hatch, fight. As hatchlings, they engage in mock battles with their nest-mates.

"As they get older, they fight with rivals for the privilege of breeding. They also fight their breeding partners to show they are worthy."

"Yes, yes, but what of the ancient ones?" *S'hyrlus* asked.

"No one knows," Cornelius shrugged. "It is not like they can communicate who is the oldest to those of us with language skills."

S'hyrlus grinned. "I'll tell you what our legends say if you wish to hear."

"You know I do," Cornelius said with more excitement than he intended, more excitement than he had experienced in many years.

"My race is much older than yours," *S'hyrlus* started, "and our legends tell us that for every one of your race that is born, a dragon is hatched.

"You were correct, as far as you went, with your knowledge of dragons. However, it is said that when a dragon becomes ancient, they seek out their counterpart from within the *Q'estirian* race if that counterpart still lives.

"It is not something that can be refused. Both are drawn together, their life paths converging. When they finally meet, they fight; they fight for their lives. Both are willing to die. Both want to live. If they fight to a standstill, the dragon will submit and allow the *Q'estirian* to mount it, and they both fly off to whatever comes after."

The crackling of the campfire was the only noise for a long time.

"Cannot a younger wizard battle the older dragon?" Cornelius asked.

"He could, but he would lose."

"Why would he lose?"

"An ancient dragon requires an ancient wizard," *S'hyrlus* explained. "A younger wizard would be no match for an ancient dragon. Dragons and wizards become more...devious in their old age. Experience has taught them well and thus become a problem for the...um...less artful."

"What happens if they both die?" Cornelius asked, finally.

"Then, they both die."

"And if the *Q'estirian* lives?"

"I do not know. The legend only covers the options I stated."

Once again, there was silence. *S'hyrlus* tilted her head, first one way, then the other, as if listening.

"I do not hear your dragon coming for you," she teased. "Not yet, anyway."

"Well, I'll be—" Irving said after long hours with his electronic notepad.

"You find something, son?" Trooper asked as he came up behind Irving.

"What did you find?" Blackwing asked, facing Irving.

"It appears that the Identifiers implanted in us turn on when they are in proximity to devices requiring their use," Irving explained. He looked around the room at all the blank faces. "You want to make a call, so you pick up your phone. The act of picking up the phone brings your ID into proximity of the device, and it turns on your identifier, allowing you to use the device.

"In the city, we were always surrounded by devices that turn on our identifiers. Out here, in the tulies, the IDs are off a large portion of the time, unless, of course, we pick up something that would require them. When you leave your phone in the living room and go into the kitchen, your identifier bleeds off energy slowly. After 10 or 15 minutes, it turns off to preserve enough power to turn on, should it be needed.

"In mine and Trooper's case, the detonation of the life-force bombs acted like an EMP and triggered a reset of all devices inside the PD. That sudden device reset forced our IDs to reset. We were transported to the storage vaults during that brief shutdown of the IDs before our IDs could regain even partial power required. Once we were in the vaults, our IDs, as they would normally do, built up power and then, since there were no devices in range of our IDs, bled that power off and then turned off."

No one said anything for some time.

"So, what exactly are you saying?" Jessica asked.

"I'm saying that we got lucky. We should've died. The only reason we didn't was only the confluence of the wildest of circumstances," Irving said.

"So, can that transit occur again?" Suzanne asked?

"Out here, away from devices and after waiting for the IDs to turn off, yes, we could be safely transported in the same fashion."

"Except the council has deemed it illegal to do so, in that fashion, again," Blackwing interjected. "If you returned to Q'estiria, you'd have to do so by the more conventional means."

"And before that could happen, I'd have to do more tests on the energies involved before sanctioning such a venture for anyone with an ID," Irving added.

It had taken several days for Cornelius and S'hyrlus to locate a tree suitable for transport to the *Eighth Plane*.

"Are you ready?" S'hyrlus asked.

Cornelius was wandering around the area nervously. "This is not a prudent action. How do we know if it is safe for us on the alien plane?"

"The point of this little excursion is to get you away from what you have grown comfortable. From the look of it, you have grown far too...comfortable." She crossed her eyes, puffed out her cheeks, and curved her arms.

"I fail to understand what you mean by those body postures. They look alien to me."

"They are things I picked up on the *Eighth Plane*. They are supposed to show how...comfortable you have become. I was mocking you a little to get you to relax. You are amplifying your nervousness over nothing. Is it safe on the *Eighth Plane*? Not particularly, but it is not as dangerous as here, in the *Seven Known Planes*. If you keep your wits, we should be fine. Besides, we have Socrates to protect us. You do trust your ambassador, do you not?"

"Of course I do. He is my great-great-grandson and the new ambassador, not to mention he is also Chief Commander; if he cannot protect us, who can?" Cornelius grinned and puffed out his chest with pride.

S'hyrlus grinned. "That seemed to calm you." She raised her hand to touch the tree trunk but stopped short of actually touching it. "Are you finally ready?"

Cornelius nodded. *S'hyrlus* touched the tree trunk. The portal opened, and both stepped through.

Once the portal closed, Cornelius looked around. "Not too different from our Plane." He breathed deep and started coughing.

"I should have warned you," *S'hyrlus* said as she pounded him on the back. "The air here is...different."

"Different?" Cornelius questioned between coughs. "I can almost chew it. It is so thick, and what is that smell? Or is it a taste?"

"You have been too long on *Q'estiria*. The air on the *Ha'Jakta Ha'Dreen B'kota* plane is far worse. Here, they call it pollen. It is what the plants spread to propagate."

"Yes, I understand. These plants should do so more...discreetly."

"I am certain that the plants here are unaware of your austere presence." She bowed and tried to stifle a chuckle.

Cornelius turned and looked at her, shocked. "Are you mocking me?"

"Of course, I am." She laughed. "You take yourself far too seriously. You need to relax."

He twitched his nose, sniffed, and tried to look severe. "If it were anyone else, I would be quite cross. Since it is you..." He laughed heartily.

5

UNEXPECTED GUNFIRE

Cornelius and *S'hyrlus* were walking through a small, wooded area. *Bang!* The loud sound made them both jump. *Bang! Bang!* Out of curiosity, Cornelius walked toward the sound. *S'hyrlus* followed close behind.

They rounded a small hillock and saw someone, or something, looking down and busy with something. As they crept closer, Cornelius suddenly found himself staring into a huge black hole. Both heard a distinctive click and saw the creature pull back something near the top of an obvious weapon. The creature was speaking, but to the pair, it was gibberish.

"Do not move, Cornelius. It is obviously a weapon, and she thinks it will be effective."

"It would probably be quite effective since it is pointing at my head. How do you know it is a female?" Cornelius asked. His hands had crept upward slightly to show empty hands.

"This is a human female. This one is called Jessica." *S'hyrlus* touched him lightly, trying to look around Cornelius' bulk.

"Is she going to harm me?" he asked.

"If you move too quickly, she could try. The weapons here are primitive and effective against their own kind. I do not know how effective they are against us."

"From my perspective, I do not doubt her resolve, and I am... reluctant...to be the test subject on the effectiveness of her weapon."

Jessica was getting in some range time when she felt the presence of the two intruders. When she turned, muscle memory took over, and the *Desert Eagle* was cocked and aimed at the head of the first of the intruders.

"Can't you read?" she said with anger and disdain. "I don't want to be disturbed. I don't want company. And I don't need protecting."

She heard the pair speak gibberish, and then her name was spoken clearly. It was then that Jessica got a good look at the couple in front of her.

"You're *S'hyrlus*, aren't you? And who is this old buzzard? What are you doing here?" She hadn't dropped her weapon or relaxed her posture. "If you move, I'll ventilate you. I don't know how effective my friend here will be, but I'm game to find out if you are."

"Jessica! Stop!" Blackwing yelled.

Her eyes darted to Blackwing.

"These two decided to sneak up on me while I was getting in some practice. They need to read the signs I posted. This is a range area and not safe for intruders."

"They can't read your signs. This is my great-great-grandfather and my mother. You should've recognized her. So, stand down."

Jessica lowered her weapon, released the hammer, and re-holstered it. "You need to inform them," she said sternly, "unless they're trying to get shot. In which case, I'll be happy to oblige."

"Venerable ancestor, excuse my friend. She did not recognize you." Blackwing bowed slightly to his great-great-grandfather. "You have inadvertently entered a dangerous area. The weapon my friend is using would be fatal if discharged so close to our skin."

"How effective would that weapon be if discharged at our leather?" Cornelius asked, curious.

Blackwing chuckled. "Unknown. However, she did offer to be part of that experiment."

"Who is she?" Cornelius said. "She is quite impressive!"

"You are an insufferable flirt," *S'hyrlus* said.

"I am allowed to appreciate beauty wherever I find it," Cornelius grinned.

After a brief conversation with the woman, Blackwing handed Cornelius an unspent shell. "That is what she is shooting. The end is the part that is propelled by the expanding gases of the chemical reaction encased inside the flat end."

Cornelius' eyebrows rose at the weight of the shell that he weighed in his hand. "Most impressive! Was she one of those that helped in the apprehension of Nighthawk?"

"Yes, as was her mate, whom you have already met. He was one of the individuals you called me to *Q'estiria* to reclaim."

"Shall we proceed to your residence?" *S'hyrlus* asked. "That was our destination until we became...distracted."

Jessica discharged a few more shots as they walked away, making Cornelius and *S'hyrlus* jump at the loud noise.

When Blackwing, Cornelius, and *S'hyrlus* entered, all the *Q'estirian* guards popped to attention. Suzanne rushed to pay her respects to *S'hyrlus*. Irving glanced at the new arrivals, but it wasn't enough to distract him from his work.

"What brings the grandfather of my grandfather to this

humble place?" Blackwing asked as he sat, being the last to do so.

"I came to see this place for myself," Cornelius said. "It was... suggested that to pass any judgments on those who live here, without experiencing this place for myself, would be arrogant."

"Besides, he was turning into an old relic in that office of his," *S'hyrlus* smirked. "He needed something to get his blood flowing once more."

"Which it is, thanks to your Jessica," Cornelius said. "I would like to see some people here and see their technology. Do they have any cities?"

"We are not far from the last populated city on this continental coast," Blackwing said.

Blackwing switched to English. "Irving, what are you working on? Cornelius would like to see some of what you're doing."

"I'm working on an app that can be used to translate documents from your language to English and to translate English to your writing." Irving brought over the electronic pad and showed it to Blackwing.

"It misinterpreted a couple of words. Mind if Cornelius sees it?"

Irving made a face. "It isn't finished, and it does have some errors, apparently."

"He just wants to see your technology. I'm sure it will impress him."

Irving capitulated grudgingly.

Blackwing took the pad over to Cornelius and *S'hyrlus*.

Cornelius looked at the presented device.

Blackwing explained: "Irving has been working on this device to translate the human language to our writing and our writing to their language. He says it is not completed yet, but he is working on it."

Cornelius nodded and pointed to the screen. "There is an error at this rune. For what purpose is this device being created?"

"We hope that it will aid those of our plane that travel to this plane, as well as the reverse."

"What about the edict against travel to this plane and the travel ban, by these...humans, to our plane?"

"Hopefully, in time, those bans will be lifted. After all, you are here, now."

"Given any thought to your *other* duties?" *S'hyrlus* asked Suzanne, shifting to the language of the nymphs.

"Other duties?" Suzanne asked. "What other duties?"

"Raising and naming *Q'estirian* younglings."

Suzanne paled.

S'hyrlus grinned. "You have not contemplated on that, yet?"

"Honestly, no, I have not. I would like to ask, why did you name him Socrates?"

S'hyrlus chuckled. "In my time, I have named many *Q'estirian* younglings." She sighed. "More than I care to think about. I visited what you would call Rome, Athens, other places, and other times in my younger days. I gave names of those I respected, or someone reminded me of someone I had known before. Should you decide to raise and name a *Q'estirian* youngling, the family name cannot be changed or modified, so pick a name that fits with the surname."

"I have noticed that some of the names on the council were... odd. I had trouble stifling a laugh at a couple of them."

"The Five Families rule the council. Their surnames are from Dragon names: Blackwing, Crowfoot, Thunderclap, Nighthawk, and Hornsdoodle. Each is revered, so which ones caused your mirth?"

"Honestly, Hornsdoodle." Suzanne tried to stifle the flush of embarrassment.

S'hyrlus smiled. "Hornsdoodle was a misinterpretation of the dragon name for *one with randomly twisting and curling horns*. A Dragon's horns are part of their defensive weapons. Most dragons have either straight or straight but twisted horns. They tend to be symmetrical. The one that became the name Hornsdoodle had non-symmetrical horns that twisted and curved. Those horns were challenging to defend against because of their non-symmetry.

"Each family has similarities inside their group, and you can see that if you look at them. The Hornsdoodle clan tends to be dissimilar to others in their clan and different from the other four clans."

"So, I should refrain from laughing at the name?" Suzanne asked.

"I would. The entirety of the Hornsdoodle clan has enormous pride in their family name and is easily offended and unforgiving."

Irving became miffed when Blackwing, and the old codger, began to talk in their own dialect. *I wouldn't mind so much if they weren't so dismissive about it.*

When Suzanne and *S'hyrlus* started with their dialect, he waved a hand behind him and walked out the back door. When he turned to see where he was going, he ran into Jessica. His hands came up to avoid running into her. As it turned out, his hands impacted her breasts.

"Hey! Watch it!" Jessica glared at him. "Can't you at least wait until we are alone before you grope me?"

"Oops, sorry, Jess."

She glared at him with her fists on her hips. "And just what, exactly, are you sorry for?"

"Sorry, I got miffed at Blackwing, both of them, Suzanne, and Blackwing's mom. I'm not sorry for bumping into you. Just sorry I did it out here...and not in private."

Jessica grinned flirtatiously.

"Did anyone say anything to you about dinner?" Irving asked.

"No, but I suspect they're gonna want Sichuan beef."

"Has anyone given you the okay to hire a cook? I'm getting tired of running to town every time I turn around."

"Would it help if we both went to town to buy dinner? We could get a pizza and go to our room." She smiled at him suggestively.

"What are you two cooking up?" Trooper asked as he came up to the pair.

"Just thinking about going for dinner," Jessica said. "Would you like to accompany us?"

"No, you two go on. The last thing youngsters need is some old codger dampening any...um...spontaneity."

"You're not 'some old codger'...not to us, anyway," Jessica said.

"Jess is right, Cap. Come with us," Irving added.

"Well, as long as I'm not in the way," Trooper smiled.

A few minutes later, the three were about to enter the restaurant that made the favored Sichuan beef when Smith approached.

"Fancy meeting you three here," Smith said as he walked up.

"You know, if I didn't know better, I'd think you were stalking us," Jessica said derisively. She fingered the grip of the *Desert Eagle* in the holster on her hip.

Smith put up his hands. "Take it easy, Jess. I'm not stalking you, and I don't want any trouble. Is it so strange? This place has the best Sichuan, after all."

"You need to make some *new* friends...to run into...by accident." She glared at Smith.

"You seem to be a burr under her saddle," Trooper said. "I'd recommend you back away slowly. She is quite capable."

"I'm looking for people to man the PD, even if it is temporary, and here are the last three members of the PD, pre-event." Smith tried to look innocent.

"You need to —"

"Hold on, Jess, I want to hear what he has to say," Trooper said and turned to Smith. "You're trying to get the PD up and running again?"

"I am, or *we* are, trying to get the political structure working again, but anyone willing to be mayor has security concerns. No one wants to be mayor for only a day or two and then be assassinated shortly after."

"Things are a bit wild here, but that's to be expected. We did have an event that significantly altered our society. What're you offering?"

"Offering?" Smith shrugged, "Just a lot of work at a thankless job for lousy pay and even lousier benefits. Why? Are you interested?"

"I don't know yet. I might be."

Smith's eyebrow rose. "I was led to believe that you weren't."

"Cap, we need to talk about it," Jessica whispered.

"Why? You and Irv have your own life. Why do *we* need to discuss it? I'm perfectly capable of making my own decisions; thank you very much."

Jessica's head was nodding while she glared at Smith. She said to Trooper: "We'll place our order and be back when it's done. If you finish your *meeting* before then, you know where to find us. Come, Irving!"

Jessica and Irving walked out of the establishment half an hour later and joined Trooper. They walked to a secluded alley before departing via the wizard-step coins to reappear seconds later at their residence.

"Jessica, are you upset with me?" Trooper asked as they walked into the house.

"With you? No. I'm upset with that slime-o Smith!" Jessica fumed.

"Why?" Trooper asked.

"I don't trust him...or anyone he works for."

"He offered *me* the job of mayor or police chief, whichever one I want. Was he serious?" Trooper asked.

Jessica's brow furrowed. "I'm sure he was. He's a Fed and thinks he can do whatever he wants and knows that anything he establishes can all go away with nothing more than a shrug, as an explanation, when cornered later."

"He seems to want the same things we do," Irving observed.

"His impetus is for *his* aggrandizement. Not for any altruistic ideal. Have you forgotten how he was ready to ventilate Blackwing?" she turned to Trooper. "Or when he pulled his gun on you in your office?"

"But if we are in charge, we can make a big difference," Trooper said. Irving nodded.

"Until such time as you would bend the rules, not that you ever did that, for someone you know." She looked sideways at Trooper. "Then the corruption would start creeping in."

Trooper looked shocked. "Are you saying I'm corrupt?"

"Not what I said and not what I meant. Besides, nobody's perfect and human nature is ever-present, whenever humans are involved."

Everyone had finished eating. The *Q'estirian* guards had returned to the bunkhouse, leaving Suzanne, Blackwing, Jessica,

Irving, *S'hyrlus*, and Cornelius enjoying the remnants of their meal enhanced by relaxation and alcohol.

"I've noticed," Irving stated, "all the guards look like Blackwing. Is that intentional?"

Cornelius' eyes flashed to Blackwing. "You allow it to speak?"

"Of course. Irving," Blackwing motioned towards Irving, "is a friend and helped capture Malthuvius and Phelonius."

Cornelius grumbled and rocked side-to-side in the throne-like, over-stuffed chair he was occupying.

"Technically, he, with Jessica, own this house, and we are their guests," Blackwing added.

Cornelius looked shocked. "They can own property?"

"Cornelius, Irving would like to know if all *Q'estirians* being similar was intentional?" Suzanne interrupted.

Cornelius' expression changed to one less confrontational.

"The similarities of *Q'estirians*, taken as a whole, are from millennia of refining the breed. The differences are exemplified in the Five Families.

"There are five families that make up the ruling council of *Q'estiria*, and each has its distinguishing characteristics. True, all are similar to the untrained eye, but all are distinctive and follow general rules.

"The taller, also known as raven-hairs, are Family Blackwing, known for their pale-blue eyes. Uniform-wise, they wear either no hatband or a black hatband."

Suzanne was interpreting Cornelius' words for Irving and Jessica.

Cornelius continued, with irritation, "Those in Family Nighthawk are known for their steel-blue eyes and a steel-blue hatband. Family Thunderclap is known for its green eyes and hatband.

"The lesser, also known as non-ravens, are generally shorter.

Those families are Hornsdoodle, known for their golden-brown eyes and dark grey hatband, and Family Crowfoot, known for their black eyes and white hatband."

Irving stared at the elder *Q'estirian* with disgust. "We are the uncivilized; the great unwashed? At least we don't group people by eye color and hatband color. As I recall, Malthuvius wore no hatband and yet had steel-blue eyes. What about that?"

"What Cornelius said was more of a general rule," Suzanne said contritely. "Malthuvius Nighthawk, though a member of the Nighthawk clan, had the choice of the color of his hatband. He chose the color that would make him adopted brother to Socrates. That would explain Socrates' reticence to injure him seriously."

"Too bad it didn't go both ways," Jessica fumed. Malthuvius didn't show any restraint.

"How ridiculous can it be? The color of a hatband?" Irving shook his head as he left the common room.

Jessica stood and followed Irving out of the room. She heard the door to their room close, and she followed, opening the door. The room was empty.

"Irving is missing!" Jessica yelled as she ran to the living room.

Everyone jumped to their feet. "Are you sure?" Suzanne asked.

"You don't think I'd notice my husband missing?" Jessica said. "I was right behind him when he left the living room."

Blackwing said something to Cornelius in their language, and both got up to investigate the last room Jessica had said Irving entered.

"Could he have used his wizard-step coin?" Suzanne asked.

"Without telling me?" Jessica asked, shaking her head. "Unlikely! We promised each other, once he returned, to tell each other where we were going if we went anywhere alone."

Blackwing reentered the living room and placed a coin in Jessica's hand.

"There's his wizard-step coin. He didn't leave under his own power," Blackwing said.

"What does it mean?" Cornelius asked Socrates in the *Q'estirian* language.

"It means that Malthuvius and Phelonius are still at large and active. We've been looking for them, and they can still strike at us when they choose."

"Do you know where they went with your...human?"

"He is not '*my human*', and I have no idea. Hopefully, *Irving* will send for me by way of his *K'obi Sha Shin J'oi Faqin T'orqute*. It is the only hope we have of finding him."

6

CALIFORNIA, HERE I COME!

I rving dropped to his hands and knees on the hard roadway and emptied his stomach's contents. The bright sunshine and hot wind caused him to sweat. He tried to look around, but the brightness obscured everything.

Where in the hell am I this time, he thought. *It is strangely quiet to have paved roads.*

"You are Irving Strange, are you not?" someone with a strange accent asked.

Irving failed to see who was talking, "That's the rumor." He shaded his eyes, trying to see who was speaking. "Where am I, and who are you?"

"Where we are is not for you to know, at present. Suffice it to say that I am Phelonius, and I have been led to believe that your family has been the thorn in my side."

"Sorry about that. I know I was transported here by wizard-step, and I know it had to have been a long way. It feels like... Northern California."

"I doubt your contriteness. I was told that you were intelligent, and it is satisfying to know my sources were not entirely wrong. If you are sufficiently recovered, we can proceed."

"Proceed? Proceed where?" Irving asked as he slowly stood.

"Onward, of course."

"Yeah, you're related to Socrates. You talk just like him."

They both disappeared.

The next time Irving materialized, there was a stench in the air. *By the aroma of the air, I'd say we were close to San Francisco,* he thought. His stomach was empty, but it still complained and threatened to empty again.

"Inform me when you are sufficiently recovered to continue," Phelonius said.

"Some water would go a long way to settling my stomach," Irving said, still standing bent over, waiting for his stomach to decide what it was going to do.

"There is no water."

"Can I ask why?" Irving asked.

"Why, what? Why is there no water?"

"Why take me anywhere? You could have taken me somewhere local and questioned me...or whatever."

"I am no fool," Phelonius chuckled mirthlessly. "Any local destination would have given you the chance to let Socrates know where you are. With each jump, we reduce the...possibility of any rescue by Socrates. Your *K'obi Sha Shin J'oi Faqin T'orqute* will not function. We are well beyond its range."

At the mention of his platinum armband, Irving chastised himself for not thinking of it sooner. *I missed the chance I had,* he thought. *I hope I have another.* He touched his band unconsciously.

Cornelius, who had been sitting with Socrates, stood. "Lady *S'hyrlus* and I should be returning. Come, my Lady," he gestured to *S'hyrlus,* who rose to take his arm.

Socrates and Suzanne were shocked into silence and could only stare at their seniors.

Seeing the couple rise, Jessica said, "Oh, hell no! Where do you think you two are going? My husband is missing, and you two ain't going nowhere until he's found." She stood, and her hand went to her holster, which was empty.

Suzanne translated what Jessica had said for Cornelius and *S'hyrlus*.

Blackwing made a gesture that indicated to Suzanne that she should stop translating. A gold coin drifted from his pocket up to his mouth as he stood, and he mumbled something, then the coin flew off toward Jessica.

"Let the coin touch your forehead," he said to Jessica. His sphere drifted toward Jessica. "This is not permanent, but it will allow you to have your say."

The coin touched Jessica's forehead and remained there. The sphere discharged a bright spark at the coin's surface and returned to Blackwing.

"That is brilliant!" Cornelius said in *Q'esterian*.

"What is so brilliant about it?" Jessica asked in a surly tone, in *Q'estirian*.

Suzanne and *S'hyrlus* looked at her in shock.

"I temporarily transferred a portion of the *Q'esterian* language to Jessica," Blackwing explained. "When the coin is removed, she will not understand us anymore. It will fall off in thirty minutes, approximately, if it is not removed."

Jessica rushed out of the room and returned with her pistol in its holster.

"Now then," Jessica said, "Let me reiterate, you two are not going anywhere until my husband is returned. Blackwing and Suzanne have been carrying the load here, and you need to help." Her hand drifted again to the butt of her pistol as Cornelius took another step.

"My Grandson can ask for my assistance any time he needs it. He has my complete confidence and support," Cornelius raved as he stepped closer to the door.

Jessica drew the pistol and pointed it at Cornelius.

"This is ridiculous!" S'hyrlus said derisively. "That weapon will not harm us!" She looked to Socrates expectantly.

"This will not help, Jess," Blackwing said soothingly. "Cornelius and S'hyrlus will help as they are able."

He turned to S'hyrlus; "I would not want to test her weapon or resolve. Her weapon is quite capable...and so is she."

To Jessica, "Irving has the armband I gave him, which means only I can use it to locate him; no one else can. Cornelius can render more assistance once he returns to Q'estiria, and Lady S'hyrlus can do more from her realm than here." He saw the barrel drop a little. "Put it away, Jess. Please?"

Jessica complied as her tears ran silently down her cheeks.

"I know she is distraught currently," S'hyrlus said. "Will she be better?"

Jessica sniffed back her tears. "Distraught? Lady, I am a whole lot more than distraught. I am mad as hell! I know shit flows downhill, but come on! First, it was Suzanne, all because of Blackwing and his private crusade, which then fell on Irv and Trooper. Now, it is back to Irv again. To be frank, I am more than a little tired of it!"

"Who is Frank?" Cornelius asked Socrates in a low, serious tone.

Jessica screamed her frustration to the ceiling with her shaking fists and stormed out.

Blackwing and Suzanne walked with Cornelius and S'hyrlus back to the Oak grove.

"What can we do to help? Your human, Jessica, seems so... upset. I would like to do something to help her," Cornelius said.

"We both would like to help," *S'hyrlus* added.

"I am working on a plan, but there are holes in it," Socrates said. "I believe Malthuvius and Phelonius are on this plane—"

"Why do you believe that?" Cornelius asked.

"Malthuvius and Phelonius are too well known to go this long unidentified in the *Seven Known Planes*," Socrates explained, raising his hand to stop objections. "Yes, they could conceal their identity through spells, potions, and disguises, but that would require them to put more effort into disguises than they are used to. Could they? Yes! Would they? Given that the *Eighth Plane* is basically cleared of humans, on this coast anyway, and they would not need to conceal themselves here, they are here."

Cornelius nodded. "How will you locate them?" he asked.

"Irving has his *K'obi Sha Shin J'oi Faqin T'orqute*," Socrates said. "You understand how they work," he said to Cornelius.

"What about those of us who do not know how they work?" Suzanne interrupted.

Socrates smiled at Suzanne. "If Irving is within two hundred miles, I would know, roughly, where he is and thus where Phelonius is. So, they are outside that range. They are here, along this coastal area where *The Event* happened, so why trigger *The Event*? Because of *The Event*, there is now a huge area cleared of humans with enormous potential for remaining concealed."

"Phelonius will disable his *K'obi Sha Shin J'oi Faqin T'orqute*," *S'hyrlus* said.

"He cannot," Cornelius interjected. "Tactically, the best he can hope for is to keep his prize outside the maximum distance and try to convince this human that trying to activate his *T'orqute* would be useless. Could he be convinced?"

Blackwing shook his head slowly. "It would depend on his level of disheartenment. He has only recently been returned to his wife, as you know. He has been told, many times, to tap it, and I would come. Phelonius would tell him falsehoods to maintain control. I do not know how long he could hold out against the onslaught from Malthuvius and Phelonius."

"If there is something that I can do to help, you have to but ask," Cornelius said.

"I could use more guards to protect the residence at this stage," Blackwing said. "I must do what I can to locate Irving, which will mean a lot of travel."

"When you find them, let me know, and I will send enough of our brothers to keep him cordoned off," Cornelius offered.

"Your efforts are appreciated, but he would escape by the time your forces would arrive. When you return to *Q'estiria*, sending more of our brothers would be a significant amount of support."

"If you need me," *S'hyrlus* offered, "I can help with transporting or communications. I am more than happy to help any way I can; just keep that deranged female away from me."

"She is not deranged," Suzanne defended. "She is hurt and in pain; most of it is emotional, but pain nonetheless."

Both Blackwing and Suzanne smiled and waved as their elders entered the vortex.

When Blackwing and Suzanne returned to the house, he stopped long enough to post one of the guards in the oak grove and called the rest to the main house.

Suzanne entered the house and called Jessica to the Livingroom, and they were joined shortly after by Blackwing and the guards,

"I need to know," Blackwing began, speaking *Q'estirian*, with Suzanne interpreting for Jessica, "how is it possible for Malthuvius, or Phelonius, to enter this house and spirit Irving away without raising any alarms?"

There was a general murmuring amongst the guards.

"It should not be possible," Blackwing continued, "at least I would have believed it would not be possible, but someone managed, somehow. Does anyone have any ideas on how that could happen?"

No one said anything.

"Since no one will speak, I will investigate, starting with the wards. I want the last three people who monitored the wards to follow me."

His body position told everyone of his anger as he left the house.

Blackwing hadn't gone far in his property circuit when he found the hole in the wards' protective shield.

"Who was the last person to check here?" he asked angrily.

No one spoke.

"By your silence, you have told me that all three of you need to be returned to *Q'esteria*. If I cannot trust—"

Blackwing was interrupted by the sound of two swords being unsheathed. As he turned to face the pair, he heard another sword drawn. When he looked, he saw that B'runix Horns-doodle had drawn his sword and interposed his body between the two attackers and Blackwing.

"I bring you to my home, feed you, shelter you, and this is how you show your appreciation?" Blackwing asked. He placed a hand on Hornsdoodle's shoulder and stepped closer to the pair. "Is your honor for sale for so little?"

Jessica sat in the living room for some time after Blackwing left the house. When her impatience drove her to action, she decided to go to her room. Suzanne followed her with her eyes.

As she closed the door quietly, she started to turn and felt something begin to touch her shoulder. She drew her pistol and fired three shots in quick succession in one, smooth, blurringly fast motion.

When the two guards heard the pistol reports, they turned towards the house. In that instant, Blackwing brandished his staff and struck the two guards' wrists, disarming them.

"Hornsdoodle, manacle them and prepare them for transport back to *Q'esteria*," he commanded. Once Hornsdoodle had the pair secured, he trotted towards the house.

When Suzanne heard the pistol reports, she ran towards Jessica's room, slamming the door open. She saw a Q'esterian lying on the floor at the door, arms crossed across his chest, groaning.

"Jessica! Why did you shoot him?" she yelled.

"Why?" Jessica said, eyes glancing towards Suzanne, "Why not? He was waiting in my room and tried to grab me after I shut the door."

"Who is he?" Suzanne asked, her own heart pounding.

"How the hell would I know?" Jessica asked. "They don't speak English, and I don't speak their lingo."

Blackwing finally reached the door to Jessica's room and shouldered his way past Suzanne. Suzanne saw his face change from concern to a smirk.

"Well, what do you know? How are you doing, Malthuvius?" he asked.

After placing manacles on his wrists, Malthuvius was dumped, unceremoniously, into one of the over-stuffed chairs, in the living room. Blackwing, two of the Q'esterian guards, Suzanne, and Jessica, encircled him.

"Explain yourself, Malthuvius," Blackwing bellowed. "Why are you in this house, and why were you in Jessica's room?"

Malthuvius glared back at the group arrayed around him but remained silent, continuing to protect his ribs.

"You should be thankful that your clothing protected your body from the puncturing Jessica's pistol is capable of," Suzanne added soothingly.

Jessica stepped forward and grabbed the front of Malthuvius' duster and pulled him toward her face. She put the barrel of the pistol under his chin. "I still want to check how bullet-proof his skull is," she said in English as she cocked the weapon.

"Now, Jess," Blackwing said soothingly. "Give him a chance to answer, and then I may consider your offer."

Even though Blackwing was speaking English, Malthuvius understood and glared at him.

"Does he understand English?" Suzanne asked, shaking her head.

"Oh, he understands, alright," Jessica sneered as she started to turn away and then spun back to strike his face with the side of the gun's barrel. "He spoke it just fine when he tortured me! The time I spent in the hospital was just so much fun," she said sarcastically.

Malthuvius struggled to maintain consciousness. Blood seeped from the corner of his mouth, and Blackwing could see the start of the massive bruise that would dominate the side of his face for a long time.

"How did you subdue him?" Suzanne asked Jessica. "His clothing, like mine, resists cutting and punctures."

"True enough," Jessica responded. "While training for the P.D., we had to wear, what they call a bullet-proof vest, and take a hit from a round. It hurt like hell; sometimes, I still feel it. I figured out a while ago that if your clothing is bullet-proof or bullet-resistant, I doubted the makers would consider the needed kinetic energy absorption and dissipation, especially if they're unfamiliar with firearms."

Blackwing looked at her with the look of someone trying hard to understand.

"The next time you get the opportunity," Jessica explained, "place your duster over a melon, pull out your sword and try to penetrate the duster. I'll bet you have a cracked and broken melon, not to mention the mess inside your duster, even though your sword doesn't penetrate." She nodded towards Malthuvius. "I'd say he has several cracked or broken ribs, tremendous bruising if nothing else."

"Are those life-threatening?" Blackwing asked.

"They can be," Jessica answered. "He needs to be tended by someone knowledgeable of his anatomy."

As if called, B'runix Hornsdoodle entered the room and stood quietly.

"Ah, B'runix," Blackwing said, "make ready to transport prisoners to Q'esteria. I, and Lady Suzanne, will accompany them. I want the rest of the guards to re-enforce the wards and seal Jessica's suite to prevent further intrusions."

"Might I ask, sir," Hornsdoodle asked, "what happened to Malthuvius?"

Blackwing smirked, "Jessica happened."

Irving sat and tapped his platinum armband absent-mindedly with his finger. *At least it is cool here,* Irving thought. *Dark and cool and a thousand miles from anywhere. At least I'm not imprisoned, but I am being held. I can go anywhere, but what does that profit me? I'd have to walk to Tacoma.* He looked around again. He was in a lower-level parking garage in San Diego or L.A.; he didn't know which.

The trip south had been long and arduous, with his stomach complaining the entire way. He'd been deposited on the street a few days ago, which was the last he'd seen of Phelonius. He had managed to scrounge some water and a few cans of food. He'd found some scrap wood to burn, but that hadn't lasted long, not even a night, and the nights were cold.

Maybe I should start to move anything I find down here, he thought. *Is it possible that I can find a vehicle? It would have to be gas-powered; an electric vehicle would be impractical. Would I be allowed to drive north? Possible. Phelonius may not know how our vehicles work. If I tell him I need it to survive here, for gathering food and water...maybe.*

He knew he would have to venture out again for water, food, and anything he could find to burn to generate some heat.

I might get lucky and find a Sporting Goods store to loot, he thought. *Some camping gear and lanterns, a camp stove, or even some dried food.* He felt himself start to smile as these thoughts filled him with the hope that he'd survive.

"It is time for us to have a chat," Phelonius said from somewhere close. Irving felt the smile, and the hope, leave him.

Blackwing, Suzanne, the three prisoners, and two guards were in the Oak grove. Blackwing, speaking *Q'esterian*, was giving him his final instructions.

"B'runix, do what you can to keep Jessica away from the alcohol. Try to distract her by teaching her *Q'esterian*. She can, in turn, teach you English." He saw Hornsdoodle about to interrupt, but he raised his hand. "I know you already have a working knowledge of the language, but she can teach you to read it and speak it." He looked at the single silver ring in Hornsdoodle's braid. "I have come to rely on you. I will be discussing your promotion with Cornelius while I am there."

With a nod from Blackwing, Suzanne opened the portal to *Q'esteria*. Hornsdoodle watched them all step through. When Suzanne entered the vortex, the portal closed.

7

BUILDING TENSIONS

P helonius transported Irving, via wizard-step, into a large, carpeted room. Irving could see out the large, polarized window onto the roofs of many lower buildings, but he could not see the ocean. He knew, from the smell, though, that it was close. He could see several taller buildings, none of which he recognized.

"Pretty posh for an interrogation cell," Irving said as he looked around the room.

"What is interrogation?" Phelonius asked. "I do not know what you mean. I had a conversation in mind when I asked you here."

"You...*asked* me here?" Irving asked skeptically. "Interrogation is a tactic used by law enforcement, or the military, of which you are both, as I understand it. The goal is to elicit useful information by establishing rapport, torture, or other means."

"Why would you believe I would torture you?" Phelonius asked without facing Irving.

"Oh? So, I can leave anytime I want?"

"Leave? Why would you wish to leave? This is such a quiet, peaceful place."

9

Irving looked at Phelonius' reflection in the transparent aluminum window and saw the smirk on his face.

"So, I can't leave," Irving said.

"You leaving would be contrary to the purpose for which I brought you here."

"And what *purpose* would that be?"

Before Phelonius answered, Irving saw his captor check his sphere, the look of self-complacency slowly disappeared.

"Bad news?" Irving asked, smirking.

Jessica was pacing the living room. "Where the hell are they?" she shouted, raising her hands to the ceiling.

B'runix Hornsdoodle, sitting in the chair often occupied by Irving, was paging through a book. "It has been two days," he said, looking over the top of cover. "I doubt they have arrived yet. Patience." His attention returned to the pages.

"Patience?" Jessica asked. "That's your advice? My husband is out there," she gestured to the walls, "somewhere, and you tell me to be patient!" She turned her back on B'runix and crossed her arms. After several seconds, her pacing resumed.

"Your scrolls fascinate me," Hornsdoodle said as he continued to turn the pages. "Are these separate scrolls? Or are they all one scroll?"

"What are you talking about?" Jessica asked, irritated. "It's a book, and it has pages; there is no scroll. Besides, you're holding it upside down." She walked over, took the book, and rotated it before putting it back in his hands.

"Fascinating," Hornsdoodle said slowly, stretching the syllables, as he rotated the book back to its original position. "These are what you use to impart your wisdom?"

"In some cases, yes," Jessica said. "Not all books impart wisdom, and some exist just for reading enjoyment, for some people. Can't we go searching for Irv? I'm getting tired of waiting."

"Reading...the art of deciphering these...runes."

Jessica laughed. "I wouldn't call it an art."

"What *would* you call it?" Hornsdoodle asked.

"A pain in the ass. A tool. A way to waste time, to me, anyway. I hate reading."

"Interesting," Hornsdoodle said as he turned a few more pages. "Is it true that the Lady Suzanne was a human?"

"Yes, she was," Jessica answered.

"As a human, what was it she did? What was her purpose?"

"She bought and sold books."

"Did she like this...reading?"

"I would think so."

"And Irving, did he enjoy...reading?"

"Probably, but he's a geek," Jessica said. "And they aren't runes. What you see on the pages are letters and words. The letters go together to form words. Words form sentences. It's how we pass on ideas, thoughts, and feelings."

"Your words...are partially understood," Hornsdoodle said, shaking his head slightly, a puzzled look on his face.

She took the book from him and got her tablet. "This is an 'A'," she said, selecting the letter.

It had been two weeks, as best Irving could figure, and he was, for the first time, exiting a shower. He had been surprised to see that the spacious room Phelonius had transported him to was a hotel room.

The hot water was glorious, he thought. *It was nice to get cleaned up after being in the parking garage for so long. It was also nice to be safe from any animals that might be rooting around. The downside is being more confined. Phelonius still hasn't given me a clue about what he's planning. There has to be a method to his madness.*

Irving went to the kitchenette across the room when he'd finished in the bathroom. *When Phelonius had left, I explored and found this room across the hall and, for privacy, use it for housing. I tried the elevator, but I can't access it or the stairs without a room key. The stairs would be a long climb. I tried to open the window, no such luck, and I tried to see the bottom floor from the window and failed to see it. I even tried all the rooms on this floor, and all the doors were locked. Not sure if that's a good thing. They could've been occupied at the time of The Event; not sure I'd like to deal with a body or three.*

His stomach growled again, and he rubbed it. He had found some minor amounts of food, but it wasn't enough.

"It is time for us to chat," Phelonius said from the doorway. Irving had left the door open, thinking he was the only one on the floor.

Irving took a deep breath and turned to face Phelonius. "You want to talk, and I want to eat. You go off leaving me here without a means for me to get food or leave this floor."

"This room was not to your liking?" Phelonius asked.

"The room is fine," Irving said, "but I need food. I tried the elevator, and I don't have what I need to activate it. It takes a room key, and I'd get one if I were registered, to get it to work."

"And what would access to this…elevator do for you?"

"It would allow me to go outside, to forage for food and other supplies, and it would allow me to secure the building."

"Secure it…against whom?" Phelonius asked.

"Secure it against anyone that still lives and comes upon this building. Secure it against vermin, rats, raccoons, that sort of thing.

Secure it against any of your beasties that may be roaming around. I'd sleep better knowing those things won't eat me in the middle of the night."

"But that would allow you to escape," Phelonius said.

"Escape? Why would I need to escape if I'm not a prisoner?" Irving asked.

"We're home," Blackwing bellowed as he entered the back door with Suzanne in his wake. The house was quiet.

"Jess must be out walking around the property," Suzanne said around his back. "We've been gone for three weeks." Suzanne shook her head. "Poor Jess. She must be out of her mind with the waiting."

"Might I enter?" *S'hyrlus* asked from the opened back door.

Blackwing and Suzanne both cleared a path for *S'hyrlus* to enter. Following close behind her was a newcomer. Suzanne stared as she followed the stranger with her eyes. They both followed the two Hamadryads into the living room.

"This," *S'hyrlus* said, indicating her companion, "is the Lady *Dar'Kyn*.

"We welcome you both to our home," Suzanne said, bowing slightly.

"What is Lady *Dar'Kyn's* purpose?" Blackwing asked *S'hyrlus*.

"Her purpose," *S'hyrlus* said, "is to free Suzanne to travel with you and be able to keep me apprised of the results of your search. I am planning to be with Cornelius, in *Q'estiria*, to keep him apprised as well."

"We just arrived, and, after some nourishment and the replenishment of my brothers, I will assign a few guards to Suzanne as we travel." Blackwing scowled. "Phelonius is for me, and I will deal with him myself. I will not allow others to intercede."

"Is your…human staying here while you are gone?" *S'hyrlus* asked.

"Jessica is not *our human*, mother," Blackwing explained. "She is not a pet. She is *K'obi Sha Shin J'oi Faqin*, as is her mate."

"Yes," *S'hyrlus* said dismissively, looking around, "so you have said. Whatever your plan is, I am offering *Dar'Kyn* to your crusade; another asset is always good."

"Come, *Dar'Kyn*," Suzanne said, walking toward the hallway. "I will find you a room to use while you are here."

Dar'Kyn dropped to one knee as Suzanne approached her and dropped her gaze. "Thankful I am, sister, for the hospitality and to be in the presence of one such as you."

After taking *Dar'Kyn*'s hands in hers, Suzanne knelt and raised her to her feet. "I am as you are. There is no need to show your appreciation in this manner. Just treat all here with respect, and all will be well."

As Suzanne was about to leave with *Dar'Kyn*, Jessica returned with Hornsdoodle in tow.

"What is this," Jessica bellowed, "a party? Well, I'll not be attending any parties while my husband is missing. And what is this?" she said, *Dar'Kyn* coming under her scrutiny. "Is *she* trying to look like you, Suzanne? Her hair is a darker auburn than yours, and her face a little longer, but all-in-all, she looks like your twin. Not much differentiation in that realm either, I see."

Suzanne scowled at Jessica. "Be nice," she started in English. "Jess, this is *Dar'Kyn*. She'll be spending some time with us while we locate Irv. She *is* part of the effort."

Jessica came over to *Dar'Kyn*. "I'm Jessica. Jessica Strange," she said, offering her hand dourly.

Suzanne started, "I'm not sure—"

"*Dar'Kyn...Trubis*," *Dar'Kyn* interrupted, "but you can call me Dar if that would be easier."

Everyone stared, mouths agape as they slowly turned toward *S'hyrlus*, confused.

"Oh, I am sorry; did I forget to mention *Dar'Kyn* speaks your language?" *S'hyrlus* said, answering everyone's unasked question.

Suzanne had gone out for a short walk after eating. A few guards followed her, as did *Dar'Kyn*.

"What was the purpose of addressing me that way?" Suzanne asked in the language of the Hamadryads, knowing no one else could understand them.

"You were the first in a long time," Dar responded.

"The first?"

"The first to become. It has been a long time, 200 years, I think, since a human has become," Dar answered.

"And how did you become?" Suzanne asked.

"I did not become. I was born to the *Sh'o Sook J'eid*."

"Born? How could you be born to something like the Hamadryad? None are born Hamadryad."

"Not in the way you are used to using that term," Dar answered. "I was...called forth, brought into being, by the Great Elm. On the other hand, you were born human and had to go through *The Becoming* to be Hamadryad. My queen/sister tasked me to help *S'hyrlus* and Blackwing because of their kindness in the past."

"That doesn't explain the bow," Suzanne said.

Dar'Kyn looked off into the distance while leaning against a small tree, "To the Hamadryad, the act of *Becoming* is something sacred. It stems from a conscious choice, in your case, to sacrifice what you are for someone else without expectations. That is an act the rest of the Hamadryad wish they had been given. Although, I think some would be surprised that they would take a pass on the sacrifice. By bowing to you as I did, I expressed my...veneration of you and your choice."

B'runix Hornsdoodle had been observing Suzanne and *Dar'Kyn*. True to their nature, the Hamadryads ignored his presence and carried on their conversation with no concern for being overheard.

When Suzanne left to return to the house, B'runix cleared his throat.

STEPHEN DRAKE

"B'runix Hornsdoodle, is it not?" *Dar'Kyn* asked in *Q'estirian*.

"Yes, it is. What has brought you to this realm?" Horns-doodle asked.

"My Queen bid me come and help *S'hyrlus*. How is it you are here?"

"I was commanded to be...here," Hornsdoodle sneered. "To help the ambassador in this...human plane."

"Your tone betrays your displeasure."

"As it should."

"You disagree with your superiors in this?" Dar asked.

"I do as ordered," Hornsdoodle replied stiffly.

Dar'Kyn turned to look at him. "In all the years I have known you, I have never heard you speak thus. Is it these humans that cause you to struggle within?" she asked.

Hornsdoodle turned his back on Dar, "If it were left to me, I would let them have this *Plane* and restrict them here. None from the *Seven* need ever venture here."

Dar'Kyn sighed. "I see your point. It is difficult to understand the reasoning of those above us."

"I read something in one of their books that explains it some-what. I do not get to blow the whistle, nor can I ring the bell, but let this train jump the track and see who catches hell."

Dar looked puzzled. "What is this train, and what is hell that you can catch? Is it something contagious?" she asked.

"I am at a loss to understand it all," Hornsdoodle said, "but I am trying. The first time I read it, I was as confused as you are. The more I observe, the more I think I understand."

"It seems that my associate, Malthuvius Nighthawk, is in poor health," Phelonius said.

"Oh? What a shame," Irving said, suppressing a grin without looking up from the desk. He was trying to get the Hotel's guest computer up and running. "And how, exactly, did you hear this bit of news?"

Phelonius looked at him. "I have my ways. It seems your mate had something to do with his...accident."

"Jess had something to do with an accident?" Irving looked stern. "If she was involved, it was no accident."

Phelonius exhaled in exasperation. "It seems he has been injured quite severely. He was taken to *Q'estiria* by Socrates to be healed. According to the report, he was trying to apprehend your mate." He looked to Irving to see the reaction.

Irving chuckled as he typed. "Sounds about right. Anyone trying to grab her will get a rude awakening. She's not one to be trifled with. She has a big gun, and she ain't afeared to use it, pardner."

"That is what I have heard as well," Phelonius said quietly.

Irving grinned. "I suppose he'll thank you for his injuries."

"Why would he do that?" Phelonius asked.

"You sent him, didn't you?" Irving asked.

Phelonius exhaled loudly. "No. The idea of apprehending your mate was Malthuvius'. I did not condone it or advise it."

Irving laughed. "So, he screwed the pooch again? You gotta love it!"

Phelonius looked perplexed. "I do not understand the idiom 'screwed the pooch'. Please explain."

Irving laughed harder. "No, I don't think I will."

"So, how are things with the *ambassador*?" Smith asked Trooper. The two were meeting to discuss Trooper's future.

Trooper set his scotch down carefully. "I'm not at liberty to say. And I believe it is none of your concern."

Smith finished his drink and held up his hand. "I wasn't trying to be nosey. I was just trying to make conversation. Given any thought to my proposal?"

"I'm leaning toward agreeing," Trooper said.

Smith was shocked. His mouth dropped open, and he seemed to freeze with his glass in the air. "Agree? With which part?" he said finally.

"I think either mayor or chief of police would suit me, as long as I get to pick who is under me."

"I need to run it by the front office, but I think they would agree with that. Do you have anyone in mind?" Smith asked.

"At some point, I would like Jessica to work with me," Trooper said. "She has some things to work out first, but I think she would be a nice fit."

"I'm thinking the same thing," Smith said absentmindedly and suggestively.

Trooper stood, took the last swallow of his drink, and caught Smith with a nice roundhouse right, knocking him off his chair. "You keep your lurid thoughts out of our conversations," Trooper said as he shook his right hand and flexed his fingers to regain feeling. "If you don't, I may have to flatten you again. And if this incident puts the kibosh on our negotiations, I don't care. In my opinion, you need me a lot more than I need you."

B'runix Hornsdoodle stood quietly before Socrates Blackwing as Socrates was reading a scroll. He exhaled loudly and rubbed his eye.

"As I said before I left, I have come to rely on you, B'runix. I spent some time with Cornelius, and he agreed that you deserved a promotion." Blackwing dropped his hand to his lap. "Our discussions became quite heated as to the level of that promotion. Since he is my immediate superior, his judgment prevailed. Congratulations. You are promoted one rank. Sorry, I think it should have been more."

"Yes, sir. Thank you, sir. Will that be all, sir?" Hornsdoodle asked stoically.

"Not quite, B'runix. I wish to inform you that you are not properly attired." Socrates smiled. "Do you mind?"

"Not at all, sir."

Socrates passed his hand toward Hornsdoodle, and the single silver band became two silver bands.

"Thank you, sir," B'runix said.

"Dismissed."

Hornsdoodle turned smartly and left the room.

Blackwing made a note in his daily report of the promotion of B'runix Hornsdoodle.

"Are you ever going to tell me why I'm here?" Irving asked Phelonius. "It's been five weeks, at least, and I still don't know why I'm here."

Phelonius smirked. "Why do *you* think I brought you here? You thought interrogation, your definition of interrogation, not mine, was the reason. Was it?"

"It doesn't appear to be the reason," Irving answered skeptically.

"It occurred to me that you knew me through the eyes of Socrates. I brought you here to show you that I am not the villain my grandson has made me out to be."

"So, what am I supposed to be, your publicist?" Irving asked sarcastically.

"I do not know what that is. I brought you here to see for yourself that I am not the villain. If you think about it, until I entered the picture, you thought wizards were fiction. Multiple Planes was just a theory. Having a mate was for someone else, not for you."

"And people I liked were destroyed and are gone forever," Irving piped in when it seemed that Phelonius had wound down.

8

THE SEARCH BEGINS

B lackwing, Suzanne, and Jessica were leaning over the table, papers strewn on the surface, when *Dar'Kyn* and B'runix Hornsdoodle entered through the back door.

"What are they trying to determine?" *Dar'Kyn* whispered in *Q'estirian*.

"I think they are trying to determine the best way to search for their Irving," Hornsdoodle responded quietly.

"Is the area to be searched so large?" *Dar'Kyn* asked.

"One would not think so, but my knowledge of this Plane is limited," Hornsdoodle said.

Dar'Kyn shook her head slowly. "This *Irving* human must be important to expend this amount of energy just to locate him."

"He is a personage of some importance, to those three, anyway," Hornsdoodle responded. "Also, it is theorized that Phelonius is with him. Phelonius *is* important to locate."

Dar'Kyn took up a position slightly behind and between Jessica and Suzanne. B'runix stood between Blackwing and Suzanne. Both observed and listened to the dialog.

"This country is large," Jessica said. "Where do you plan to start searching?"

"I've only been in the Tacoma area. What should I expect?" Blackwing asked.

Jessica produced a graphic on an electronic pad. "This," she started, "is the area affected, as best as we can figure, by *The Event* caused by Phelonius."

"What are these darker lines?" Blackwing pointed to the screen.

"Those are the State borderlines," Suzanne said. "As close as Jess and I can figure, the affected area in Pacific-Coast Washington is roughly 25,000 square miles," she said, indicating the area she was describing. "Pacific-Coast Oregon, approximately 30,000 square miles, and Pacific-Coast California, approximately 82,000 square miles."

"As you know from living here," Jessica said, "PC Washington is rather wet. The further south you travel towards PC Cali, the climate becomes warmer and dryer. By the time you get to the southern-most part of PC Cali, it is close to desert conditions."

"Jessica and I are assuming," Suzanne said, "that Phelonius is within *The Event* area else why cause *The Event*? If he is outside that area, it becomes increasingly less likely that you will find Irving."

"Knowing Phelonius," Blackwing said, "he is within the affected area, and there is a high probability that he is in PC California. He does prefer a warmer, dryer climate."

"And if he is not?" Hornsdoodle asked. "For all we know, he could be in town, north of here, or anywhere inside the affected area."

"For those of us who don't understand their function," Jessica said, "How do the *K'obi Sha Shin J'oi Faqin T'orqute* work?"

Blackwing glared when he caught Hornsdoodle rolling his eyes in an all-too-human response to Jessica's question.

"As I told you when I gave them to you," Blackwing explained, "once you tap the *K'obi Sha Shin J'oi Faqin T'orqute* three times, I am alerted via my sphere. What I didn't tell you is that I am the only one able to reset them once you tap them."

"But Phelonius would know that and would remove it from Irving's arm," Jessica said. "Then what?"

"As long as you wear it, the *K'obi Sha Shin J'oi Faqin T'orqute* is powered by you, using your life-force," Blackwing said. "Should Irving remove it, Phelonius can't remove one given by someone else, and he had tapped it, it will continue to...transmit, would be the closest term, and I can still locate it."

"For how long?" Jessica asked, not sure if she wanted to hear the answer.

"It would eventually drain after being removed, but I would be able to locate it after five years," Blackwing said. "True, it does fade, but it would take a long time to fade to nothing, ten years maybe."

Jessica seemed to cheer a little.

"As long as Irving remembers to tap it," Hornsdoodle added. Blackwing, Suzanne, and Jessica glared at him. "Phelonius is no fool. He knows that you are aware of his preferences and, tactically, he should go somewhere you wouldn't suspect."

"Tactically, you could be correct," Blackwing said. "If information were his goal, he would do that. I'm not sure that information is his goal. It could be something else."

"What else could be his purpose of absconding with your Irving?" *Dar'Kyn* asked innocently.

"I wish I knew," Blackwing said softly, "I wish I knew."

"Hornsdoodle was testing my patience," Suzanne said as Socrates looked around the early morning scenery. They had left the following day after the table discussion.

"He wasn't out of line," Blackwing said. His attention

seemed, to Suzanne, divided. "He was pointing out the weaknesses in our plan. It is part of his duties to present alternate theories. He wasn't trying to hurt Jessica's feelings."

"It was difficult to keep my temper," Suzanne said. "Where are we, and what are you looking at?"

"We're a fair piece north of Seattle," Blackwing said. "By looking all around, I'm looking for a signal from Irving's *K'obi Sha Shin J'oi Faqin T'orqute*." He tapped his eyepatch. "This is tied to my sphere and will give me direction if the signal is present."

As Suzanne looked around, she could see the Sound in the distance. "What are you going to do about the Olympic Peninsula?" she asked.

"What is the Olympic Peninsula?" Socrates said, still scanning.

"It is land on the other side of Puget Sound and goes to the Pacific Ocean," Suzanne said. "Since you can't wizard-step across large amounts of water, we can't get there from here."

"Where *can* we cross?" Socrates asked.

"When we turn south again, we can cross to the Peninsula a little south of Olympia."

"How big is *Puget Sound*?"

"I'm not certain. I know that residents and visitors traveled it with huge ships that floated on the water. Where we are, the Sound is wide. It narrows the further south we travel."

"More delays!" Socrates spat. "It can't be helped. I'd rather eliminate the possibility of Phelonius being in the north than ignore it and not be sure."

"There are no guarantees that Irving tapped his *K'obi Sha Shin J'oi Faqin T'orqute*."

"True, but I'd rather be doing something than doing nothing. Irving deserves the best we can do."

Dar'Kyn and Hornsdoodle stood behind Jessica, B'runix's arms crossed on his chest. Socrates and Suzanne had just left. Jessica was still watching the spot where they had disappeared.

"What is she doing?" Hornsdoodle whispered in *Q'estirian.*

"She is wishing that she was going with Socrates and Suzanne," *Dar'Kyn* said. "It is not an easy thing to wait. Sometimes, the imagination plays on the mind with all of the unspoken fears."

"What can be done to ameliorate her despondency?" Hornsdoodle asked.

Dar'Kyn's eyes narrowed as she turned to look at Hornsdoodle. "Nothing can be done, but the waiting." She continued to look at him. "You almost sound as if you were concerned. That is out of character for your kind."

"Forgive me for leaving you with that impression," Hornsdoodle said. "I was looking for a way to improve her mood. It is exhausting to watch these...these *humans* when they are so..." he stopped, shaking his head.

Dar'Kyn exhaled loudly. "I understand."

Jessica was still focused on the spot where Blackwing and Suzanne were standing. *Finally,* she thought. *The search has finally started. I was beginning to think they'd never start. My poor Irving, out there, somewhere. What is Phelonius doing to him? Why was he taken? I expected one of them to try for me, but why Irving? In many respects, Irving is an innocent. Why did it take Blackwing so long to get motivated? Irv is his friend, too. I'd think he'd be chomping at the bit to get Irving.*

Jessica turned and walked back to the house. She didn't notice *Dar'Kyn* and B'runix fall into step behind her as she passed them.

When Jessica entered the house, she gathered her electronic tablet and sat at the table.

"B'runix, can I get your help?" Jessica asked, motioning him to a chair.

"I will if I can," B'runix said as he seated himself.

"Close your eyes and imagine you are Phelonius," Jessica said. "What would motivate you to take Irving? What would be the purpose of it?"

"I...I do not understand what you want," B'runix said.

"What part don't you understand?" Jessica asked.

"*Imagine*? What is *imagine*?" B'runix asked.

"Hmmm...," Jessica paused. "The word '*Imagine*' is defined in many different ways. I want you to form a mental image of being Phelonius. Try to think as he does. He is *T'et Faqin Q'estirian*, as you are. I can't imagine what he would want with Irving, so I'm asking you, as a *Q'estirian*, what could be the reason?"

B'runix stared stoically at Jessica for a while before he spoke. "No one can think like someone else. To you, we may all look alike, but we are not the same. I am offended that you fail to see our...individuality."

Jessica pulled her hand down her face in frustration and took a deep breath. "Calm down," she said after exhaling loudly. "I meant no offense. What is your function here?"

"You know perfectly well what my function is," Hornsdoodle said peevishly. "Security, personal as well as grounds."

Jessica perked up. "When you inspect a building, how do you determine where to place the barriers to make it more secure?"

Jessica sat and patiently listened while Hornsdoodle explained, in painful detail, everything he knew about securing a facility or a person. However, he did not hint at or state that he "imagined" or "tried to get inside" someone else's head.

Jessica said after a long pause, "You are *Q'estirian*." Hornsdoodle nodded. "Just as Phelonius is *Q'estirian*." He nodded again. "Why would he take Irving?"

"I have no idea why," Hornsdoodle said, "Why are you

insisting that I know what Phelonius thinks? I have no idea what he thinks or how he arrives at his decisions." Hornsdoodle paused and glared at Jessica. "Frankly, I do not care what you think, or even if you think. I do not like you or your kind and dislike this *Plane*." He stood to go. "Do not leave this building. My brothers will prevent it." He scowled at Jessica and left the house.

Jessica was dumbfounded. Her mouth hung open, not believing that anyone would talk to her with such disdain. "What the hell just happened?" she asked. "Was it something I said?"

"I-I do not know," *Dar'Kyn* stammered as she sat heavily. "As a general rule, B'runix is far more tolerant. In all the years I have known him, I have never heard him talk so…disrespectfully."

Jessica, the first to recover, stood and went to the kitchen for a drink. She started to pour and stopped herself, thought better of it, and set everything back on the counter. She went to the kitchen door and tried to open it. The door refused to budge.

Jessica's profanity assaulted *Dar'Kyn's* ears as she passed her on the way to the front door. It refused to open as well. She stepped to the side of the door and tried one of the windows. Nothing seemed to open.

Jessica returned to the dining room and stood behind one of the empty chairs.

"Nothing opens," Jessica fumed. "We're trapped in here."

"Are you sure?" *Dar'Kyn* asked as she stood and went to the back door. It opened easily for her, but as she stepped out, one of the guards stationed at the back door stepped into the kitchen, *Dar'Kyn* stepping under his raised arm.

When *Dar'Kyn* exited the door, the guard followed her, closing the door behind him.

Dar'Kyn sought out B'runix. She found him in his office in the barn.

"What are you doing?" *Dar'Kyn* asked as she entered.

B'runix stood and closed his office door. "I am trying to fulfill my duties with as little frustration for myself as possible," he said, his back to her.

"You accomplish this by imprisoning her inside her house?" *Dar'Kyn* asked.

B'runix turned to face her. He saw her flashing eyes; her hair had more flame color than a few minutes before. "She is not... normal. How can someone be inside someone else's head? I answered her questions, but she refused to accept my responses. She was insinuating that I am Phelonius, or his twin."

Dar'Kyn glared. "She is distraught at the absence of this Irving. To her, she fails to understand the why. After a brief exposure to her, I can tell she will not let it continue without trying to solve it. To her, it is all a puzzle to be solved. Your response to her was extreme and unacceptable."

"Unacceptable...to whom?" B'runix glared at *Dar'Kyn*.

"What will happen when Socrates hears of this, which he certainly will?" she asked.

"From you? The *ambassador*," B'runix spat, "left me in command during his absence. As the commander, I decided to keep this...*human* confined...for her safety."

"Not from me. Probably from Jessica via Suzanne. For how long?" *Dar'Kyn* asked.

B'runix turned his back to her to look out the window and waited for many seconds. "She is...an *irritant*. She will be confined until such time as she stops being an irritant."

"It appears to me that you do not like this Plane," *Dar'Kyn* said. "I tend to agree with you, to a point. The residents on this Plane were better behaved 3,000 years ago...or thereabouts...I become confused with the amount of time passed since I was last here."

"You spoke correctly. I grow weary of this Plane. I would be content to return to the *original Seven Planes*," B'runix said.

"*Original*...how do you know *this* Plane is not part of the original? Do you have any particular information that is not available to our learned contemporaries?" *Dar'Kyn* asked.

"*Learned* contemporaries," B'runix sneered. "Nothing *learned* about them. There is an idiom here that seems to fit, 'educated idiots', I think it is. But to answer your inquiry, no, I do not have knowledge others do not have. To my mind, there are only *Seven Known Planes*. This one is not worth the losses we have had here. These...*humans* are not worth having around. *P'koosh F'aeul* every one."

"I disagree. I think I am starting to get used to Jessica, and Suzanne began as a human here. There are very few worthy ones, but a significant number," *Dar'Kyn* said. "What are you going to do about this...*situation* you find yourself in?"

B'runix quickly glanced to the door. "I will do my duty, as I see it, until the *ambassador* returns."

Dar'Kyn nodded and left the office. Once outside the office, she strolled to the house and was allowed entry by the guard at the back door.

As she entered the house, Dar saw Jessica pacing across the living room. She was wearing her holster.

"I was able to speak to Hornsdoodle," Dar said, eyeing the impressive bit of iron at home in the holster.

"And what did Mister Asshat have to say?" Jessica asked calmly.

"He has informed me that he finds you irritating." Dar looked at Jessica's grin.

"And what, pray tell, is the length of my incarceration?" Jessica asked. Her hand drifted to the pistol's handle and rested there.

"You are to remain inside the house until B'runix determines that you are no longer an irritant."

"He's in for a very long wait," Jessica said. She pulled the pistol and spun the cylinder before placing it in the holster. "He sticks his nose inside the house, and you'll need to return him to wherever they took Malthuvius." She paused for a few seconds. "Or you can leave him here to suffer. Either is fine by me."

Dar'Kyn looked around the house and saw no sign that Jessica, as she called it, had been chatting with Jack.

"How are you going to get out of here?" Dar asked.

"Any way I can," Jessica said. "When he locked me in here, he cut off the *Q'estirian's* food supply."

"I would not count on that," *Dar'Kyn* said. "*Q'estirian's* are notoriously patient and are known to have their own supplies. True, they are cut off from the human food they had become used to, but they have access to their own foodstuffs."

Jessica scowled at *Dar'Kyn*. "Whose side are you on, Dar? The time has come for you to pick a side. Until today, I would've thought B'runix, and the rest of the *Q'estirians*, were on our side, but now, I'm not so sure."

"I am as surprised at B'runix's attitude as you are," *Dar'Kyn* said. "Given that, I was sent by *S'hyrlus* to assist Socrates and Suzanne in their quest for Irving. I was not sent to, as you say, 'Pick a side'."

Jessica, still scowling, said, "I understand the difference. Can I at least count on you not to run to B'runix and his charges? Can you keep things I say to yourself, or do I have to treat you as a spy?"

Dar'Kyn looked grave. "Being human, you are unaware of certain expectations. All *Q'estirians* know what happens if any *Sh'o Sook J'eid* becomes injured."

"What does happen? I'm more than a little curious."

"Whoever is responsible will forfeit any aid from any *Sh'o Sook J'eid*," *Dar'Kyn* said with an air of preeminence.

"For how long?" Jessica asked.

"Forever."

"Is that a promise? So, if I clocked you," Jessica was rubbing her knuckles, "you'd leave me alone? Would you pick up your toys and leave this Plane?" Jessica was advancing slowly toward *Dar'Kyn*.

"Yes, I would," *Dar'Kyn* said as she retreated from Jessica's continuing advance. "I would see to it that every *Sh'o Sook J'eid* be precluded from assisting anyone on this Plane. That means that Suzanne would not be allowed to help Socrates while he is on this Plane." *Dar'Kyn* bumped against the wall. Jessica towered over her. She had to look up to see Jessica's face. "Hurting me is not recommended," *Dar'Kyn* whimpered.

Jessica scowled down at the diminutive female. "Be sure to tell those that would care that you sided against a single, human female and sided with a dozen big, bad *Q'estirians*." Jessica took in a deep breath and let it out slowly. "Get out of here and leave me alone," she said as she turned away.

Dar'Kyn scrambled for the back door.

9

ESCAPE AND EVADE

I n a dimly lit warehouse, clangs of metal on metal broke the silence that was prevalent elsewhere. The sun was close to the horizon and would be disappearing before long.

Irving and Phelonius circled each other, swords drawn. Periodically, Irving would press the attack with flurries of slashes to the head and waist alternately. Phelonius parried each attack easily.

Once Irving had finished his attack, his front foot slid back slightly. Phelonius pressed an attack. Irving managed to parry each attack with his sword. After a parried low strike, Phelonius slid his blade between Irving and his sword, stopping the point a fraction of an inch from Irving's lower jaw. Irving and Phelonius froze for a second and then backed away from each other.

"Good! You are improving," Phelonius said, drying the sweat on his face and neck with a towel.

"Thanks, Phelonius," Irving said as he dried sweat from his face. "Still have an issue with that last move of yours."

"You will figure it out...eventually. Either that or it won't be an issue."

"Won't be an issue?" Irving asked.

"You will square off against someone, and they will shove a

sword into your brain...and that will end it being an issue for you. Still wearing that old arm bracelet, I see."

"Armband, and yes. I'd miss it if it weren't there." Irving tentatively touched the armband.

"In all the time you have been here, has the...individual that gave you that come for you?" Phelonius asked, indicating the armband.

"Not that I've noticed."

"Is that contrary to what you were told when given it?" Phelonius asked,

Irving frowned. "You know it is."

"Seen anything of anyone from before?"

"No," Irving said, looking more dejected.

"How long has it been?" Phelonius asked.

Dar'Kyn paced in the woods, not far from Jessica's firing range. *What am I to do,* she thought. *I know I am to report to Lady S'hyrlus on Q'estiria. But what am I to report? True, the human, Jessica, was intimidating me. I know she is capable of great violence and had sent Malthuvius home with severe injuries. Was being threatened by a human a sufficient reason to report the incident? Hornsdoodle. Hornsdoodle was another matter. He has taken his role too far. He cannot imprison Jessica without cause. It is her house, after all. Suzanne had explained it to me before she left with Socrates. I know I should report it, but is it enough to warrant disturbing Lady S'hyrlus and Cornelius Blackwing?*

On one of her trips amongst the trees, *Dar'Kyn* was shocked to see Jessica walking towards her.

"How...how did you escape?" *Dar'Kyn* asked. "I am surprised, pleasantly so, but still surprised. How did you get out of your house?"

Jessica glared. "*Pleasantly* so? I don't think it's a *pleasant* surprise, but that is on you. How did I get out?" Jessica grinned mirthlessly. "I don't think I'll tell you until I know which side you're buttered on."

Dar'Kyn looked shocked. "I-I do not understand. I am not buttered."

Jessica looked skeptical. "That remains to be seen. You have a long way to go before I can trust you, just so you know."

"What does that mean?" *Dar'Kyn* asked.

"It means I'll keep my own counsel," Jessica snapped. "I'll keep you in the dark until you decide whose side you're on. What have you done, so far, to screw things up?"

Dar'Kyn looked puzzled.

"You didn't tell anyone that I was a prisoner in my own house?" Jessica asked. Dar shook her head. "You didn't think it important enough to let Cornelius know?" Dar hung her head. "If I was Cornelius, knowing that one of my trusted soldiers had slipped a gear would be important." Jessica shrugged. She took off her backpack, opened it, and started searching inside. She found something that smelled good and stuck it in her mouth before shouldering her pack.

"Where are you going?" *Dar'Kyn* asked.

"Away. Question is, what are *you* going to do?"

"Might I...come...with you?" *Dar'Kyn* asked haltingly.

Jessica had her right hand in her pants pocket, looking at the pitiable, young female. *Well, she seems young...how old is she?* After a definite hesitation, Jessica held out her left hand, Dar took it, and they both disappeared.

Irving awoke, sat up, and looked around the darkened room. He felt sweat run down the side of his face. Not finding a clock, Irving got up and went to the kitchen. He found a glass and filled it with water.

Was that real? He thought. *Was it a dream, or had I been sword fighting with Phelonius?* He hung his head and tried to remember.

True, Phelonius has been pleasant, which is a surprise, but would he trust me with a sword in close proximity? I'm not sure if he would trust anyone that close with a sword unless he has no doubt that I'm no threat to him, sword or not.

After taking a drink of water, he found a towel and dried his face. As he progressed to drying the back of his neck, he looked around the room. It wasn't completely dark, drapes pulled, and night outside, but the moon was full and bright. Some of the light peeked through the breaks in the heavy drapes.

Jess would have liked the moonlight, Irving thought as he drank more water. His left hand drifted to the band, his finger tapping it absent-mindedly. *I wonder what she's doing tonight. Does she even know that I'm gone? How come no one has come looking for me? Hell, maybe they are. How would I know? I'm out here in the desolation area. I only think I know where I am. I could be almost anywhere.* Irving chuckled. *Maybe what I'm doing now is all a dream. When dealing with wizards, your reality can become skewed.*

Jessica and *Dar'Kyn* reappeared in a dark area. Dar looked around but could see nothing as Jessica took something out of her back pocket and snapped it. A warm, blueish glow began when she shook it.

"Where are we?" Dar whispered.

"A place that's safe from Asshat Hornsdoodle," Jessica said.

"B'runix. His name is B'runix, not Asshat," Dar said, which brought a glare from Jessica.

Jessica dropped the chemical light stick as she shrugged off her backpack. She found a corner near the light and sat with her pack behind her.

"You don't see any stars, even though it's nighttime?" Jessica asked as she frowned at Dar. "Does the air smell fresh and clean? Do you hear any of the small noises that permeate the night?"

"No, I do not," Dar said, "and there is no need to be snide. I am not familiar with the things and places of this Plane."

"We're in a sub-basement, and I'm very familiar with its floorplan." Jessica closed her eyes, crossed her arms, and tucked her chin.

"What is...sub-basement?" Dar asked innocently.

Jessica chuckled. "A sub-basement is an underground story located below the main basement."

"We are...underground?" Dar asked, awestruck and disbelieving.

"Yes," Jessica answered, "quite far underground. We probably could've landed upstairs, but I don't know if Asshat has been here before, and I didn't want to tip off anyone, or anything, that might be around."

"Might I ask what your plan is?"

"You can ask," Jessica responded without opening her eyes.

"How did you manage to exit your house without one of B'runix's men seeing you?" Dar asked after it was apparent that Jessica wouldn't answer her previous question.

"You can ask that, too," Jessica said. "Now, pipe down. Morning is going to be busy, so get some rest."

Socrates Blackwing had built a fire and was reclining close to it. Suzanne was kneeling, warming her hands.

"Something is bothering me," Socrates said. "How did you know about the wizard-step limitations and water? I don't recall ever mentioning it, yet you knew."

"Do the Hamadryads know your limitations?" Suzanne asked.

"They should. The *spell* originated with them."

"So, why wouldn't I know it?" Suzanne asked. "I can speak *Q'estirian* without being taught, not to mention opening portals. When I was...transformed, knowledge was imparted to me. I have no idea what that knowledge is or what it pertains to, but like speaking *Q'estirian*, I'll know it when I hear it or need it.

"I don't know how else I'd know that larger bodies of water, lakes, oceans, and some rivers, block the energy flow from the planet that you rely on to wizard-step."

Suzanne looked at the fire questioningly. "How did I know that? I didn't know until just this second. I hate it when that happens." She paused for a while and then continued, "How is it that Phelonius could capture Irving and move him out of range of the *K'obi Sha Shin J'oi Faqin T'orqute* or your ability to detect it?"

Socrates looked uneasy. "I have no idea how it was accomplished. The...incantation that activated the *K'obi Sha Shin J'oi Faqin T'orqute* was explicitly designed to be used inside a specific range. Exiting that range should not be possible without me knowing, but it is a fact, apparently. He would have to move outside the 200-mile limit quickly.

"The wizard step is the same idea as the seven-league boots from your folklore. Instead of 7 miles, my wizard-step is 100 miles, if I understand what you call a mile. Since we started searching, I haven't been able to go the full range."

"You have to know what you're stepping on to go the maximum distance," Suzanne inserted. She hit her forehead with the heel of her hand, "Stop it, stop it, stop it." After a pause, she said, "Sorry. This flood of information is going to make me crazy."

Socrates looked at her, concerned. "You need to relax, Suzanne. I know it is...difficult to handle the flood of information, but you must relax. It's part of why you were sent to me when you were. I had the same issue when this," he pointed to his patch, "was first given to me."

"So, *S'hyrlus* knew this would happen?" Suzanne asked.

Socrates glanced at her. "It has been so many years since a human was—"

"Changed? Converted?" Suzanne interjected with some pique.

"I was going to say metamorphose, to become one with the elite ranks of the *Sh'o Sook J'eid*," Socrates explained. "I believe the Lady *S'hyrlus* was expecting the deluge your mind is currently trying to come to grips." He was rubbing her arm lightly. "I had to be trained to use my eye and the sphere in concert. The volume of information passed into my mind was overwhelming. I found the key to dealing with it was to relax and not focus on any one thing; let it wash over you. Hopefully, you can absorb it and sort it out later."

Suzanne grinned sardonically. "We are quite the pair."

Sitting on the roof across the street from the P.D., Jessica periodically poked her head above the tall parapet.

"What are you doing?" *Dar'Kyn* asked. "What is your plan?"

Jessica glanced at her companion and noticed that she wasn't crouching, the parapet being taller than Dar was. It was getting close to dawn, and they had been in their position for several hours. It had taken the pair two days to get this far.

"I'm waiting to see if the hovercars on the roof of the Police Department are being monitored or guarded," Jessica explained. "*My* plan is to obtain one of the hovercars to aid us in our search for Irving."

Dar looked at her blankly. "And what will that gain us? Why are you being so...covert in your acquisition? You were...police? Police, were you not? Were you not authorized?"

"I *was* a cop, and I *was* qualified and authorized," Jessica looked across the street again, "but then I *wasn't* a cop at the time of *The Event*. I was a Special Diplomatic liaison to the ambassador at that time, and I'm uncertain that I still have my authorization.

"I'm trying to be *covert* because it's easier to ask forgiveness than permission, sometimes, and I don't want to be questioned or followed."

Jessica glanced over the parapet again. "I still don't see anyone around over there. Doesn't mean they don't have surveillance cams." She took several deep breaths, exhaling through her mouth, before taking out her coin. Dar grasped her upper arm as they both disappeared.

Less than a second later, Jessica and *Dar'Kyn* reappeared on the roof of the PD. Jessica, staying low, trying to keep out of the line of sight of the surveillance cams, opened one of the hovercars and dove inside. As she seated herself in the pilot's seat, she reached across the cabin and opened the passenger door.

"Move your ass, Dar!" Jessica yelled harshly. "Either move it, or I'll leave you here! Move!"

Dar said nothing. She trotted over to the hovercar while the fans were whining up to speed. She climbed in, and Jessica reached across her to shut and latch the passenger door.

"Fasten your harness," Jessica said as she put on the pilot's monocle/headphone/microphone unit.

Dar'Kyn was trying to figure out the harness as the hovercar started to gain altitude. Jessica again reached across her to fasten the safety harness and put the secondary monocle unit on Dar's head.

"It is very noisy!" *Dar'Kyn* shouted, trying to make herself heard over the piercing engine noise.

Jessica pulled her headphone away from her right ear and glared at *Dar'Kyn*. "No need to shout, you brainless twit! Just talk normally into the microphone," she said, indicating the microphone part of the headgear.

Dar looked sheepish. "Certainly is noisy," she said into the microphone.

"It is, and there's nothing to be done," Jessica said sharply. "Now, shut up while I herd this thing in the proper direction."

Dar'Kyn sat back and watched outside the window on her

side and the windscreen. After a few minutes, she asked. "How do you know which direction you need to go?"

"I don't!" Jessica said brusquely. "We're heading south, mainly because any direction is better than sitting at home with my thumb up my ass, doing nothing."

"Attention! Attention hovercar November-2-2-5-7-9-0-Tango-Ex-Ray," came over the earphones within thirty minutes of their take-off.

Dar'Kyn gripped the arms of the seat and looked over to Jessica.

"Shit!" Jessica cursed, "Shit, shit, shit." She took the craft off autopilot and took control. She jerked the controls into a steep, banked dive.

"Evasive action is not required, Jessica Strange, and will do you no good."

The mention of her name triggered her memory, and she could place the voice.

"What would you suggest, Mister Smith?" She said his name with as much disdain as she could muster. She leveled the craft and resumed the course she'd set. She looked out her window and saw another hovercar come alongside. "How did you know it was me?"

"I do have you on video stealing that hovercar from the roof of the Tacoma PD, not to mention that yours is the only aircraft off the ground in several hundreds of miles. Who's the kid?"

"Who my passenger is doesn't concern you," Jessica sniped. "What are *you* doing up here in a Tacoma PD hovercar? Seems to me that you're just as guilty as I am. I ask because I'm sure you have better things to do than to follow me."

"I'm a Federal Agent," Smith responded. *"I'm allowed a certain...latitude to do whatever it takes to accomplish my mission, including shooting you down unless you land."*

99

"I think I'll pass on your invitation," Jessica said as she throttled up and pulled back on the dual controls, gaining altitude.

"*It wasn't an invitation*," Smith replied. "*It was an order. Land now!*"

Jessica glanced to her scopes via the monocle, pulled one control lever back, and pushed the other lever forward, causing the craft to roll.

The acrobatic maneuvers seemed to go on for hours, though they only lasted minutes. At one point, Jessica looked at Dar and noticed a slight green tinge to her skin and grinned as she continued her evasive actions.

Socrates and Suzanne were standing close to some trees on a streambank. Both were shading their eyes from the sun's glare as the two hovercars streaked southward.

"Wow!" Suzanne said. "They certainly are in a hurry."

"What are those?" Socrates asked.

"Hovercars. Used mostly by the police in most Metropolitan Areas. They're used to transport people via the tops of buildings."

"I don't envy those inside," Socrates said. "I think I'd be ill with some of those maneuvers."

"The pilots are well trained and are used to it," Suzanne said. "I'm surprised to see those vehicles burning up the sky since *The Event* decimated us."

"I wonder who they are and where they're going," Socrates said. "As long as I've been here, on this *Plane*, I don't think I've seen such machines flying through the air. I had no idea that was possible."

Suzanne stared at Socrates. "For me, flying is something so ubiquitous that it seems strange to know someone unfamiliar with it. We've had it for at least a hundred years."

"For my people, flying is a dream," Socrates said, awed by the disappearing craft.

"If you don't stop, I'll have to shoot you down," Smith's voice came to her headphones.

"Take your best shot!" Jessica challenged. She saw something small detach from the larger blip that was Smith's ship.

Jessica rolled and dived her craft. The craft buffeted by the air passing by the windscreen.

Dar'Kyn's stomach complained about the dramatic maneuvers. More than once, she saw the ground coming swiftly to meet them, just to be torn away and their craft skimming the surface of a wide strip with other vehicles on it. There was a low explosion behind them.

More than once, during their maneuvers, Jessica and Dar saw their adversary through the windscreen, just to see him execute evasive maneuvers of his own.

"If I had a missile or a gun, I'd shoot his ass down," Jessica said, forgetting the mic would activate with her voice.

"Think so? I don't. Now, land! While you can," Smith commanded.

Jessica exhaled loudly, knowing the mic would pick it up. She flipped the switch that killed the transmission but allowed her to talk to Dar. "I'm out of ideas, Dar. Do you have any thoughts?"

"You have your gun," Dar suggested.

Jessica smiled mirthlessly as she reactivated her microphone.

"Okay, Smith," Jessica said finally. "You win. Landing." She cut the transmission.

10

NO NEWS IS GOOD NEWS

Cornelius Blackwing was sitting at his desk, trying to reduce the amount of paperwork accumulated on it.

The knocker sounded. "Enter!" he yelled without looking up. "Yes? What is it?" He had heard someone walk in, but no one answered. He looked up and saw *S'hyrlus* walk across to her favorite chair and exhale loudly. "I am too busy to go off on some *adventure* today. I have not caught up, nor recovered, from our last one," he said, continuing his paperwork.

"Maybe not, but it was fun anyway," *S'hyrlus* said. "I know you enjoyed it, even though you complain now."

Cornelius paused and looked toward the far wall. "Yes, I quite enjoyed it," then he cleared his throat and glared at *S'hyrlus* briefly before scowling and turning again to his work. "What is it?"

"What is what?" *S'hyrlus* asked.

"Why are you here?" Cornelius restated his question with irritation.

"Have you heard from the *Eighth Plane*?" she asked.

"Not a word, you?"

"Nothing and that concerns me. To my thinking, we should

have heard something. Even if it was the standard 'Nothing to report at this time'."

"The only message I want to receive is the expected 'mission accomplished'," Cornelius said somewhat snappily. "My people know what they are doing, and I expect them to perform admirably."

"I know how they were trained," S'hyrlus said. "I have had a hand in establishing some of their training regimens, just as you have. I would feel better if someone would report something, anything."

"Socrates said something to me on his last visit. Something the people of *Plane Eight* say or did say." He stopped scribbling on the parchment as he squinted at the far wall trying to remember. "'No news is good news', I think it went, "

"How is that helpful?" S'hyrlus asked. "Personally, I think they are all insane."

"Who is insane?" Cornelius asked as he picked up another parchment and looked at it from arm's length.

"The *Eighth-Planers*," S'hyrlus said.

"Of course," Cornelius said.

S'hyrlus frowned. "Cornelius, there is an old dragon here to see you. He says he has an appointment," S'hyrlus said.

"Have him come in and sit down. I will be with him in a minute." Cornelius was writing and then sat up. "Wait. What?"

S'hyrlus laughed.

Jessica set the hovercar gently on the ground but didn't cut the fans. They were idling.

"*Cut the fans*," Smith's voice said over the headphones, "*and step out, both of you.*"

"What are you going to do?" Dar'Kyn asked.

"See this switch?" Jessica cut the microphone on her and Dar's headset. She pointed to a switch on the dash. "When I tell you, push it into this position." Dar nodded. "For now, though," she clicked the switch, and the high-pitched whine of the fans began to lower.

As the rpm's dropped, she saw Smith's hovercar land alongside her own. She unlatched her door, opened it a little, and put one foot out. She unlatched the strap on her holster and started to stand. "You stay put! No matter what! Understand?" Dar nodded in agreement.

"Step out, Jessica, and keep your hands where I can see them," she heard Smith's voice over the headset.

Jessica looked across to the other hovercar. She saw Smith standing on the ground, gun drawn and resting the butt on the roof of the hovercar, with the vehicle and the pilot side door between them. Jessica activated her microphone. "You gonna shoot me as soon as I stand?" she asked over the headset as she pulled her firearm.

"Not unless I have to," came across the headphones. Jessica could hear Smith grinning. *"Where is your artillery?"* Smith asked.

"What *are* you talking about?" she asked.

"The piece you took off me, for starters, needs to hit the ground," she heard. *"And where is your passenger? Thermal readings indicate you have a kid in the car. Have them exit, now!"*

"Okay, okay! Just cut your thrusters!" Jessica took a deep breath and let it out. *"Dar'Kyn,* now," she said in even tones, as calmly as possible.

The fans were gaining in rpm's again as Jessica whipped around toward Smith's vehicle and fired three quick rounds. The first caused Smith to duck behind his hovercar without getting off a shot first. The other two rounds hit the center fan on the side closest to her, which started to smoke slightly.

By the time Smith could get above the roof of his vehicle, Jessica was inside her hovercar, heading south after a steep climb and roll maneuver that placed her above and behind before burning up the sky going south.

Smith got inside his hovercar and noticed a flashing red light on the dash. *Nice,* Smith thought. *I seemed to have underestimated you yet again, Jessica. One-shot to make me take cover so you could damage my vehicle so I can't follow—all in fractions of a second. I should've thought of that myself.* He knew he could follow Jessica, but he wouldn't be able to match her speed. Essentially, he would be limping after her. He shook his head in admiration.

When Jessica and Dar were heading south once more, Jessica looked at her fuel levels and frowned.

"What is it?" Dar asked.

"Fuel," Jessica said. "We're about out. That dogfight cost us miles. I'll have to set down in Portland and refuel."

"How long will it take to get there?" Dar asked.

Jessica glanced around and did some mental calculations and then said, "At this velocity, less than thirty minutes to get there and land. It's getting dark, so we'll have to settle in for the night. The car has to cool down before I can refuel it, and we don't have the equipment to fly at night. Wouldn't want to hit a mountain."

"How do you know where to land to get this *fuel* you seem to need?" Dar asked.

"Easy," Jessica said. "The only place we can get the fuel is at the Portland PD roof-top staging."

"Roof-top staging?"

"The same type of place we...acquired this car," Jessica smirked.

It was dusk by the time Dar and Jessica landed.

Socrates and Suzanne were sitting at their campfire after placing the wards. "Where are we?" he asked as he sat.

"According to your requirements for safety reasons,"

Suzanne said, "we're on the Washington side of the Columbia River. We're not far from Portland. We should be past it relatively early tomorrow."

"How long will it take to search this area?" Socrates asked as he popped some of his dried beef into his mouth. He had some in his other hand for Suzanne.

"We're doing the same zigzag search pattern as we've been doing?" Suzanne asked. She saw him nod. "Oregon, from the coast to the mountains, narrows as we travel south. The time required will become shorter as we won't have to zigzag as much as we did in Northern Washington."

"I know it seems tiring, but I don't want to miss something," Socrates said. "I don't want to miss Irving in some out-of-the-way place, hidden there by Phelonius..." Socrates' voice just trailed off to nothing.

"What is the procedure to secure Phelonius?" Suzanne asked.

"There will be no...securing him," Socrates said. "I am to terminate him."

"I knew it would probably come to that," Suzanne said.

"*S'hyrlus*?" Socrates asked.

Suzanne nodded. "On my last...summoning."

"What is it you're not telling me?" Socrates asked.

Suzanne chewed her lower lip. "If I could tell you, I would," she said after a long pause,

"Does it have anything to do with the *Sh'o Sook J'eid Plane*?" Socrates asked. "You know, the one that the rest of the Seven Planes don't know about."

Suzanne looked shocked.

"For as long as I can remember," Socrates said, "there has been this *Great Debate* about where the *Sh'o Sook J'eid* go, to train and to refresh themselves; the place of safety for them to relax. The current consensus among those who have voiced an opinion is that they have a *Plane* of their own...somewhere. Is that what you're not telling me?"

Suzanne glanced to the ground as she nodded.

"Don't worry too much over it all," Socrates said. "If there are things that you're not to tell me, then don't. There are things about my kind that we don't tell others. Do what you know to be correct. It's all you *can* do, no matter who says otherwise."

Neither said anything else.

Phelonius and Irving had spent the day scrounging the area in ever-widening circles to see what they could use. Irving managed to locate more food, stored in cans and jars, and some weapons. He did not attempt to conceal anything from Phelonius.

"What is that?" Phelonius asked while they were in a deserted market.

"This?" Irving responded by shaking the jar. "Pickles. Cucumbers fermented in a seasoned brine." He opened the jar, pulled one out with his fingers, and offered it to Phelonius, who skeptically took it. He then got one out for himself and bit the end. It made a satisfying crunch.

Phelonius copied him and then screwed up his face. "Bitter," he said, his face in a frown.

"I'd say they were more sour than bitter, but that's just me. Pickles are, what we call, an acquired taste. Most people either love them or hate them, and by the expression on your face, I'd say you hate them." Irving chuckled a little. "That means there are more for me. It also means you probably won't like sauer-kraut either."

"You...enjoy these...pickles?" Phelonius asked, handing back the rest of his. "And what is this sauerkraut you mentioned?"

Irving took the pickle and put it back into the jar. "Yes, I enjoy them here and there and once in a while." He walked down the isles a few more feet and handed a different jar to Phelonius. "Sweet pickles. They may be more to your liking. If not, then more for me. Sauerkraut is fermented, raw, shredded cabbage that is salted and flavored. As a general rule, it's what I would call sour. Most people either love it or hate it."

"Humans are just so...strange," Phelonius said as he opened the jar.

Smith managed to nurse his crippled hovercar back to the Tacoma PD roof-top staging area. He managed to land just before dark.

Made it, he thought as he touched down and killed the fans. He relaxed into the seat as the fan's rpms dropped, evidenced by their whine reducing. *Didn't think I would make it, but glad I did. Woulda been a long walk otherwise. Do I take another hovercar to Yakima to get the rocket launcher and controls refitted, or do I forgo the rocket upgrade to resume the pursuit? The refit will put me a couple of days behind Jessica. Taking another hovercar and pursuing her will only put me an hour behind her. She's going in the general direction we need her to go already.*

Smith closed his eyes and slept in the hovercar's pilot seat.

Dar'Kyn curled up in the rear bench seat and looked to be asleep. Jessica had the navigation portion of the autopilot displayed and was trying to plan out her course.

Knowing what I do of Phelonius, Jessica thought, *and knowing Socrates, Phelonius took Irving somewhere in California. He likes the heat and the dry. He hates the rain, so Oregon and Washington are out of the question. He has to be in the depopulated areas; otherwise, why bother to depopulate those areas.*

Jessica looked at the potential refuel points in Oregon as her planned course took her south. *Portland to Eugene to Ashland to Redding to Santa Rosa to Salinas to Pismo Beach to Long Beach, to*

San Diego, Jessica thought. "A lot of stops, but that can't be helped," she said aloud.

"A lot of stops?" Dar asked from the back seat.

"Yes, we're limited to approximately 150 to 175 miles, depending on weather conditions, before we need to refuel. Those towns are big enough to have Police Departments large enough to have roof-top staging areas for hovercars. And the stops will allow us to travel to the California-Mexico Border, effectively covering the area of *The Event.*"

"How is that significant?" Dar asked.

"Somewhere," Jessica said, "I'm hoping to find Irving and rescue him inside this depopulated area. I thought you knew that?"

"I did," Dar said. "Sometimes, I find it helpful to remind myself of my ultimate goal, to keep my focus on it. I wanted you to restate your goal to see if it had changed since we left...Tac-oo-ma. At what point are we picking up Socrates and Lady Suzanne?"

"Tacoma. What do you mean, pick them up?" Jessica asked. "I'm not planning on picking anyone else up. If Suzanne and Socrates are searching in a southerly direction, it's the first I've heard about it. Do you know something I don't?"

"How would I know anything?" Dar asked, shrinking back a bit. "I've been with you since you left your house."

Jessica looked at *Dar'Kyn* skeptically. "Is that why I'm feeling led, or is it herded?" Her eyes narrowed.

"I have no idea what you are referring to," Dar said. "I am just...how you say...just along for the ride."

Cornelius and *S'hyrlus* quietly emerged from the massive oak close to Socrates' and Suzanne's residence. They were stunned by the silence.

"Hmmm, we are not expected?" Cornelius asked *S'hyrlus* in Q'estirian.

"No, we are here to gather the latest information on the search, not for pomp and circumstance," *S'hyrlus* responded.

Cornelius frowned a little. "A little pomp and circumstance once in a while is not a bad thing," he said ruefully, eliciting an eye roll from *S'hyrlus*.

"There should be guards patrolling the property," *S'hyrlus* said as the pair walked towards the house. "We should have been challenged by now. There is something not quite right about all this."

"I agree," Cornelius said, "there should be patrols. I do not have a good feeling about this."

"Should a guard be posted at the rear door of the residence?" *S'hyrlus* whispered when the backdoor was visible. Cornelius nodded, took *S'hyrlus'* hand, and the pair disappeared.

They reappeared in the living room of the house. *S'hyrlus* was facing the table and saw Hornsdoodle sitting in a chair with his boots on the table. She tapped Cornelius, and he turned.

"What is the meaning of this?" Cornelius roared.

A startled Hornsdoodle fell backward, the chair clattering as it hit the floor.

"Where is Socrates?" Cornelius yelled as Hornsdoodle scrambled to his feet.

"Where is Lady *Dar'Kyn*?" *S'hyrlus* asked loudly to be heard over the din of the scrambling Hornsdoodle on the hardwood floor.

"Pardons, sire," Hornsdoodle managed breathlessly, coming to attention. "Lady *Dar'Kyn* and the human, Jessica, escaped. Socrates and Lady Suzanne are not on the premises. They are searching for the human Irving."

"How could they *escape*?" *S'hyrlus* asked. "Is this not her house? Saying she escaped would indicate that she was imprisoned…in her own house. Explain, please."

Hornsdoodle looked flustered as he tried to think of an answer.

"Speak up! Answer Lady *S'hyrlus*," Cornelius bellowed.

"After Socrates and Lady Suzanne left to search for Irving, Jessica became...unruly and unreasonable," Hornsdoodle said. "Because of her behavior, I had to...confine her to the inside of this structure."

"Do you consider her being uncooperative with you as being unruly and unreasonable?" *S'hyrlus* asked snippily.

"Being responsible for the security of the ambassador's residence," Hornsdoodle said with fluttering eyelids, "I do not consider Jessica's opinion as relevant. She is, after all, merely human."

S'hyrlus smirked. "Merely human? Tell me, Hornsdoodle, what was her function here?"

"She was a special diplomatic liaison to our ambassador, a position created for her by the ambassador," Hornsdoodle stated flatly.

S'hyrlus nodded. "And what was her function before there was an ambassador?"

"I have no information on that subject," Hornsdoodle said dismissively.

"They did not explain that part of her history to you?" *S'hyrlus* asked.

"They did not," Hornsdoodle said, looking down his nose at *S'hyrlus*.

"I am sure Socrates explained it to you," *S'hyrlus* said. "Before she knew Socrates, she was a member of this Plane's local security forces, what they call police. From my understanding, she managed to attain a trusted position and was one of few humans to survive Phelonius' attack. Not to mention that she was also, as was Irving, *K'obi Sha Shin J'oi Faqin* to Socrates, the ambassador, and your immediate superior." She turned her back on Hornsdoodle.

"What I want to know, Hornsdoodle," Cornelius roared, and

Hornsdoodle shied away from the verbal assault, "is who told you that putting your feet on someone's table was acceptable behavior? If it were my table, you would be guarding the porcine pens until you were as old as Syn'Chin Hornsdoodle, grandfather of your grandfather."

B'runix Hornsdoodle remained stoic.

"Nothing to say?" Cornelius asked as he paced in front of Hornsdoodle. After a brief silence, he said, "You are to call your second in command and relinquish your position. Additionally, you are demoted two ranks."

"Yes, Sire," Hornsdoodle responded with a bow and down-cast eyes. "I will return to *Q'estiria* as soon as I can make—"

"Oh, no!" Cornelius interrupted. "You do not get off the hook so easily. Lady *S'hyrlus* and I must find Socrates and Lady Suzanne. We will need a guide. Until further notice, you will accompany us and act as a guide or anything else we need you to do."

Hornsdoodle started his pleas, "But Sire, I—"

"But nothing!" Cornelius roared. "You have disrespected Socrates, Lady Suzanne, Lady *S'hyrlus*, and myself! Not to mention what Jessica and Lady *Dar'Kyn* will have to say on the matter when I ask them."

The color drained from B'runix Hornsdoodle's face.

11

RESUMING THE SEARCH

Cornelius looked out at the rain-soaked foliage. In the distance, he could see a meandering river, one that he was sure their path would cross.

"Everything is so green here," Cornelius said to the person coming up behind him. He hadn't turned to see who it was. "Do you know what this place is called?"

"I have no idea," came *S'hyrlus'* lilting tone.

Cornelius turned slightly with a grin. "You know, your voice has always made me smile," he said. "So, are we lost?"

"Not lost," *S'hyrlus* said. "Socrates and Suzanne must be traveling quickly. I was hoping to cross their path long before now."

"Do we know where they are going?" Cornelius asked.

"It appears they are heading to this...Kalif-orn-ia," Hornsdoodle said, cringing a little that he had answered without thinking.

Cornelius glared at Hornsdoodle for his assumption of familiarity. "If they are going to this place called Kalif-orn-ia, how will we intercept them?" he asked *S'hyrlus*, without looking away from Hornsdoodle.

"Personally," *S'hyrlus* answered, "I have never been to… Kalif-orn-ia, so we are destined only to follow."

Cornelius broke his glare with Hornsdoodle and meandered around. "How far behind are we and is there a way to close the distance?" he asked.

S'hyrlus walked up to stand next to Cornelius. "The only way we could get closer is for Socrates to slow down, and for the oak trees, we use to travel to be closer than those passed. Then we may be able to intercept him and Suzanne. Otherwise—" she shook her head slightly.

Smith was finally on his way. It took several hours to prepare and install the needed satellite-based scanner from the damaged hovercar to the new one. He had opted for an undamaged vehicle over the need for the missile launcher. Display and power connections needed to be jerry-rigged, but, finally, he was heading south, fiddling with the controls to pick up the tracker signal on Jessica Strange. When he picked up the signal, he saw she was between Eugene and Ashland, Oregon. Unconsciously, he smiled. *Now, Miss Jessica, I'll be catching up to you*, he thought. *It'll be sooner than you think and when you least expect it.*

Dar'Kyn sat in the backseat of the hovercar, watching Jessica. Dar was confused by the inappreciable adjustments and her constant monitoring of the craft's indicators.

"Where are we, now?" Dar asked.

"Not far from Ashland, Oregon," Jessica said without turning around.

"That means nothing to me," Dar said. "How will you know where Irving is? What is to stop you from going past him?"

Jessica's mouth hung open. She was silent and unmoving for a long time.

"Now is a hell-of-a-time to ask that!" Jessica said. "I would've appreciated that little tidbit of a question before we left the house."

Dar looked at Jessica and smirked. "You are teasing me, right?"

"Not really, no, not teasing," Jessica replied, chagrinned.

"Well, who knows," Dar said. "Things may yet work out. I know you think you are the only one looking for Irving, but I do not believe that to be so."

Jessica looked at the indicators. "I wish I had your optimism," she said under her breath as she prepared to land in Ashland.

"What is this place?" Socrates asked. He was standing on the broad ribbon of asphalt that ran north and south. The pair had repeatedly returned to it in their search.

"Mount Shasta is what we call the mountain. We are in California," Suzanne answered.

"You've been here before?" Socrates asked.

"No, but I have seen pictures and read books referencing it," Suzanne said. "They didn't do justice to it, though."

Socrates looked perplexed for a few seconds. "Ah," he said finally. "I understand the idiom, even though the idiom is confusing."

"Any indicators?" Suzanne asked.

"As a matter of fact," Socrates said, surprised, "there is. Some distance behind us. I have no idea who it is, it's either Jessica or Irving, but the indication is there."

"So, what are we doing?" Suzanne asked. "Do we wait here for them to catch up, or do we proceed and ignore it for now?"

"What would you suggest?" Socrates asked.

Suzanne was quiet for some time. Finally, she said, "If it's moving towards us, it could be Jessica. She could be trying to find us, but it's more likely that she is looking for Irving on her own. Jess was quite upset when we left her at home.

"If it's Irving and it moves away from us, then we missed our target and might as well turn around and head back unless... Irving isn't the only target. In which case, we'd have to wait until Phelonius strikes again.

"Those are the options as I see them. It's up to you to develop a plan from that information."

"No recommendations?" Socrates asked.

"I would recommend we wait and see. The indicator will disappear, move closer, or move away. Develop a plan once you determine what it's doing."

"I agree," Socrates said.

Dar'Kyn was becoming impatient. Jessica had landed their craft in Redding, California. "What are you waiting for?" Dar asked as she paced the roof area.

"Like I've told you before," Jessica said from the open door of the hovercar, "this craft generates a lot of heat as it passes through the air. It's about as aerodynamic as a rock. Since the fuel is of the hydrogen fuel cell type, I prefer refraining from detonating it. That tends to ruin your day."

"If this craft is so inefficient, why do you insist on using it?" Dar asked.

"Way back in the Dark Ages," Jessica began, "ninety years ago or so, the people decided that liquid fuels were bad for the environment. This...monstrosity, and its inefficiencies, were the result. The people, who didn't like or appreciate the police, decided that ground cars that used liquid fuels were outdated and opted for electric vehicles that required long periods to recharge, to be plugged into coal-burning power plants, and thus, making things worse.

"The police complained long enough that they were awarded these…these…things that are only marginally safer than flying a bomb. Seventy or so years before that was this event called the Hindenburg incident. It was an airship that emulated, either by accident or intent. As an airship, its lift was derived from hydrogen.

"When our so-called modern scientists were reminded of this, their comment was something along the lines of 'that was then, this is now', as if chemistry or physics had changed dramatically. Besides, if only cops had them, only cops could be hurt if something went boom.

"It wasn't long until we had our own modern Hindenburg event. Can you guess what caused it?"

Being only marginally fluent in English or understanding some of the words Jessica used, Dar could only shake her head side-to-side.

"Fuel. Specifically, the changing out of the fuel cells while the skin of the ship was still hot. So, with that said, if you wish to change the fuel cells, just let me get clear before you do."

Dar'Kyn saw Jessica get comfortable in her pilot seat, leaning back and closing her eyes. Not knowing what else to do, Dar walked the roof's perimeter.

Jessica changed the fuel cells and was finishing closing everything up.

"Hello, Jessica," Suzanne said.

Jessica, startled, turned to see her friend standing there. "Where did you come from?" she asked snippily.

"The same place you did. Tacoma," Suzanne said. "We weren't far north of here when you flew over."

"How did you know I flew over?" Jessica asked skeptically.

"You do know that Socrates can track you via your armband," Suzanne said. "He doesn't always bring it up or use it, and sometimes I think he forgets. My question is, why are *you* out here?"

"I got tired of just sitting around," Jessica said, "doing nothing while everyone else was out here. And then there is the Hornsdoodle incident."

"What is the Hornsdoodle incident?" Suzanne asked as Socrates walked up behind her.

"It's part of why I'm out here instead of at home," Jessica said.

"I'm not too concerned, at this point, as to why she's here," Socrates said. "My concern is can she get me higher off the ground."

"I'm sure she can," Suzanne said after Jessica nodded.

"That would help," Socrates said. "I wouldn't have to zigzig across the landscape."

"Zigzig?" Jessica asked.

"He means zig*zag*," Suzanne said.

"Yes, zigzag," Socrates said. "Being higher would eliminate the need to zigzag." Socrates looked sheepish: "Besides, I've never flown in a machine before."

It wasn't long before the hovercar, with Jessica at the controls and three passengers, lifted off the roof of the Redding Police department and turned southward.

———

Irving was on the roof, sitting under the solar panels that covered it. He was facing east, towards the rising sun, and was sitting in the Lotus position. His meditations were disturbed.

"I'm trying to meditate here," Irving said without opening his eyes.

"It was not my intent to disrupt your thoughts," Phelonius said.

Irving opened one eye. "Of course, you meant to disturb me. You want what you want when you want it." Irving straightened his legs slowly.

"Sometime in the next few days, we will be going to the beach that is long," Phelonius said.

Irving looked at Phelonius, puzzled. "The beach that is long? You mean Long Beach?" he said finally.

"That is what I said," Phelonius snapped. "Why do you continuously correct my speaking?"

"It would help if you would apply the corrections I give instead of discounting them," Irving snapped. He could see Phelonius' face redden with anger. "What's the matter? Are you going to turn me into a rat, lizard, or something similar? I know you can but doing so would not be in your best interest."

"Why do you insist on tempting me to vent my anger at you?" Phelonius asked through gritted teeth.

"After all this time, after all the time we've spent together, and you still don't understand?" Irving asked.

"What is it I do not understand?" Phelonius asked, seething. "Enlighten me!"

"You absconded with me to enrage Socrates and any other allies he happens to enlist," Irving said. "I realize my role is to be the bait...the live bait...for your little trap. You have kept me alive and whole, so Socrates will know it's me. I know you won't transmute me into any other creature because they won't recognize me."

"I know all that," Phelonius said. "You were going to tell me what I do not understand."

Irving smirked and said, "I correct you, so you don't sound like an idiot. You may have abducted me, but I can appreciate your particular point of view, and I don't want others to think badly of you and associate me with you."

Phelonius' eyes narrowed as he looked at Irving's smile.

S'hyrlus turned away from the large oak with a frown.

"What is wrong?" Cornelius asked.

"I have been leaving a message with the oaks for Suzanne," *S'hyrlus* said as she sat on the ground.

"What kind of message?" Cornelius asked, sticking a blade of grass into his mouth.

"I want Suzanne and Socrates to slow their traveling," *S'hyrlus* said, looking at a huge sign. "San...ta...Ross...a. What is that?" she asked Hornsdoodle. "You understand these creatures."

"My understanding is not much better than yours," Hornsdoodle said as he stared at the sign. Suddenly his hat fell forward off his head. He turned to see Cornelius standing behind him. Hornsdoodle rubbed the back of his head, frowning.

"Her title is *Lady* to such as you!" Cornelius said roughly. "Have you forgotten all your training?" When Hornsdoodle looked, he could see Cornelius' anger and returned it with a scowl.

"I have not been struck in that fashion since I was a youngling at the academy," Hornsdoodle said sternly and quietly. "I would warn you not to strike me thus again."

"I struck you in that fashion because you *act* like a youngling, newly arrived to the academy," Cornelius explained. "You do not like being stricken in that fashion, then stop acting in a way that will get you struck like that. Only you can change it!"

Cornelius turned his back on Hornsdoodle.

Cornelius, you are pushing him too hard, S'hyrlus thought, watching the interchange. *He will lash out at you at the first opportunity. I would tread lightly if I were you.*

S'hyrlus wandered off to locate an oak.

To Jessica, the hovercar seemed sluggish with the additional passengers as they traveled southward.

I hope Smith doesn't pick now to poke his ugly face into our business, Jessica thought as she watched all around the craft directly and through feedback via scanners and gages. *The last time he poked his nose in, he tried to shoot me down. We won't fare well if he picks now to have a dogfight. It's all I can do to keep us airborne.*

"I've noticed you look all around," Socrates asked. "Since *The Event,* there has been very little traffic."

"Our buddy Smith tried to shoot me down a few days ago," Jessica said. "I'm trying to watch for him, or anyone else who may get the same idea, and watch the highway down there," she nodded toward the ground, "to keep us from getting lost."

"Oh. I didn't mean to distract you," Socrates said. "I can appreciate the need to maintain your focus."

"Before *The Event,*" Jessica said, "a trip like this would have been handled by computers tied into radar. Based on our destination, our fuel consumption would have been monitored and refueling locations laid out; an academy trainee and a chimpanzee could have piloted this trip, and he could've left the trainee behind.

"Currently, though, most of the computer network is inoperable, mainly because it is unmanned. Machines being run by computers made too many people nervous, so the designers opted for *some* minor human control. As it applies to this hovercar, a human must sit in this seat and handle the controls. Another human can sit where you're sitting and operate the secondary controls, but one must be in this seat."

"So, I couldn't fly this...vehicle?" Socrates asked.

"Why? Do you want to?" Jessica asked, startling Socrates. "I don't think you would be able to, but since the designers didn't know of your characteristics, I doubt they could have designed your...differences out. We could try and see."

"And how would we do that?" Socrates asked.

"On either side of your seat are the controls," Jessica said. "Just pull them up until they snap into place." She waited for him to snap the controls into place. "On my set," Jessica continued after the other controls were locked; she indicated a button on her left-side stick close to the throttle, "I have this switch to allow someone in training to fly and let me take back control of the craft if things went sideways.

"The controls are two throttles, activated by rolling the hand-grips, and two-directional sticks. Equally, rolling on the throttles increases the fan speeds and increases altitude...distance from the ground. Letting go of them would make them go idle. Rolling on, increasing one more than the other would cause you to turn to the opposite of the faster throttle.

"Pushing the yokes forward equally would make the craft go forward. If they're in the middle, it is more of an idle position. Pulling back acts as an airbrake."

"It all sounds complicated," Socrates said.

"It is," she agreed, "but not overly so. The craft somewhat helps the pilot by not letting you do things that would result in an unsurvivable impact with the ground."

Socrates shook his head. "You do the flying. I'm busy trying to locate Irving.

"If you ever want to learn, just let me know," Jessica said.

A while later, Jessica breathed a sigh of relief as they landed in Santa Rosa. "We need to have a conversation," she said to Socrates.

"About what?" Suzanne asked.

"This vehicle is not built for dogfighting while transporting a full complement of passengers," Jessica said. "It wouldn't take much to ground us in the middle of nowhere. Too much weight."

"I like this mode of travel," Socrates said. "If we run across Smith, I'll deal with him. In the meantime, we can all help by paying closer attention to the surrounding airspace, leaving you free to concentrate on flying. How long will we be here?"

"Depends on how long it takes the vehicle to cool down enough to refuel it, a couple of hours at least," Jessica said.

Everyone nodded their understanding as they exited the hovercar.

An hour later, Suzanne and Socrates came over to the car to talk to Jessica.

"What other stops are you planning?" Suzanne asked.

As a response, Jessica pulled up the course she'd initially set. "There you go, even though I don't understand why," Jessica said.

"There was a message from S'hyrlus," Suzanne said. "She and Cornelius were here already and want to link up. I wanted to let them know where we are and where we were heading."

Jessica exhaled loudly. "This hovercar can't handle that many. It was already too sluggish with the rest of us. I doubt it would get off the ground with two more."

Suzanne smiled. "You misunderstand. We want to meet with them to compare notes and devise a plan of some sort."

"Making a plan is different than following a plan," Jessica said. "A plan would've been nice before we all started."

"According to your flight plan, we are going to Salinas and then Pismo Beach?" Suzanne asked.

"Yes," Jessica said. "We can't get to Pismo Beach much before tomorrow, though. Cool-down time and I can't fly at night."

"That will work," Suzanne said as she and Socrates left.

"So, what is the plan?" *Dar'Kyn* asked from the backseat of the hovercar.

Has she been here the entire time, Jessica thought. *Did I forget about her?*

"You heard Suzanne as well as I did," Jessica snapped.

"You did not understand me," *Dar'Kyn* repeated. "*They* have their plan. *You* have your plan. I heard *their* plan. What is *your* plan?"

"I haven't formulated one yet," Jessica said as she turned to refuel the craft.

THE CALM

I t was close to midday when Jessica set down the hovercar at the Pismo Beach PD staging area. After Jessica cut the fans, it took a few minutes before the cabin was quiet enough to talk.

"How long will it be until you can proceed?" Socrates asked.

"I need to wait on the cool-down, change out the fuel pod, and do a preflight checklist," Jessica said. "If it were up to me, I'd stay here the night and head out at first light."

"Where will you be?" Socrates asked.

"Right here," Jessica said. "I'm not planning on going anywhere else. I want food, something other than the energy bars I grabbed and stuffed into my pack. I want a shower and sleep the night in a bed, but things are what they are..." She shrugged.

"I don't understand," Socrates said.

"I've never been here before," Jessica explained. "I would like to be able to tell you that I'll be at the Marriott, but I don't even know if this burg has one. And how would I get there if they did?

"We've been lucky so far. I'm sure someone else is still roaming around out there," Jessica gestured to the part of the city they could see, "and I don't want to run into them. We already know Smith is still creeping around, somewhere."

Everyone exited the hovercar.

"What is that water called?" Socrates asked as he pointed to the west.

"That," Suzanne said, joining him, "is the Pacific Ocean."

Jessica and *Dar'Kyn* joined the couple at the roof's edge and looked westward.

"Does that sign say 'Edgewater Inn'?" Jessica asked as she shaded her eyes with her hands.

"I believe it does," Suzanne said.

"I think I'll just jump over and see what I can find," Jessica said with a grin. She had her jump coin out and turned to *Dar'Kyn*, "Coming?" she asked.

Dar walked to her, took her hand, and the pair disappeared.

Since she was unfamiliar with the area, Jessica took four jumps to get to the parking lot of the Edgewater Inn. She was a little surprised to see Socrates waiting for her.

"Are you afraid I'd leave you here?" Jessica asked irritably.

"No, just seeing where we can find you, should we need to," Socrates said. "I agree with you that we don't know who else is out there, wandering around, you know, like we are." Socrates grinned.

"Why is that?" Jessica asked. "According to Suzanne, you can track me anytime you want. Was she lying to me?"

"No, she wasn't lying," Socrates said. "I try not to track you unless I have to. I should have been doing it when Irving was taken, but I try to give you as much privacy as possible."

"Well, not that it's any of your business; I'm planning on finding an empty room and taking a shower," Jessica said sarcastically. "After that, I'll see if something is available to eat and then off to bed. Does that meet with your approval?" Jessica glared at Socrates; she saw his expression change from a mirthful grin to an unreadable stoic.

Socrates disappeared.

Dar'Kyn and Jessica had just finished eating. Jessica had raided a small local store for canned goods, can-opener, bottled water, plastic eating utensils, and shampoo. She'd made sure a few cans of fruit were included in the haul. When they found a room that suited them, Jessica opened a can of peaches and gave the can to *Dar'Kyn* while she went in to take a shower.

"You owe Socrates an apology," *Dar'Kyn* said as Jessica exited the bath.

"Why is that?" Jessica asked as she adjusted the towels wrapped around her torso and hair. She went to the bathroom sink, where she had a can of stew warming in hot water while she showered.

"He has been doing what he can to find your...Irving," Dar continued when Jessica once more exited the bathroom. "He has exhibited patience on an unimaginable level." Dar took another bite of peaches.

"Why do you say that?" Jessica asked brusquely while she opened the can and picked up a plastic fork. "This whole ordeal is his fault. Why should I apologize?"

"How is it *his* fault?" Dar asked.

"If he wouldn't have come here, none of this...this..." she gestured with her fork while chewing, "would have happened. Ergo, *his* fault!"

"Your reasoning's are flawed," Dar said, shaking her head a little while she fished out another piece of peaches. "He had no say in coming here."

"So you say," Jessica said.

There was silence for some time.

"Would it be wrong of me to blame you for something someone else did 200 of your years ago?" Dar asked finally.

"I wouldn't care if you blamed me for anything," Jessica said. "For it to bother me, I'd have to be concerned with your opinion. I'm unconcerned with everything unless it is required to find my husband and take him home."

Dar looked at Jessica. "No matter how anyone else feels?" Dar asked. She shook her head. "Are you sure you are not a *Q'estirian*? You are as ill-natured and as insolent as most *Q'estirians*. If you would go there, you would fit in."

Smith was watching the satellite scanner screen as he landed in San Diego. The blip he was following had been at Pismo Beach for hours.

I'm tired, Smith thought. *To catch up to Jessica, I've been landing and taking off again as fast as possible. I even managed to put two cells in series to extend my range.* He rubbed his upper arm and the platinum band unconsciously while watching the screen. His fingertips making contact with the band under his shirt sleeve brought back the memories of his Faustian bargain. *I didn't sell out humanity*, he rationalized. *I was ensuring humanity's continuance.* He snickered to himself. *The power of one being to depopulate the entire west coast, hundreds of millions of people, is nothing to take lightly. Phelonius, alone, managed it. I couldn't have that kind of power released against the rest of my country.*

This older one, Socrates Blackwing, is another powerful being, though not as powerful as Phelonius, or so I'm told. But he can do tremendous damage unless I assist in bringing down this pretender ambassador, so Phelonius can remove him from our reality, whatever that means.

Smith tried to put those thoughts out of his mind as he set an audible alarm on the scanner and busied himself with replacing the fuel cell. *I hope Jessica isn't helping Socrates Blackwing*, he

127

thought as he made the connections. *I had considered asking Phelonius for her as part of the price for my help, but her skills and value were unknown, beyond the puerile, that is.*

Once the fuel cell was swapped out, Smith reentered the pilot position and checked the alarm on the scanner to be sure that it wasn't discontinued when the active cell was switched. Seeing all was as he had intended, he settled in for the night. *Jessica is very desirable*, he thought. *A tasty morsel.*

While Jessica slept, Dar was sitting in a chair looking out the window through the small part in the heavy drapes. *I can feel the tension in the air*, she thought. *They can all feel it. It will not be long before this affair is ended and resolved.*

Dar heard Jessica moan and her breathing change, and then she rolled over. *I find myself identifying with these humans*, she thought. *They have short, miserably little lives, and they deserve whatever peace and happiness they can find or that life in this realm will allow them to find.* "Huh," she said quietly. The speaking of it shocked her. *Am I starting to let them get me involved with their petty lives*, she thought. She sighed. *I suppose I am, a little anyway. I wonder what their reactions will be when all is revealed?*

She turned to look out at the empty parking lot, or that is what Jessica said it was called when she asked before sunset. She noticed it was getting light. *I have spent this night watching over my friend.* This thought shocked her. *Friend? Is this rude, uncouth, surly creature, my friend? I do not recall ever having a friend of any kind before. She tried to intimidate me, but I was fearful of her weapon more than her. Was Jessica's anger generated by the gun, which is what she called it, she carried? I will have to monitor her when her weapon is not readily available.*

Dar could hear the slight noise Jessica made while she slept. She could see one of her arms over her head when she looked over. The other arm was under the covers somewhere. *I will be unconcerned about what the others think when the reveal happens, except for this one. I do not like it, but there it is, just the same.*

When Phelonius and Irving had arrived in San Diego, Irving was granted leave to find a room with a bath and kitchenette. It wasn't that he was given permission; Irving's consent was assumed.

As Irving wandered around, he saw a building with "Holiday Inn Express" on the side. "I may not be a genius, but I did spend the night in a Holiday Inn Express," he chuckled. "Nah, too easy!" he said, shaking his head. "I'm not that easily entertained." Irving took a few more steps, "Careful, Irv. You're already talking to yourself. Better not answer yourself, too." He laughed. "Sorry, could you repeat that?" He laughed harder.

It took some time before he could restrain his laughter. "Irv, I'm worried about you," he said in a severe tone.

"Where are they now?" Phelonius asked loudly.

Smith jerked himself awake after being startled. "They are in Pismo Beach." He rubbed his eyes. "They've been there a little more than a day." Smith forced his eyes wide, trying to force the sleepiness from his brain.

"Are you sure this thing is working? Why would they be there so long?" Phelonius asked as he peered at the screen. "What are they waiting for?"

"All good questions," Smith agreed, "but those answers are beyond the capabilities of this equipment. All I can tell you is the location of the bug I planted years ago. And it's in Pismo Beach.

"Have you heard from your other comrades?" Smith asked as he glanced sideways to Phelonius.

"You are either assuming I have other comrades or trying to

elicit information from me," Phelonius said as he glared at Smith. "Which is it?"

"Just trying to make conversation," Smith shrugged and returned his attention to the screen.

"You have never struck me as someone who indulges in idle conversation," Phelonius glared.

"Uh hem. Where is Irving?" Smith said quickly, trying to change the subject. "Should he be allowed to wander around on his own?"

"He is not, as you say, wandering around," Phelonius said. "If I need him, I call him, and he comes to me. If I do not, he is free to indulge in some freedom. He is allowed to find food and shelter."

"You make him sound like a dog," Smith said with a chuckle. "Here, Boy! Sit! Speak! Go fetch!" Smith started laughing heartily. He glanced at Phelonius and saw no delight, just a cold, hard stare. Smith choked off his laughing into a cough. "It makes me feel good to see that high-IQ, over-educated—"

"I find him…interesting," Phelonius said, interrupting Smith. He then looked at Smith with disdain. "I find you…useful, for the time being."

"Does he have one of these?" Smith asked with an air of superiority as he rubbed the band around his bicep.

"He does," Phelonius said. "However, his is not mine. I have tried repeatedly to induce him to remove it, as that is the only way it can be removed, by him or the band's owner. Until he removes the one he currently has, he cannot accept one from me." There was a long pause. "And before you make some imbecilic suggestion, forced removal would result in death for anyone who attempts it. Either from the band, the band's owner, or —" Phelonius glared at Smith again, "me."

Smith felt a chill run down his spine.

Cornelius watched *S'hyrlus* walk around, touching substantial oaks in a small grove. When she found one that met her needs, she waved for Cornelius to come to her.

"Walk past this tree slowly," she directed. "It has to recognize you."

"Any tree that fails to recognize me cannot be that well-informed," Cornelius quipped.

"Of course," *S'hyrlus* said, "but then they do not get out much."

"Why am I doing this?" Cornelius asked.

"You saw me touch other trees," *S'hyrlus* said. "I sent Suzanne a message to transport to you via the trees. For that to happen, the tree needs to recognize you. It already knows its location. Thus, it will lead her here."

"Is that all there is to it?" Cornelius asked.

"For her to come here, yes," *S'hyrlus* responded, "but she has to do the same with Socrates so that we can return to him."

"Sounds complex," Cornelius said.

"The explanation is more complex than the action," *S'hyrlus* said, "as it is with most things."

Cornelius nodded. "Hornsdoodle!" he yelled.

Hornsdoodle was within earshot and came to Cornelius when he called.

"Your choices are come with us or return to *Q'estiria*," Cornelius explained.

"And how am I to return to *Q'estiria*?" Hornsdoodle said. "I have no means to transit the barriers."

"You could go to the vaults," Cornelius said.

"Is that not the way Irving went to *Q'estiria*?" Hornsdoodle asked.

"Yes," Cornelius said smiling, "and he was no worse the wear for it."

Hornsdoodle dropped his gaze. "I will follow you and Lady *S'hyrlus*," he said.

"Are we set yet?" Socrates asked. He'd been watching Suzanne trying to select a tree. He guessed it would be used to transport Lady *S'hyrlus* and Cornelius to their location.

"Almost," Suzanne answered. "I've never done this before, so I'm trying to be as precise as possible."

"I don't understand," Socrates said. "You transport me all the time. What's so different with this one?"

"When I transport you from this plane to *Q'estiria*, we travel from this plane to another plane, to *anywhere* on that other plane. This time it's different. This time has to be precise. We are on the same plane as Lady *S'hyrlus* and Cornelius. If I tried and conditions were not optimal, I could end up anywhere."

"She sent me instructions to use Cornelius and you as the destination targets."

"Can't you just leave the portal open, once there, for the return?" Socrates asked.

"I can and probably would," Suzanne said, "in any other circumstance, but Lady *S'hyrlus* wants to use this as practice."

Socrates chuckled. "I'm sure Cornelius would balk at this if he knew."

Suzanne laughed. "I'm sure he would, which is why I'm not going to tell him."

"And neither am I," Socrates said as the portal opened.

"Well, that worked," Suzanne said. "I can see Lady *S'hyrlus* and Cornelius on the other side. I'm off!" She stepped through, and the portal closed.

"What exactly is the purpose of this?" Cornelius asked *S'hyrlus* as she approached. She had been talking to Suzanne, trying to calm her.

"She needs the practice," *S'hyrlus* said, indicating Suzanne with a nod. "This type of transport needs to be precise."

"She has transported Socrates to *Q'estiria* without incident," Cornelius said.

"That was different," *S'hyrlus* said. She turned to see Suzanne coming to her. "This has upset her greatly. Please do not add to her distress."

"I don't know what it is, Lady *S'hyrlus*," Suzanne said quietly. "I've never had this kind of issue before."

"Have you tried clearing your mind first?" *S'hyrlus* asked.

"I have," Suzanne said. "I know it is not that hard. It is as if —" she broke off suddenly. She said nothing for a while. "How independent are our skills?" she asked.

S'hyrlus looked questioningly and shook her head slightly.

"Can our powers, for lack of a better word, be interfered with?" Suzanne asked.

"What is it you suspect?" *S'hyrlus* asked.

"To put it another way," Suzanne said, "can Hornsdoodle interfere with my ability to transport?"

S'hyrlus leaned to look around Suzanne at Hornsdoodle. "He should not be able to, but he could. Part of his training was to take care that the *Sh'o Sook J'eid* not be interfered with in any way. That is not to say they do not have the capability to do so."

"Are we ready to leave yet?" Cornelius asked as he strode up to *S'hyrlus* and Suzanne.

"We probably would have been there already," *S'hyrlus* said, "but Suzanne thinks her abilities are being interfered with...by Hornsdoodle. We have no proof, at this point, just suspicion."

"When Socrates and I transported Phelonius," Suzanne said, "Socrates had fitted restraints that blocked his access to *The Source*. Can you do something like that to Hornsdoodle?"

Cornelius smiled as he glanced towards Hornsdoodle. "As the Lady Suzanne wishes," he said with a slight bow.

"Hornsdoodle!" Cornelius bellowed as he, Suzanne, and *S'hyrlus* turned towards Hornsdoodle.

133

They all saw Hornsdoodle wizard-step away.

Suzanne walked over to the tree and immediately opened a portal. She saw Socrates on the other side. "Let us proceed!" Suzanne said and motioned to Cornelius and *S'hyrlus*.

The pair preceded her through the portal.

"I was beginning to be concerned," Socrates said as the portal closed.

"About what, my son?" *S'hyrlus* asked.

"To me, it did seem that Suzanne was gone an unusually long time," Socrates said. "I thought there could've been an attack by Phelonius on either her or one of you two."

"There was," Cornelius said. "It just was not the kind of attack I was expecting."

Socrates' raised his eyebrows.

"No, I was not expecting that kind of attack," Cornelius said, "and I am considering changing the training regimen to keep the possibility of it uppermost in our minds."

THE STORM BEGINS

P helonius, Smith, and Irving were gathered around a small fire. They were all sitting on the curb, watching the flames just onto the roadbed from the gutter.

"Where are we?" Irving asked quietly. He didn't like being out in the open at night.

"San Diego," Smith answered as he stretched his legs toward the fire. "Where have you two been holed up anyway?" he asked as he retracted his legs.

"I have no idea," Irving said

"That is a good thing," Phelonius said. "If I wanted you to know, Smith, I would have told you."

"I was just making conversation," Smith said.

Irving looked to Phelonius, and Phelonius looked to Irving.

"Hahaha," Irving laughed heartily.

"I find your remark...off-putting," Phelonius said with a smirk and a dour expression. "I doubt you say anything; how did you put it, making conversation?"

Someone standing in the dark said something that sounded like gibberish to Smith, but Irving recognized it, even though he didn't understand what was said.

"I am B'runix Hornsdoodle," he said in *Q'estirian* as he took off his hat and bowed, one leg forward and bent at the waist, arms extended.

"What is it you require, Hornsdoodle?" Phelonius asked.

"I seek Phelonius Blackwing. I may have information he would find useful," Hornsdoodle said.

"I am Phelonius," Phelonius said. Hornsdoodle's shocked expression caused Phelonius to grin. "What is your information, and what is the price of it?"

"The price is nominal, for one such as you. The information concerns Cornelius Blackwing," Hornsdoodle said.

"Hmm. What is this nominal fee?" Phelonius asked.

Hornsdoodle inhaled deeply and let it out slowly. "I find myself stranded on this...this *Plane*. I require transport to any of the *Seven Known Planes*."

"And you believe I can arrange transport for you?" Phelonius asked. Hornsdoodle nodded. "And if I cannot arrange transport? What then?"

B'runix's expression changed to one of concern. "I do not understand."

"Like you," Phelonius said, "I find myself on this *Plane*, except I have no intention of leaving."

B'runix looked shocked. "I did not mean for you to transport me, just to arrange the transport."

Phelonius chuckled. "What is your information? I will agree to your price if I find it worthy."

B'runix looked to the other people present.

"Pay no attention to those two," Phelonius said. "They do not understand our language."

"Are you certain?" B'runix asked. "That one stands *Sha Shin* for Socrates Blackwing, the pretender ambassador. His mate is credited with capturing Malthuvius Nighthawk. He is quite intelligent."

136

"Both of them are human," Phelonius said dismissively. "Relay your information. Ignore the humans."

Hornsdoodle leaned in closer to Phelonius. "Cornelius Blackwing is on this Plane and is near, and the Lady S'hyrlus is accompanying him."

"Hmmm," Phelonius said. "A member of the council on this *Plane* in contravention of the council's mandates." He grinned broadly. "I wonder if the rest of the council is aware.

"Any other information you wish to pass along?" Phelonius asked.

"Socrates Blackwing is also close at hand, and he is traveling with the Lady Suzanne," Hornsdoodle said.

"I do not recognize Lady Suzanne?" Phelonius asked as he shook his head slightly. "Anything else?"

Hornsdoodle nodded his head towards Irving. "His mate is also nearby."

"Young Hornsdoodle," Phelonius said. "I did not seek you out. You found me. Why?"

"Primarily," Hornsdoodle said, "because I despise this *Plane* and everyone on it. It is my opinion that these...humans are not worth dying for, and we should never have come here. They have...tainted our kind."

"B'runix, you interest me," Phelonius said. "I do not agree with you, but your thought processes...or lack thereof...fascinates me."

B'runix glared at Phelonius.

"Firstly, B'runix," Phelonius said, "you brought me nothing I did not already know. Listing the *Sh'o Sook J'eid* is meaningless. You know as well as I that they are precluded from interfering in any altercation. That is their protection and why harming one is punished so severely.

"Secondly, I prefer those who detest this *Plane* and would ban it. They have no idea the rejuvenation of their life that is possible here."

"I gave you the information I have," B'runix said.

"Is it my concern that what you offer is worth nothing?" Phelonius said. "I am curious to know of your fighting skills, though."

"And who is it you wish me to fight?" Hornsdoodle asked.

"If it were up to me, I would say this one," Phelonius said, indicating Smith, "but then there would be the refusal and the pleading, generally making a fool of himself. So, if I am to know, it will either be Irving or me. You choose."

"I have faced him before," Hornsdoodle said, shifting to English. "He is no challenge to me. The other one might be more of a challenge."

"As I said, Smith is a coward," Phelonius said. "I am not in the mood to see such a one cry and grovel. I am looking for entertainment." Phelonius smiled. "I take your shift to their language as you warning them what is happening. Are you trying to undermine me?"

"What kind of fighting are you wanting?" Hornsdoodle asked, ignoring Phelonius' question.

"Since you will be going against humans, swordplay," Phelonius said. "I do not want you to injure my prizes unnecessarily. I need to assess their skill compared to yours." Phelonius shrugged.

"And if I decline?" Hornsdoodle asked.

Phelonius' grin widened. "Then you will battle me."

When Jessica awakened, she saw *Dar'Kyn* sitting in a chair, watching her. She fell back onto the bed. "Don't start, Dar. I haven't even had my coffee yet."

Dar looked at her with a puzzled expression, "What is coffee?" she asked.

"It's a drink, usually hot. You have it when you need a jolt of caffeine," Jessica said.

"And what does this...caffeine do?" Dar asked.

"For some of us, it gets our hearts started in the morning," Jess explained. "Some people drink it all day long, so they stay alert. Others drink it out of boredom." Jess sat up quickly. "What are you doing here?"

"I was sent to escort you to the meeting," Dar said

"Meeting? What meeting?" Jessica asked as she got to her feet and pulled on her clothes.

"There is a meeting with Socrates, Cornelius, Lady Suzanne, and Lady *S'hyrlus*," Dar reported.

"And where is this meeting being held?" Jessica asked as she tied her hair back.

"I do not know what it is called, thus the need for me to escort you," Dar said.

"Well, if I see a store that has coffee, we're stopping," Jess said as the pair exited the room.

They hadn't gone far when Jessica saw a restaurant, glass front facing the ocean.

In a corner booth sat Socrates, Suzanne, Cornelius, and *S'hyrlus*. All were fascinated with watching the waves on the beach.

"What are the chances of getting some coffee," Jessica asked as she approached the booth.

Suzanne said, "Help yourself. We have to plan, so we'll be here a while."

"Does anyone else want coffee?" Jessica asked as she walked behind the counter. Hearing no reply, she proceeded to the walk-in freezer, selected the 16-ounce, pre-brewed coffee, and popped the heat tab on the bottom of the disposable cup.

As she walked back to the front, she could smell the coffee

heating. When she got to the counter, she set the cup on the counter, removed the lid, and savored the smell of the hot beverage wafting up. She leaned on the counter, not far from the rest of her companions, and took the first tentative sips.

Dar'Kyn climbed, with difficulty, and sat on top of the counter next to Jessica. She strained her neck to be able to smell the beverage. "That does smell tantalizing," she said.

Jessica looked sideways at Dar and slid the cup over to her. "It's hot, so be careful," she said.

Dar took the cup and tried to raise it to her lips, but the steam coming off it prevented it.

"We humans blow lightly over the top of the cup to cool the liquid enough to sip a little," Jessica said. She took back the cup and demonstrated, then passed the cup back to Dar.

Dar mimicked her friend and took a tentative sip, making a face. "Bitter?" she asked.

"It can be," Jessica responded and headed back to the freezer. She returned a minute later with a light-brown, steaming cup. "You might like this better," she said as she removed the top and set the cup on the counter in front of Dar.

Dar took a sip and smiled. "That is better. Why is mine in a light-brown cup, and yours is black?"

"Mine is called black coffee," Jessica explained. "Yours has creamer and honey. They went to a representative-colored cup when reading fell out of favor."

It wasn't long after dawn that Irving faced Hornsdoodle. Hornsdoodle had his sword and was taking a few practice swings.

"Do not unnecessarily harm him," Phelonius said to Irving as he handed him a sword.

Irving nodded his understanding as he grasped the sword.

"I have instructed him to refrain from injuring you," Phelonius continued, "but I would advise you to be ready for anything."

Irving nodded again as his hand caressed the grip of the familiar blade. This was his blade whenever he and Phelonius sparred.

Phelonius moved equidistant between the combatants. "This is training only," he said. "Consequently, I expect restraint and control." He pointed to Irving and received a nod.

"I object to this," Hornsdoodle said when Phelonius pointed to him. "I have trained with this one many times before. He is not up to the basic skills we expect from younglings."

Phelonius glared at Hornsdoodle. "You will either fight him or me," Phelonius said. "Pick now, or I will."

Hornsdoodle shrugged and started to circle Irving. Irving crouched and held his blade-tip shoulder high and the hilt low. Hornsdoodle made a half-hearted lunge, which was parried easily by the central ridge of Irving's sword just enough to be certain Hornsdoodle's sword missed. Hornsdoodle withdrew.

The pair circled each other slowly. Periodically, Hornsdoodle would thrust only to have his sword slide down Irving's sword ineffectually. Finally, Hornsdoodle brought his sword down towards Irving's head. Irving's sword met the other's blade, letting it slide down towards the hilt, but Irving slid toward Hornsdoodle and punched him in the face.

"Foul!" Hornsdoodle yelled as he backed away, rubbing the side of his face. "He committed a foul!" he repeated, pointing his sword at Irving.

"What is this foul you say he committed?" Phelonius yelled at Hornsdoodle.

"You stated the rules, and this was to be a training match," Hornsdoodle said. "In all my training matches, I have never been struck."

"Yes, it is a training match. Were you cut?" Phelonius asked. "He struck you with his hand while you have a sword. You say you have never been struck while in training? Maybe you should have been. Continue!"

———

From the moment Irving squared off with Hornsdoodle, he felt intimidated. After all, he had never achieved anything close to a win with a sword against any of the *Q'estirians*. When Hornsdoodle's blade first pressed against his, he noticed that his wrist was stronger. His arm felt stronger.

Irving saw Hornsdoodle circle him, and he copied the action. Hornsdoodle caused his blade to drift toward Irving's blade as if they were drawn together magnetically. As soon as the blades touched, Hornsdoodle made a few testing strikes towards Irving's head and knees, alternating. Irving met the testing strikes, making the blades ring, and deflected them easily. After two or three, he forced Hornsdoodle's blade down, stepped in, and brought his left elbow into play, striking toward Hornsdoodle's head. As Irving hit Hornsdoodle's jaw, he stepped behind Hornsdoodle and turned to face him, ready for anything. A brief smirk crossed his lips, seeing the tall *Q'estirion* stumble and drag his blade on the pavement.

"Foul!" Hornsdoodle yelled. He had switched hands and was probing his jaw while flexing it.

Phelonius sighed audibly. "What is it now?" he asked as he strode over to a mid-point between Irving and Hornsdoodle.

"You need to instruct the human that this is training, and it is considered a foul to strike your opponent," Hornsdoodle said curtly.

Phelonius cocked his head to one side. "Excuse me. I don't think I heard you correctly. I…what was it…*need*? Did you say I *need* to do something?"

Hornsdoodle shifted his weight from one foot to the other, still caressing the side of his jaw. Phelonius walked up to Hornsdoodle scowling, and Hornsdoodle instinctively raised his blade defensively.

"*I* do not *need* to do anything," Phelonius said tensely. "You will refrain from calling foul for your perceived slights." Hornsdoodle's blade drifted towards Phelonius. "If you do not wish me to respond, I would suggest you get control of that blade." The sword moved away from Phelonius. Phelonius turned and walked toward Irving.

Irving had maintained his stare even as Phelonius approached. He came to a stop slightly on Irving's right.

"About one more, I would say," Phelonius said quietly before continuing. "Continue!" he yelled a few steps past Irving.

Irving prepared to continue his training.

"Seek," Phelonius whispered to Smith.

Smith grinned and nodded.

Jessica and *Dar'Kyn*, both carrying a cup of coffee each, joined the others. Suzanne and *S'hyrlus* raised an eyebrow at the sight of *Dar'Kyn* and what she was drinking. Suzanne glanced at Jessica.

"She wanted to know what coffee was," Jessica said with a shrug.

"Uh-hem," Socrates cleared his throat. "What is the next place on your predetermined course?"

"Long Beach," Jessica said as she sat on a table with her feet on the bench seat. Dar jumped up and sat beside Jessica. "It's about 169 miles. Being at the edge of the operational safety range, I can only carry myself and Dar. No other passengers."

"Luckily, the distance isn't beyond our step range," Socrates said. "Initially, I'd thought to approach every possible hiding place en masse. Having to split up could be problematic."

"I believe," Cornelius said, "that Jessica and *Dar'Kyn* are quite capable of defending themselves. At least for as long as it would take us to step to their location. It should not take us too long."

S'hyrlus nodded her agreement.

"Jessica, you proceed to Long Beach with *Dar'Kyn*, and then use your coin to call me to you," Socrates said. "We will be there in no more than a couple of minutes. So, when you get there, call for me. Don't do any scouting, and no heroics!"

Jessica put her hand on her chest and looked innocent. "Heroics? From me? I wouldn't think of it!" she said.

"How far do we have left to go?" *Dar'Kyn* asked as she finished her coffee. She was sitting in the front with Jessica and was shaking one foot.

"Not too far. About," Jessica looked at the radar screen, which had just started to beep. "Shit! Another craft is coming in, fast too." She heard Dar's harness click.

"Well, how about that!" came over the headphones. *"And they say miracles never happen!"*

"Smith?" Jessica asked.

"And she still remembers my name! I am impressed!" Smith said.

"I'm about out of fuel and am not in any mood to chitchat," Jessica said.

"Figured you might be. You are, however, at the end of the line," Smith said.

"What's that supposed to mean?" Jessica asked.

"It means you can land anywhere you like, but I have the refueling location mined. I'll set it off if you go closer than a couple of miles."

Jessica cut the mics. "I swear I'm gonna kill that sonofabitch if it's the last thing I do!"

"We have trouble?" Dar asked.

"Ya think!" Jessica snapped. "If I don't set this thing down, he'll blow the refuel, stranding us here." She was looking frantically for a place to set the hovercar down. "We'll have to find a way to get this thing refueled," she said. *If we survive,* she thought.

Jessica had located a large parking lot littered with only a few vehicles and started her descent. She heard the low fuel alarm when she was 10 feet off the surface, and she set the vehicle down and cut off the engines.

"You stay here," Jessica told Dar. "If it's safe, I'll come back for you."

Jessica unlocked and opened her door. As she did, she was hit with a blast of hot wind. She exited and closed the door without looking back.

"That's far enough," Smith said from behind Jessica.

Jessica tried to look over her shoulder towards Smith, presumably. "What is it you want?" she asked.

"I want to collect what you owe me," Smith said.

"What is it you think I owe you?" Jessica asked.

"I think you owe me for all the humiliation I've had to endure," Smith said.

Jessica couldn't see Smith but could tell he was grinning by the tone of his voice. "Pretty pleased with yourself, aren't you? So, are you *sure* you want to collect for the humiliation? Wouldn't you rather have the humiliation continue?" She heard Smith's teeth grind. "I can see to it that your humiliation continues for a long time."

"Shut the fuck up, you bitch!" Smith spat. "I'm going to rid myself of—"

Jessica turned suddenly and grasped his wrist and the gun in it as she hit his jaw with an elbow. The blow caught him just under the ear. She heard a snap and felt his temporomandibular joint give way. She felt a sharp pinch on the web of skin between thumb and forefinger. Instinctively, she had grabbed the gun close to the hammer. The intense pain was from the hammer being released.

"You asshole! You tried to shoot me!" she said tensely. She yanked the pistol from his grip, opened the hammer to free her hand, and shook it. "You know, that fucking hurt!"

Smith tried to rush forward as Jessica popped open the cylinder to check if the gun was loaded. She closed the cylinder. She saw him and kicked his knee to the side, and Smith dropped and rolled over onto his back, holding his knee.

Jessica walked over to the sobbing Smith and pointed his gun at his head. "I can't miss from here," she said. "You shoulda left well enough alone."

There was a loud report and an unsightly red smear on the pavement.

14

THE EYE OF THE STORM

I rving and Hornsdoodle continued their training match after Smith was dispatched. Neither knew what Phelonius' plan entailed. Irving was doing what Phelonius instructed him to do and trusted in the knowledge that Phelonius needed him intact.

After parrying a few more of Hornsdoodle's strikes, Irving stepped in and struck Hornsdoodle's nose with his free hand, breaking it.

"Foul!" Hornsdoodle screamed again as he backed away, covering his face with his free hand. Blood was spewing from his nose, and Irving saw Hornsdoodle's eyes swelling.

"I would advise you to protect yourself," Phelonius warned. "The human that you despised and regard as a weak fool has the opportunity to send you to your long-dead ancestors."

"I protest the foul blows he has struck!" Hornsdoodle said. "I am having difficulty breathing, and I find it difficult to see. This match has gone far beyond any training."

"What do you propose to mitigate those foul blows?" Phelonius asked.

"You have disrespected me!" Hornsdoodle yelled.

Phelonius laughed. "True! What do you propose to regain your...honor? Are you challenging Irving to an *actual* duel? I

STEPHEN DRAKE

would be careful. He has already shown you the effectiveness of your sword training." Phelonius grinned. "Or are you challenging me?" he asked, looking sideways, and smiling at Hornsdoodle.

Irving stood to the side, watching Hornsdoodle.

After a few minutes of silence, Phelonius motioned for Irving to come over to him.

"Irving, kill him," Phelonius whispered.

"I was waiting for you to tell me that," Irving said. "I have to decline."

After shooting Smith, Jessica was standing over his body. After holstering her pistol, she quickly searched Smith's body and removed his pistol and holster. As she turned away, she spit on the body.

It wasn't long before Jessica opened the door of her hovercar. "It should be safe to come out," she said to *Dar'Kyn*.

"What about that Smith character?" Dar asked as she exited the hovercar.

"He won't be bothering us anymore," Jessica said as she secured the second holster on her opposite hip in a cross-draw. "This car is so low on fuel, and I don't want to risk flying it to the refuel station. I did search Smith but found no means to detonate any mines he said he'd placed."

"Not that I would know what a dee-tone-ater would look like, so where does that leave us?" Dar asked. She had walked around to the left side of the hovercar. She saw Smith's body lying where Jessica had dropped him as she looked around. "Did you terminate him?"

"Yes," Jessica said. "It gave me no pleasure. Smith had been a burr under my saddle for some time.

"We need to try to locate Smith's hovercar. He may have a

148

detonator in it. He could have also been lying about mining the refuel station."

"Why would he lie?" Dar asked.

"Smith was trained to lie," Jessica said. "When he said he mined the refuel, did I know, with certainty, that he hadn't? No, I chose to err on the side of caution. He knew I would, so his bluff, if that's what it was, worked, and we landed. I'm uncertain about going close to the refueling area unless we find something electronic that could be used as a detonator. If he has one, it wasn't on his person, that leaves his hovercar."

Suzanne, Socrates, Cornelius, and S'hyrlus were waiting for a signal from Jessica. Cornelius and S'hyrlus were waiting outside the restaurant at a table. Socrates and Suzanne stayed inside. Socrates looked to be meditating, though Suzanne figured his stillness was related to monitoring Jessica's signal.

"I take it that you haven't received anything from Jessica," Suzanne said.

"I'm not just monitoring for Jessica," Socrates answered without opening his eyes. "I'm also monitoring for Irving."

"Have you figured out how to handle Phelonius when we catch up to him?" Suzanne asked.

Socrates frowned. "Not yet. I'm well aware that there will be all the Blackwings, currently living, all in one area."

"There are only three of you?" Suzanne asked.

"Currently." Socrates nodded.

Suzanne frowned and remained quiet for some time.

Dar was the first to find Smith's hovercar parked between tall buildings not far from his body. As she approached, she heard a beeping coming from the interior. She left to bring Jessica to the find.

Dar was first to return. She heard the beeping getting louder and more frequent.

"What did you do?" Jessica asked, irritability apparent as she approached. The beeping grew louder and increased in tempo.

"What do you mean?" Dar screamed to be heard over the beeping.

"You must have touched something to sound an alarm like that. What did you do?" Jessica yelled.

"I touched nothing!" Dar yelled. "This...alarm...was already sounding when I found the vehicle." She pressed her hands against her ears in an attempt to reduce the alarm volume.

Jessica frowned and motioned for Dar to follow her.

As the pair moved away, the alarm seemed to slow and reduce in volume.

"That's interesting," Jessica said.

"What is?" Dar asked.

"It appears that the further away we move, the quieter the alarm becomes," Jessica said.

"Not exactly," Dar said. "When I found the vehicle, the alarm was sounding, but it was not as rapid nor as loud. It became louder when you approached."

"Hmm. A proximity alarm," Jessica said, nodding. "You go over by the vehicle and wave if it gets louder or more rapid. I'm going to start removing things I'm carrying or wearing until it stops getting louder."

Dar complied without argument.

Jessica removed the recently liberated pistol and holster, taken from Smith after he was dead, and started toward the hovercar. She hadn't taken half-dozen steps before Dar signaled. She returned to her previous position and removed her pistol and holster and retrieved the other pistol and holster. When she was ready, she started toward the hovercar. She received no signal from Dar after a dozen steps.

Jessica returned to the location of her favorite pistol and stood there looking at it. After thinking about the situation, she pulled the gun, laid it aside, and draped the empty holster over her shoulder. Jessica started toward the hovercar, expecting a signal. After a dozen steps, she received no sign, and she motioned for Dar to come to her.

"We need to return to our hovercar," Jessica said after Dar had reached her. "I need tools. There seems to be a tracking device somewhere in my pistol, and I need to find it."

Phelonius walked up to Hornsdoodle and held out his hand.

Hornsdoodle looked chagrinned, hung his head, and handed Phelonius his sword.

"B'runix Hornsdoodle," Phelonius said as he took the sword and handed it to Irving, "you have been found to be faithless and a danger to your brothers. I take custody of you as I have assumed charge of your sword." He placed a coin on Hornsdoodle's wrist. "This will separate you from the *Source*. Do I need more to restrain you?"

B'runix shook his head.

"Do I get his sword?" Irving asked. "I did defeat Hornsdoodle."

"No, you didn't," Phelonius corrected. "You refused to take his life. If you had, you would have won his sword. At best, Hornsdoodle defeated himself."

"But—" Irving started.

Phelonius gave Irving a glare that said, leave it alone and motioned for Irving to come closer.

"This may help protect you from what is coming," Phelonius said as he pressed a gold coin to Irving's forehead.

Irving reached up and felt the bands of gold go around his head, just above his ears, and across the top of his head, in a version of a stylized helm.

"Prepare for transport," Phelonius said to Irving.

"Are we proceeding to Long Beach or somewhere else?" Irving asked.

"I have determined that all will come to fruition at the beach that is long," Phelonius said as he glared at Irving.

Irving chuckled as the trio disappeared.

Jessica and Dar had returned to their hovercar and opened the back door. Jessica began to take her Desert Eagle apart, placing the parts on the floor mat. Dar was watching over the back of the front seat.

"What are you looking for?" *Dar'Kyn* asked.

"I've had this gun apart many times," Jessica answered without looking away from her work. "Even though I've taken it apart, cleaned it, and put it back together, I've never taken the gun down to the frame. Most of the time, it isn't needed unless something breaks.

"Hello! What have we here?" she asked when she removed the grip from the frame.

"Did you find something?" Dar asked with a significant increase in curiosity.

"There is a heavy, grease-like substance in a small hollow on the inside of the grip," Jessica explained as she selected a cleaning patch and wiped the grip with it. "Run this over to Smith's hovercar to see if it trips the alert," she said, handing the patch to Dar.

Dar'Kyn took the patch and left. Jessica cleaned everything and assembled the gun.

She had inserted the cylinder, loaded it, shut the back door of the hovercar, and walked behind the vehicle.

"Oh, shit," she said as Phelonius, Hornsdoodle, and Irving appeared close to Smith's body. She ambled toward them, hand on her pistol.

Phelonius looked up as Jessica approached.

"Did you...dispatch him?" Phelonius asked, indicating Smith with a twitch of his head in Smith's direction. Jessica gave a single nod. "Ahhh...that is a shame," Phelonius sighed as he turned back toward Smith. "He was...helpful," he paused for a long time, "but it is just as well. He was close to the end of his usefulness."

Dar came bounding up, startling Phelonius. An energy ball flew from him, hitting Dar. It propelled her backward out of sight.

"Hey!" Jessica yelled and started to draw her weapon.

Phelonius had another energy ball ready to throw at her when both froze. "Have a care, human," Phelonius warned, "of the beasts you deign to entertain."

"I'm sure she didn't know," Irving said as he interposed his body between the two.

"Irving," Jessica said, "get out of the way."

Phelonius smiled. "Kill her," he whispered to Irving.

"That would be a terrible idea," Irving said, shaking his head. "All I have is a sword...and we humans have a warning about knives and gunfights."

"I do not understand," Phelonius whispered.

"A sword is, essentially, a big knife, and the warning is 'Don't bring a knife to a gunfight'. Meaning you'll be outmatched."

"I will not be outmatched, as you say," Phelonius said. "You may be, but I still insist you kill her."

Irving sighed. "Alright, just remember you asked for this." He drew his sword, assumed a guard position, and walked slowly toward Jessica.

"Irving," Jessica warned, "I will shoot you if you try anything with that pig-sticker."

Irving maintained his approach and gave her a little wink before he was close enough to strike. He stopped.

"Irving," Phelonius warned. "Do as I requested."

"No, I don't think so." Irving relaxed and turned around. He assumed a guard facing Phelonius.

Phelonius frowned.

Socrates, Cornelius, Suzanne, and *S'hyrlus* materialized some distance away at an angle that allowed everyone to see everyone else.

"Phelonius Blackwing," Socrates yelled as he stepped forward, "In the name of the council—"

"What!" Phelonius interrupted, "You will subdue me? Would you subdue your grandsire for that bunch of ineffectual cowards?"

"Ineffectual?" Cornelius said. "You will submit to the council's appointed enforcer and me. I am the head of the council and your grandsire. Do not force us to…insist you submit."

"Ha, ha, ha," Phelonius laughed maniacally. "I hope you do not mind if I try to stop laughing first? You are both old! Old and impotent, while I am young, young and vibrant.

"As a matter of housekeeping," Phelonius motioned for Hornsdoodle to walk toward Socrates, "I have uncovered dissension in your ranks. Thank you, I believe is the idiom."

As Hornsdoodle moved past Socrates, Cornelius transported Suzanne, *S'hyrlus*, and Hornsdoodle behind Jessica's hovercar.

"Keep him quiet and out of the way," Cornelius told *S'hyrlus*. "I would suggest you two *Sh'o Sook J'eid* stay behind cover." Cornelius disappeared and reappeared next to Socrates.

"Ever the gallant, Cornelius," Phelonius said, shaking his head slightly. "You truly are a relic." His hands clapped loudly, and he said, "Are we all prepared?"

Phelonius stepped back and began launching energy balls toward Socrates and Cornelius.

Jessica saw Phelonius turn toward Irving. She tried to get to her wizard-step coin. An energy ball hit Irving in the head just as Jessica touched Irving and squeezed the coin, causing both of them to disappear.

Irving and Jessica appeared behind Jessica's hovercar. Irving was trying to get the gold helm off his head.

"Get it off," Irving screamed, again and again, panic edging his voice.

Jessica tried to pull it off Irving's head but failed. Suzanne and *S'hyrlus* did what they could. None could remove the helm.

After Irving had quieted, Jessica sat with his head in her lap. As she stroked his chest to try to relax him and let him know he wasn't alone, she noticed that he was aging at a phenomenal rate.

"I'm sorry, love," she whispered. "We can't remove the helm, and it seems to be aging you."

"Phelonius, it must be," Irving said. "I feel like I am being wrung out. You know, when you look at a beautiful sunrise, you don't expect it to look back...I didn't expect you to look back, but I'm glad you did."

"So am I, love," Jessica whispered. A tear fell on Irving's cheek. As she watched, she saw wrinkles appear and Irving's hair thin and gray.

"I love you, my wife," Irving whispered.

"I love you, my husband," Jessica whispered. Irving tensed and then went slack; his breathing stopped.

As Irving's body continued to wither, the helm fell from his head. When it did, the helm returned to the shape of a coin, and Jessica bent to retrieve it.

"Stop!" Suzanne yelled.

"Do not touch it!" *S'hyrlus* shouted.

As Jessica watched, the coin flew toward Phelonius.

"Phel...own...ee...us!" Jessica screamed as she got to her feet and checked both *Desert Eagles* for readiness.

Socrates and Cornelius had their hands full battling Phelonius after Irving and Jessica disappeared. Both Socrates and Cornelius had no idea how long Jessica had been gone, and both were surprised to see her materialize behind Phelonius.

Bang, bang, bang, they heard. They saw Phelonius stagger from the rounds impacted to his back. *Bang, bang.* They saw Phelonius stumble forward as his knees were hit.

"Okay, you sonofabitch," Jessica said, holding one of her pistols to Phelonius' head while sitting on his back. "I'm real interested in finding out if your shit-filled head is bulletproof."

"Jessica, don't!" Socrates said as he ran up to the pair.

"Why not? He killed Irving. Why does he get to live?" Jessica asked without looking at Socrates. She felt Phelonius twitch. "Twitch again, fucker, and I'll end you...right here, right now!"

"If you think ending Phelonius will bring back your Irving, then go ahead," Cornelius said.

Socrates glared at Cornelius. "That isn't going to help the situation, Cornelius."

"And why not? He is outside of the council's edicts and outside the human's...what were they called?" Cornelius paused.

"Laws?" Jessica asked.

"Yes, laws," Cornelius said, "He is outside of the human laws. If Jessica is willing, she can do everyone a favor and end Phelonius, here, in the *Faewyld.* That is not what it is called here. This wild area...," Cornelius paused again.

"The frontier?" Jessica finished.

"Exactly! He does have many followers in the *Seven Known Planes.* If we take him back, there is the chance that he will be released," Cornelius warned.

"Every time I end a life, it weighs on me," Socrates said. "It drags my spirit down. The days seem darker, and the nights seem longer and colder. I wouldn't wish that on anyone, let alone a friend."

Jessica shook her head. "You two are confusing me. Irving

died because of this scumbag. He has caused no end of pain and suffering. Who has a greater right to terminate him than me?"

Dar'Kyn came over to Jessica. "Jessica, you do what you feel is right," Dar said. "If you feel it is correct to eliminate him, do so."

Jessica's muscles tensed. "He'll just get off if I don't," she said through clenched teeth.

Dar started to laugh. To everyone, Dar's laugh seemed strange and discordant. None of them had ever heard Dar laugh.

"I can assure you, he will be paying for his crimes for a very long time," Dar said after getting control of her laughter. "Socrates was correct. Ending a life wears on the spirit. If you feel you need that kind of perpetual pain, then, by all means, do it." She paused. "However, if you wish Phelonius to suffer, suffer as he deserves, for the rest of his days and then some, then tell me that is what you want, and I will arrange for that to happen."

"How can you?" Cornelius said. "If you," he looked her up and down dismissively, "tried to take him, he would escape. You are not physical enough to restrain him."

"He needs to be convicted by a trial," Socrates said. "We have our assumptions of his guilt, and those facts we do have, need to be presented to judges, and they need to determine the appropriate punishment. Who are we few to pass that kind of judgment on anyone?"

Dar looked sideways to the *Q'estirians*. "Jessica, you are *sha shin*, to the *Q'estirians*. You have earned the right to end the one that forever killed your joy. I understand your pain, the pain now, and the pain that comes later. In this, we are sisters. The Ladies Suzanne and *S'hyrlus* are not your sisters, not in this. I am not arguing either option is preferable. I leave that to you. It is *your* choice."

Silence seemed to go on forever.

"If I choose to have him suffer, Dar, what do I do next?" Jessica asked, turning slightly toward her. "I'm not letting him up without some sort of restraint."

A sad smile dominated *Dar'Kyn's* face. "Do nothing, my sister. Your efforts will be sufficient. Is that what you choose? Eternal suffering?"

Jessica nodded.

Dar stepped away from the rest and whistled.

To Jessica, the whistle sounded like someone whistling and humming simultaneously, but by multiple individuals. The notes were strangely unmelodious. The notes grated on the nerves and seemed to reverberate throughout the world. Everyone but Dar clamped their hands over their ears.

Everyone turned to look at the western sky. Something dark hung on the horizon and blotted out the setting sun, turning the air cold.

15

THE PASSING OF THE STORM

W hen Irving became too uncomfortable with his head in Jessica's lap, he got to his feet.

"Are you doing okay?" a young man, sitting on the hood of the hovercar, asked.

"Yeah, I guess so," Irving said as he brushed himself off. "I feel...funny, though."

"Can I ask your name?" the young man asked as he slid off the hood to his feet.

"Irving. Irving Strange," Irving said, sticking out his hand.

The young man took his hand. "Phil," he said.

Irving turned around and saw Jessica still sitting on the ground with his head in her lap. "I'm dead, aren't I?" Irving asked.

"You got it right off," Phil said. "Sometimes it takes a while."

"Am I supposed to move on?" Irving asked after a long pause.

Phil nodded. "When you're ready. There's no rush. Let me ask, *Elysian Fields*, *Valhalla*, neither, both, or something else?"

"I don't know. I never really gave it much thought. Where am I supposed to go?" Irving asked.

Phil looked at Irving for a bit before answering. "I'd say you are more *Elysian Fields* than *Valhalla*. The *Elysian Fields* is a nice place, and always just the right temperature, soft, sweet grass on which to lay. You'll like it there."

"Will my wife be joining me there?" Irving asked.

"I have no idea. That is above my paygrade," Phil chuckled.

"I understand," Irving said. "Well, we may as well be moving on."

"As you wish," Phil said as he took Irving by the elbow.

They both disappeared.

Jessica, looking past *Dar'Kyn*, watching the darkness coming their way from the west. The wind was picking up as it approached.

Dar'Kyn knelt and turned Phelonius' head so he could see.

"They come for you," Dar said.

"Who comes?" Phelonius asked.

"Three daughters of Nyx," Dar answered. "The *Erinyes*. They come for you, and they are your escort to Tartarus."

"I won't let him go," Jessica said.

"You have no choice now, Jessica," Dar said. "This is what you wanted. They will take him from you no matter how tightly you hold him, but you will not be harmed. He will not escape, not even if you release him now."

Socrates and Cornelius moved toward Jessica's hovercar, where *S'hyrlus* and Suzanne held Hornsdoodle. They were mesmerized by the approaching darkness and the coldness that preceded it.

"You cannot do this!" Phelonius yelled, trying to be heard over the wind. "Grandsire! You can stop this!"

Cornelius bowed his head and strode over to *Dar'Kyn*. "Is there any intercession allowed?" he asked Dar.

"His guilt is not in question," Dar said. "There is no

bargaining or intercession. His myriad victims' blood screams out. I am surprised you cannot hear them."

Hornsdoodle, Socrates, Suzanne, and *S'hyrlus* were mesmerized as the darkness dropped and seemed to pick Phelonius, *Dar'Kyn*, and Jessica up with invisible hands.

They heard Phelonius scream as he was engulfed. They saw Jessica and *Dar'Kyn* set on the ground as the darkness withdrew to the west.

They all watched as the darkness retreated and the last vestiges of sun and heat returned.

It took a few seconds before Jessica recovered enough to bend closer to *Dar'Kyn* and ask, "Who *are* you?"

Dar turned a little to look at Jessica. "I am who I said I am. *Dar'Kyn* Trubis, and I am Hamadryad-sister of the Lady *Ptelea* of the Elm Grove."

Jessica looked skeptically at Dar. "And what else?" she asked.

"What do you mean, what else?" Dar asked.

Jessica turned toward Dar and bent down. "I'm willing to bet that if I asked Lady *S'hyrlus*, she'd be unable to explain what we all just witnessed, and she's seen a lot. You want to keep it to yourself, that's fine. But I'd like to suggest you get a whole lot better at spinning that yarn." Jessica turned and walked to her hovercar.

As she rounded the front of the hovercar, Jessica stopped at Irving's body and covered her face with her hand.

Suzanne came over and put her arm around Jessica's shoulder. "He was a good friend," she said quietly.

"He was naive, nerdy, silly, brilliant, and a love all at the same time," Jessica said around her silent tears. After a long pause, she continued, "I never felt loved, appreciated, wanted, or needed as he managed to make me feel even though I fought it at every turn. I knew that if I gave in, he would make me happier than I have ever been, and that's the damnable misery of it all."

Dar'Kyn had silently followed Jessica. She knelt, touched Irving's head, and closed her eyes. After a bit, she rose and stood quietly behind Jessica.

Finally, Jessica tore herself away and checked in the luggage area of the hovercar. It took her a while, but she found a heavy-duty body bag. She walked around to Irving's body and prepared him for transport.

"Have you decided what you're doing with Irving's body?" Suzanne asked.

"I would like to bury him somewhere on the property at home," Jessica said. "He always loved that place."

Suzanne nodded. "Yes, he'd like that. On another matter, Cornelius and Lady *S'hyrlus* are transporting Hornsdoodle back to *Q'estiria*, and they will be returning after he is incarcerated."

"Why will they be returning?" Jessica snapped. "As far as I'm concerned, they can all stay away."

"Socrates and I would like to help you with Irving's body," Suzanne said softly, "if you'd let us. He was our friend, too."

Jessica and *Dar'Kyn* were in Smith's hovercar, with Irving's body in the luggage area, a few hours later. They were on their way back to Tacoma.

"It's been hours," Jessica said. "Are you going to just sit there all the way home? Sit there and look out the window?"

"What is there to say?" Dar asked without turning from the window.

"You could try telling me who or what you are," Jessica said. "It isn't like there is anyone to overhear. And don't try to feed me that innocent line of yours. I was a trained observer, and I watched *S'hyrlus'* reaction, and she was as shocked as the rest of us."

Dar said nothing for a long time. "I am not ignoring you, Jessica," Dar said finally. "I am trying to decide how much to tell you. Sometimes, I think the information would console you, and other times, I am not sure."

Jessica said nothing. She knew when not to press for information, and she felt Dar was on the verge of full disclosure.

"What I told you already," Dar continued, "was true. I am *Dar'Kyn* Trubis, Hamadryad-sister of the Lady *Ptelea* of the Elm Grove, but that is not all." Dar sighed deeply. "I must insist on your total discretion," she said, turning to Jessica. Jessica nodded without turning toward Dar. She sighed again. "I am also Harpy Corps, Second Class...under *Tisiphone*."

"Not to sound uncaring or rude, but...so?" Jessica asked. "I understand that there is some significance to that, but it's beyond me."

Dar sighed deeply, again. "Depending on your source, *Tisiphone* is one of the Erinyes."

"Umm...still not registering anything here," Jessica said.

"The Erinyes are probably better known to your kind as... um...the Furies." Dar looked at Jessica and saw her shrug. "The Furies are the three daughters of Nyx, and they are goddesses of retribution and vengeance whose job it is to punish those who committed heinous crimes."

"Daughters of who?" Jessica asked.

"Nyx," Dar said. "Nyx is the goddess of night."

"And who is this *Tisiphone*?" Jessica asked.

Dar exhaled loudly in exasperation. "*Tisiphone* is one of the Furies dealing with retribution for murder."

Jessica was silent for a long time. "And how long have you had these delusions?" she asked.

After refueling, Jessica and Dar were sitting in a hotel room they managed to find.

"Why did you think me knowing would be comforting?" Jessica asked after she was snuggled under the covers.

"You saw me touch Irving's head?" Dar asked without turning to look at Jessica.

"Yes, I saw that, and I just thought it was something religious," Jessica answered.

"It was, but more," Dar said. "There are things I gave up by joining the Harpy Corps. One of the abilities I gained was the ability to check a recently passed spirit by touching."

"So, what did you find by touching Irving?" Jessica asked after a brief pause.

"He was not there," Dar said. "He had already moved on."

"Moved on…to where?" Jessica asked.

"To wherever," Dar said. "What we have in that compartment of the hovercar is a husk, a shell, something your Irving has sloughed off so he can move onward."

Dar could hear Jessica crying again, but she remained stoic and didn't turn around to look at her.

After refueling the hovercar and finding someplace for coffee, the pair were off again.

"Sorry for implying you were delusional," Jessica said. "From my perspective, what you said about the Furies and being a member of the Harpy Corps—"

"Second Class," Dar interrupted.

"Yes, Second Class," Jessica chuckled at the correction. "Anyway, to me, it all sounds crazy."

"Crazier than knowing wizards and Hamadryads?" Dar asked.

"Good point," Jessica said, chagrinned.

"When I first came to your *Plane*," Dar said, "I had heard of things that, at the time, I thought were unbelievable."

"You mean back when Phelonius took Irving," Jessica said. "Yes, I suppose everything here was crazy to someone like you."

"No, way before that," Dar said good-naturedly.

"When exactly was that?" Jessica asked.

"Never mind," Dar said seriously. "We are not supposed to talk about that. Not with your kind, anyway."

Socrates and Suzanne returned to an empty house, and it was evident to Suzanne that no one had been inside for quite some time. She could see dust everywhere.

"I want to hire someone to help keep the place clean when we are out and about," Suzanne said.

"We were looking into hiring someone to cook for us," Socrates said, "maybe we could hire one person to do both jobs?"

Suzanne grabbed a hand towel and started dusting the table and chairs. "How did Phelonius spirit Irving away so quickly?" she asked as she worked.

Once one chair was dusted, Socrates sat and produced two tankards. "If you start at that far wall and take a step," he said as he handed one to Suzanne, "look around a second, then step again; it would take you a while to get across the room. If you start at the far wall again and run, you'd cover the same distance but significantly faster.

"What I think is, Phelonius had traveled up and down the coast so many times that he selected distinguishing landmarks within the limits of the wizard step that he could run, each step in the stride being a new wizard step. It would take him no time to get outside the range of Irving's *K'obi Sha Shin J'oi Faqin T'orqute.*

"Most of the time, we use the wizard step to get somewhere faster, but we're limited to reference points that are familiar."

Suzanne looked grim as she sat and sipped from the tankard.

"For Phelonius to gain that level of familiarity, how long was he here?" Suzanne asked.

Several hours after leaving Long Beach, sunset was upon Jessica and Dar.

"I assume we will be stopping for the night?" Dar asked without looking at Jessica.

"Yeah, we're going to layover here in Santa Rosa," Jessica responded.

"Are we getting a room?" Dar asked.

"We can look around and see what we can find," Jessica said. "I know you've grown accustomed to Hotel coffee."

"Actually," Dar said, "I prefer what you call *Diner* coffee. Motel or Hotel coffee is...what is it you call it? Rot the gut?"

Jessica smirked. "Rotgut. I call it rotgut. Anything strong enough to dissolve a spoon is rotgut."

A few hours after finishing the refueling of the hovercar, Jessica and Dar walked into a room that looked to be dusty but clean otherwise. At least, no one died in the room at the time of *The Event*.

Jessica threw back the covers, stripped off her clothes, climbed into bed, and turned out the light.

Dar had already gotten a cup of warm coffee and sat in the dark. *Sleep well, my friend. I will watch over you and wake you should the need arise,* Dar thought without averting her eyes from the window and the moonlight on the overgrown lawn. *I know she is in pain, and I know she acts braver than she is. She should know that she is not as alone as she believes.*

Dar then heard Jessica's labored breathing and a snuffle once in a while. *Jessica's tears cannot wash away her sorrow; only time can do that. There is nothing to be gained by choking back your tears, Jessica. You are alive, and living is difficult, as it should be.*

Eventually, Dar heard Jessica's breathing slow and even itself out. Dar knew Jessica was finally asleep.

An hour after daylight, Jessica and Dar walked into the deserted diner. Jessica hopped the counter and searched for coffee makings.

"Are you sure this coffee will do for you?" Jessica asked over her shoulder. "I was beginning to think you liked coffee made with hot water from the tap."

"I find the evening coffee satisfactory, just not preferable," Dar said from the counter. She was sitting on a swivel stool and was spinning the full 180 degrees of travel. "I much prefer the morning coffee."

Jessica paused and looked over to Dar. "You do know this little ritual won't be continued when we get to my home in Tacoma, don't you?" she asked.

"Why is that?" Dar asked.

"Because I don't have this kind of setup, and I won't be taking you into town every day," Jessica said.

"Why will you not take me to town?" Dar pouted. "We are partners, are we not?"

"We are for the next few days," Jessica said irritably. "Besides, taking you into Tacoma would raise more questions than I care to deal with."

She took two mugs of hot brown liquid to the counter and started to sip.

"I got your first one; you can get your own if you want more," Jessica said after a few sips. "I ain't no damned waitress, you know." She sipped more coffee. "I have a question."

"Ask your question," Dar said.

"What are you going to do for coffee when you return to your *Plane*?" Jessica didn't look at Dar.

"Unknown, at this time," Dar said after a short pause. "I am considering taking this...coffee to the rest of the *Seven Known Planes*. I think others would appreciate the flavor."

Jessica looked at Dar, disbelieving. "I think I need to research coffee when I get home. I guess I've taken it for granted and know next to nothing on the subject."

Jessica and Dar were sitting in the hovercar, with the doors open, waiting for it to cool enough to refuel.

"You've been uncharacteristically quiet since we were in Santa Rosa," Jessica said. "We're now in Ashland, any comment?"

"I do not know what you want," Dar said. "When I have nothing to say, I listen rather than talk. Far too many talk incessantly and say nothing."

"Agreed," Jessica said. "You said something about being a member of the Harpy Corps—"

"Second Class," Dar interrupted.

"Yes, Second Class," Jessica continued. "And you said you're still Hama...something."

"Hamadryad," Dar corrected.

"Do the leaders of those two...tribes, groups, whatever, know about your dual loyalty?"

Dar looked at Jessica skeptically. "Confidentially, yes, they do." Dar took a deep breath. "I am not supposed to disclose this, but there are always several Hamadryad that fail to...fit in, I think is how you would say it. I do not act as Suzanne, Ptelea, or even *S'hyrlus*."

"You are unique, I'll give you that," Jessica interrupted.

Dar looked peeved and continued, "When that occurs, they are...reassigned. Lady *Ptelea* knows I serve *Tisiphone*, and she does not know details about what those services are or what they entail."

"How about *S'hyrlus*?" Jessica asked. "Did she know about the Harpy thing before she brought you here?"

"I did not discuss such things with Lady *S'hyrlus*," Dar said carefully. "It was not something that would be discussed between us. Lady *S'hyrlus* had gone to Lady *Ptelea* and expressed a need for help apprehending Phelonius. I became aware of the need and, with Tisiphone's leave, offered to help in any way I could, and here I am."

"Didn't you send Phelonius to Tartar sauce...or something like that?" Jessica asked.

"Tartarus," Dar corrected peevishly. "It is a place of punishment for those such as him."

"If it's a place, he'll escape...somehow," Jessica said.

"Never. No one has ever escaped yet," Dar bragged. "Not since its creation. *Tartarus* and *Elysian* are two distinct *Planes*, and access to them is by another *Plane* that we call *Hades*, and yes, Cerberus guards the entrance."

"A three-headed dog is guarding the entrance to Hades?" Jessica asked disbelievingly.

"He is not really a dog, as you know them, but he does have three heads," Dar said.

After a long pause to think and absorb the information, Jessica continued. "Why tell me anything if you're not supposed to disclose it?"

Dar exhaled loudly. "I know you are not ready to hear it, but if you ever become...disillusioned with this life," she circled, arms extended, "the Harpy Corps would embrace you."

"I'm not ready to become a Hama-whatzits like Suzanne," Jessica said, shaking her head.

"Not all in the Harpy Corps are Hamadryad," Dar explained, "and we have none that have *Become*, as Suzanne did. Put another way, you seem to be pretty good in a fight, and we could use you."

16

TURNING THE PAGE

Two days after Suzanne and Socrates returned home, someone knocked at their back door.

"Greetings," Suzanne said, in English, as she swung the door wide, seeing who it was.

Being the first one through the door, Cornelius shook her hand limply and squeezed past her into the dining area to join Socrates. *S'hyrlus* took her elbow and gently guided her to the table. When Suzanne tried to close the door, she glimpsed two…others.

"This is Synkyn and Tynkyn Broadstone," *S'hyrlus* introduced the two creatures, speaking the Hamadryad language. "They are twins and have agreed to make the trip to this…outland for cooking and keeping the ambassador's residence," she said smiling.

One twin went into the kitchen and rummaged around the pots and pans. The other twin ran a finger over the top of the baseboards and stifled a sneeze at the dust she found there.

"I do not think we would fit in here," the twin in the kitchen said. "They do not have a proper cooking stove, no kindling or wood box, and who makes the deliveries? I will not chop wood!"

"Agreed," her sister said. "This place has more dust than the trail from *Q'estiria*."

"The one to *Sha'tukassia Breen*?" the sister in the kitchen asked.

"No, the other one," came the response.

"The *Barren Lands* are dusty!"

"As you can see," *S'hyrlus* interrupted, "they are *Grum K'sha U'ien*, and being twins, they have a distracting manner of speaking."

"And what is wrong with the way we speak?" the one in the kitchen asked.

"I can understand my sister perfectly," the one in the living room said.

"As can I," her sister added.

"So, any fault would be...elsewhere," the other sister replied.

S'hyrlus stood. "Stop!" she yelled. The twins became quiet. "That is better," she said as she sat. "They may be a bit...irritating, but being *Grum K'sha U'ien*, their skills, and their references, are impeccable."

"But how will I tell them apart?" Suzanne asked, leaning in to whisper her question.

"That is something you would have to solve for yourself," *S'hyrlus* said.

"Does this belong to you?" Socrates asked as he led one of the twins by the ear.

"Let go of me, you...you *Q'estirian*," the twin said, scowling at Socrates.

S'hyrlus smiled. "Not anymore. They belong to the Lady Suzanne and you."

Socrates scowled at *S'hyrlus* then turned it to Suzanne.

171

"Socrates," Cornelius said from behind him, "let Lady *S'hyrlus* and Lady Suzanne handle this business with the *Grum K'sha U'ien*. The cooking and cleaning do fall under their purview, after all."

Socrates turned to look at Cornelius. "That may be true, but chaos in my house will not be tolerated! These two seem to be the very definition of chaos."

"That may be true," Cornelius said, "but leave it to the ladies to sort out."

<hr/>

"Can the four of us sit and quietly see if we can reach a consensus?" *S'hyrlus* said, switching back to the Hamadryad language. "This," she turned toward Suzanne and lifted a hand, palm up, "is the Lady Suzanne, and she is consort to the ambassador, who happens to be my son."

The twins turned to look at Socrates and then to Suzanne, awestruck.

"A Hamadryad —" Syn said.

"Bearing a *Q'estirian*—" Tyn said.

"We have never heard—" Syn said.

"Of such a thing!" Tyn finished.

"Well, I did not bear him of my body," *S'hyrlus* corrected.

Syn nodded her head. "It is as I was telling you, Tyn. Liars, thieves, and unsavory."

Tyn nodded. "I think we should have no truck with the likes of these...creatures." Both twins got to their feet.

S'hyrlus chuckled. "I can see now why you two have no sponsor." She steepled her fingers and stared at the result.

"What is that supposed to mean?" Syn said.

"I think we have been insulted!" Tyn said.

"I am sorry, Suzanne," *S'hyrlus* said. "I should not have wasted your time with these two. They appear to be lazy and unwilling to work."

"Now, you just hang on there," Syn said, standing.

"How dare you speak such slanders!" Tyn protested, standing.

―――――――

"Cornelius," *S'hyrlus* said, shifting to *Q'estirian*, "what was the sentence for these two?"

Suzanne saw the twins blanch.

"I have it here, somewhere," Cornelius said as he searched the pockets of his duster.

"Was it not 60 years in the vaults?" *S'hyrlus* said.

Cornelius found a folded parchment, unfolded it, and skimmed it. "60 years in the vaults and 100 years in the household of the council's choosing." He began to fold the parchment. "That is usually in *Ho'teth'sei*, these days. They have the greater need." He put the parchment in his inner pocket. "Why do you ask?"

S'hyrlus' eyebrows met above her nose as she grinned. "I was checking my facts, thank you," she said, looking to Syn.

―――――――

"Well?" *S'hyrlus* said, switching back to the Hamadryad language. "Shall I speak to Cornelius about your intractability?"

The twins sat begrudgingly.

"Um...also, I am not technically the property owner," Suzanne whispered to *S'hyrlus*. *S'hyrlus* placed her hand on the table; her pinky finger touched Suzanne's pinky.

"There is no need to go into those details at this time," came to Suzanne's mind. *"Especially not in front of these two."* *S'hyrlus* moved her finger, breaking the rapport.

―――――――

Once, the Tacoma police captain, Marshall Trooper, spent his time talking to the street people, as it was all that was left in Tacoma after *The Event*. Most people thought he was just a strange-looking hermit and left him alone. Others bent on preying upon others found the old man to be most capable.

Today, Trooper entered his favorite eatery, there were only two in the city, and this one was the best, in his opinion. As he rounded a corner in the tiny foyer, he saw a big man holding a sawed-off 12 gauge at the counter girl.

"Hey, ya, Pete!" Trooper greeted the owner in his usual manner. "I'd like some coffee over here." Trooper moved to an empty booth in the back of the main dining area and sat so he could see the door and the counter.

The startled gunman swung the shotgun towards Trooper. "What the hell are you doin' here, old man?" the gunman asked.

Trooper looked behind him and then turned back to face the gunman. "Oh! You mean me. Sorry, it just startled me that someone would actually notice me, most people don't."

"So? Answer me, what are you doin' here?" the gunman repeated,

"I come here mostly for the coffee. Sometimes I get a meal when I can," Trooper said coolly.

The gunman laughed. "What's stoppin' me from sendin' you straight to hell?"

Trooper shrugged. "Nothing, I guess. But you see this?" Trooper turned his head so the gunman could see the scarred face and thin hair. "Somebody already tried. They ain't here, I am."

The gunman smiled. "You're runnin' your mouth kinda reckless."

"Am I?" Trooper asked. "I don't think so. You see, I know things you don't."

The gunman grinned. "Like what?"

Trooper sighed. "I know that Pete, there, has a .45 and will open up your chest with it if you shoot me."

"Anything else?" the gunman scoffed.

"I know that I can go from here to you before you can blink," Trooper said calmly.

"No shit?" the gunman asked disbelievingly.

Trooper nodded, "No shit."

"You know, old man, you're scaring the shit right outta me," the gunman said with a grin.

"I know," Trooper said seriously. I can see you starting to shake already. What's worse, I can smell the fear coming off you from here."

The gunman started to look around for an escape. He licked his lips nervously.

Trooper stood slowly. "Okay, this is how it's gonna go down. I'm gonna count to three; then I'm going to pick you up off the floor."

"Awfully sure of yourself, ain'tcha?" the gunman asked as he glanced around. "Anything I can do to stop ya?"

"Well, you could lay that shotgun on the counter and walk outta here. That way, I can get my coffee and continue on with my day," Trooper said.

The gunman could feel how heavy the shotgun was getting. The tension was starting to make him shake.

"Last chance," Trooper said. "Put the gun on the counter and leave, now!"

The gunman was weighing his options.

After what felt like an eternity, Trooper said, "Okay, this is how you wanted it. Are you ready?"

The gunman dropped the shotgun on the counter and ran out.

Pete picked up the shotgun and made it disappear under the counter, and said, "What was it you wanted, Marsh? Just coffee? No breakfast?"

Trooper sat back down at his table and exhaled loudly. "Not today, Pete. Somewhere I gotta be in a bit."

"Doris! Get the man his coffee, and be quick about it," Pete said to the counter girl. "And make sure it's on the house!"

Thirty minutes after the confrontation, Trooper left the small café and walked to a deserted alley; he turned down the alley and disappeared before he got to the end.

He reappeared in a familiar room inside the borderline set by Federal Health officials in D.C.

In the room was the gunman he'd just confronted in the café.

"That was an excellent job, Trevor," Trooper said. "The patrons were terrified."

Trevor was removing the cheap, theatrical makeup he used to disguise his features. "I don't know what you're up to, but you do know someone is going to call your bluff one of these days."

Trooper smiled. "Are you sure it's a bluff? I'm trying to get elected to police chief or mayor. To do that, I need people to know who I am and what I've tried to do to better their lives. After 20 years on the force, no one knows who I am.

"Currently, the city is hanging in limbo. No one is trying to cross the quarantine border, start up a business, or do anything productive. The Feds supposedly sealed the city, but they haven't been here for months. We've been living here for months, and I have not seen a single Fed."

"So, what's your *Master Plan*?" Trevor asked sarcastically.

"At some point, soon, I hope," Trooper explained, "I want to go around to all the people I can find with a petition to make me temporary mayor so we can get the city opened up."

"What's in it for us?" another big man asked as he entered.

"Hey, Bill," Trevor said. Bill waved but kept his attention on Trooper.

"My goal is to have a productive city. One that is safe for people again," Trooper said. "Several undesirables would disappear if we had a Police Department or just a police presence."

"Yeah, I get that," Bill said. "But what's in it for us?"

"Depends on what you want," Trooper said, looking sideways at the two men.

"How long can you stay?" Socrates asked Cornelius. They had gone for a walk in the trees and sunshine.

"Not long," Cornelius said. "I wanted to talk to you about something important. I am getting old and would like to step down from the council, and that would mean that the seat, our family seat, would fall to you."

Socrates started to shake his head until Cornelius put up a hand.

"I will not be stepping down tomorrow, not even this...what you call a year."

"But you are not that old," Socrates said sadly.

Cornelius grinned. "I appreciate the thought, but we both know the truth of the matter, and I do not wish to die in the council seat. That would be...unseemly, I think is the word.

"I had hoped that your father would have survived to take my place, but there is no one else."

"Is there a specific procedure that needs to be followed?" Socrates asked.

Cornelius laughed heartily and slapped Socrates on the shoulder. "We are *Q'estirians*; of course, there are procedures. We have procedures for everything, or that is the way it seems."

Socrates exhaled loudly. "I do not seek your council seat, but I will serve until such time as I am not needed."

Cornelius smiled. "I know. I know your heart in this matter. It is much the same as mine was, long ago."

"Since you bring this up now, what is to happen to *B'runix* Hornsdoodle?" Socrates asked. "To my knowledge, we have not had a defection. What is the price he must pay?"

Cornelius sat on a log, hands on his knees. "What do you

think should happen? Did he defect, or did he refuse to be here, on this *Plane*? I have talked to him, and he did admit to giving information to Phelonius, but he did it to get home. He wanted to get away from here and never return." Cornelius paused for a long time. "How would you punish him?"

Socrates thought for a few seconds. "I think I would research the books in your office to determine what his punishment would be."

"That," Cornelius said as he stood, "is an excellent idea. When can you leave here to begin your research?"

Socrates' mouth dropped open. "I do not see how I can do that at this time. Jessica is bringing Irving's body here for their ritual for the fallen. And who would take my place here?"

"Are you so busy that one of the guards could not do your duties here?" Cornelius asked.

"I am here to pay homage to your Irving...sorry to Irving. He did fall in the battle with Phelonius, and he was an innocent, but he paid the price to keep others safe."

"There is the matter of Suzanne," Socrates said. "She was counting on things getting somewhat back to normal. I do not think I could get to *Q'estiria* in less than a full phase of their moon."

"You sound like you are never coming back," Cornelius said. "You will return if the Fates allow. I do not know when, but you will return. As far as Lady Suzanne is concerned, I have tasked *S'hyrlus* with breaking the news to her, and I am sure she will be thrilled to go."

Socrates did a double-take. "You, Grand Elder, do not know Suzanne!"

A day after Syn and Tyn had arrived, Suzanne heard the roar of a hovercar passing over the house. Everyone except Syn and Tyn followed the sound out the back door.

They saw the hovercar settle in the open area through the grove's trees. Everyone moved toward the craft.

Just as Suzanne reached the craft, Jessica made her way towards them, and Dar fell in behind Jessica.

"Jessica," Socrates said, "since I'm not familiar with the human ritual for Irving, what can I do to help? What would you require of me?"

"The normal funerary requirements, nowadays, is an exceedingly hot fire. They did away with burials some time ago. Irving was always terrified of being burned up, so, a hole 3'x9'x6'," Jessica said.

"Any particular place?" Suzanne asked.

"The clearing, I guess," Jessica said. "Irv always liked coming out here to sit and think."

"Anything else?" Socrates asked.

"I suppose Trooper should be here," Jessica said as she walked toward the house. "He should be asked, anyway. If he wants to decline, then that's fine with me."

When Jessica reached the back door, she opened it and entered. She saw two diminutive creatures scurrying around and chattering to each other, and they took turns chattering at her.

Dar looked up at Jessica and tried to stifle a grin with various degrees of success.

Jessica heard Suzanne clap her hands loudly from behind her, and the turmoil stopped.

"What's up with Frick and Frack, Suze?" Jessica asked, scowling.

"This is Syn and Tyn," Suzanne said. "They're here to help with the house cleaning and the cooking."

"Well, that gibberish might be all well and good for you, but I can't understand a word!" Jessica said. "And I suppose they will be here when you all go off on some adventure or something?"

"That would be the point of having household staff," Suzanne said. "Maybe Socrates can come up with something?" She looked to Socrates for help.

"I'll see what I can do," Socrates said. "Now, then, Does Irving's...funeral have to be completed by a certain time? Dark of the moon, by sundown, anything like that?"

"No, Irving wasn't religious," Jessica said. "I'd say in the next few days, would be best." She put her head down on the table and exhaled loudly.

Dar came over and gently rubbed Jessica's shoulder.

Trooper walked through the deserted Tacoma PD building. He had heard that the Feds were maintaining surveillance, but no one had seen any Federal Law Enforcement officers.

As he wandered through, it seemed strange that he was the only person in the building. He had spent 20 years entering at all hours of the day or night, and he had never known it to be so empty.

Eventually, Trooper made his way to his office.

"It has been a while, Trooper," Socrates said as Trooper made his way to his desk.

"Yes, Socrates, it has been a while," Trooper said as he sat tentatively behind the desk.

"What I meant was it has been a while since you've been out to see Jessica," Socrates corrected.

"Jessica and Irving don't need some old coot coming around," Trooper said. "They made that apparent a while ago."

"I'm here to inform you that Jessica has requested you to come out tomorrow before noon," Socrates said as he got to his feet. "I can take you there now if you like."

"Jess and Irving don't need me," Trooper said, shaking his head.

Socrates exhaled loudly. "Irving died, and Jessica requests your presence."

Trooper tried to stand but fell back into his chair. "He's what?"

"He died a few days ago, in California," Socrates replaced his hat on his head. "I'm leaving now. Am I taking you with me, or do I tell Jess that you'll be along if you feel like it?"

Trooper got to his feet and tried to remember if he had what he needed. "I'm not sure I can. Can you take me? I wouldn't want to put you out."

Socrates smiled compassionately as he took Trooper's elbow, and both disappeared.

CLEARING THE AIR...SOMEWHAT

A t the appointed hour on the appointed day, the grave had been dug, and Irving's body, still in the plastic body bag, was placed in it. Those friends and family that had gathered huddled under umbrellas, trying to stay dry in the heavy mist that plagues the Pacific Northwest. The mist and the umbrellas seemed to be required for the mood of the event.

"You were a good man," Jessica said, speaking only loud enough that those close to her could hear. "You were a better man than I probably deserved." She sniffed back tears for a few seconds. "I will never forget you." She turned away from the grave with Dar patting her shoulder in consolation.

"You were a good friend," Suzanne said when Jessica had finished. "We all valued your friendship and your loyalty."

"You were one of the most trusting humans I'd met," Socrates said. "You were tougher than some I've met, but there wasn't any brutality. You were intelligent and passionate; I was glad to know you and call you friend."

"Irving was a mass of contradictions," Trooper said. "He was the most intelligent person in the room and, at the same time, the most naive. He always expected others to be as intelligent as he was but didn't take offense if he had to explain things to you. He always thought I was smarter than I actually was. I'm going to miss that."

Trooper stepped in to whisper to Jessica when the after-funeral reception had moved inside, "What would you say about coming back to work?" He was balancing a plate in one hand and trying to drink with the other.

"I need to grieve, first, before thinking about coming back to whatever work you find for me," Jessica said. "Speaking of which, I'll be bringing in the hovercar Smith commandeered. I figure it has enough fuel to get back to the P.D."

"I'm not worried about it," Trooper said. "You can hang onto it if you need to use it. Call it a perk of the job." Trooper grinned.

"What job?" Jessica asked. "I know of no job with a hovercar as a perk."

"We can talk about perks later," Trooper said. "Who is your diminutive friend?"

Jessica looked down at Dar, who had come over to her unnoticed. "This is Dar'Kyn, and she is a friend," Jessica smiled quizzically. "One who was there when I needed her."

"Far be it for me to say anything about your friends," Trooper chuckled.

"Really? You always seem to have an opinion about everything any other time," Jessica remarked. "Why refrain now?"

"I don't want to get into it," Trooper said. "I'm going to be opening the P.D. building. You can find me there most days."

Jessica's eyebrows raised, "What are the Feds going to say about that? I haven't heard anything about the C.D.C clearing downtown of the lockdown."

"I haven't seen a Fed since Smith," Trooper said. "Smith was the one that told us that downtown was closed, and I haven't seen another Fed since. This city can't remain locked down. They won't do anything, then we will."

"Careful, Captain," Jessica said. "You're starting to sound like a politician."

"We will soon be leaving," Cornelius said, in *Q'estirian*, as they finished breakfast two days after Irving's memorial.

Socrates raised his eyebrow as he looked to *S'hyrlus*.

"We have a determination at the *Sh'tuk Q'estiria Faqin*," Cornelius said, looking to Socrates.

"No offense, but does Cornelius speak for you, Lady *S'hyrlus*?" Socrates asked.

"He does," *S'hyrlus* said, "at this place and time. It could change at any time, though; it is nothing permanent."

"Excuse me, my lady, am I required at this...determination?" Suzanne asked.

"It is not for me to say," *S'hyrlus* said, glancing at Socrates.

Jessica was looking around at all the others. "Can't you speak English when you're here?" she asked angrily. "At least speak it when I am around," she said, shaking her head. "That's the least you could do."

"Sorry, Jess," Suzanne said contritely, in English. "Cornelius and Lady *S'hyrlus* were just informing us that they need to go to *Q'estiria*, and Socrates needs to go with them. I was just asking if I'm required to go as well."

"You can go, Suzanne, if that's what you'd like," Socrates said in English.

"If Suzanne is required to give testimony," Cornelius said in *Q'estirian*, "she can be sent for."

"Cornelius, we have been asked to speak English in Jessica's presence," *S'hyrlus* said in *Q'estirian*. "It is the least we can do," she finished in English, smiling at Jessica. "She *is* one of our traveling companions."

Cornelius pressed the left side of his chest with his right

184

palm. "Please, excuse," he said as he bowed his head slightly. "I sometimes forget that I am in your domicile."

Jessica scowled at Cornelius, "And what am I supposed to do with all of you gone? Am I to stay here with Frik and Frak?"

"Synkyn and Tynkyn…Broadstone," *S'hyrlus* interjected.

"Whomever. And what about the rest of the 'wiz squad'?" Jessica continued. "Are they all going? Please, say yes."

"What is this 'wiz squad'?" Socrates asked Suzanne in an aside.

"She is making a rude remark about the security here," Suzanne explained quietly to Socrates.

"As a general rule," Suzanne said to Jessica, "if Socrates and I are both here, the complete security complement is. If Socrates is not here, half of them will travel with Socrates.

"There will be at least two of the *Q'estirian* security here at all times. Do I have that correct, Socrates?"

Socrates nodded. "We need the security on this *Plane*," Socrates said. "Maybe not as many, but that is something we can discuss when we are here again."

"What about Frik and Frak…sorry, Sinkin' and Tinkin'?" Jessica asked. "Are they permanent fixtures here? I still think you made up their names."

"Am I wrong in assuming you would like us all to leave?" Suzanne asked.

"No," Jessica said, "I just need to know when I can come back. Why would I stick around with no one here to talk to?" She stood after banging her hands on the table, making everything on it jump.

"Don't leave," Suzanne said as she stood when Jessica did. "We need to hash this out, Jess."

"What's there to hash out?" Jessica said as she started toward the back door. "It's your house. I'm the one that doesn't fit in." She could feel the tears threatening to run as she grabbed her jacket and opened the back door.

Before she could take a dozen steps, Dar was standing in front of her.

"Whaddya want?" Jessica sneered.

"You and I need to say our goodbyes," *Dar'Kyn* said. "I will be leaving with Lady *S'hyrlus*. She is, as you say, my ride."

"So long, farewell, auf wiedersehen, goodbye," Jessica said as she tried to step around Dar.

"Not so fast, Jessica," Dar insisted. "You need to consider what we discussed. If you need me, just tell any Hamadryads you see, and they will get the message to me."

"And if I don't see any Hama-whatzits?" Jessica said, tears rolling down her cheeks, her back to Dar.

"Can you wait long enough for Socrates to make us something to contact each other?" Dar asked. "I do not want to lose track of you."

"You don't?" Jessica said. "You could always stay until Socrates comes back. I'm sure Suzanne would see that you get where you need to go."

"I am sure she would try," Dar said. "But I have a job to do, one that I think you know is important, and I have a report to make."

"Well, then, I'll see ya when I see ya," Jessica said using the wizard-step coin.

When Dar entered the house, after Jessica's departure, all was silence.

"I take it Jessica left?" Suzanne asked, finally.

"Yes, she left in great pain," Dar said.

"I don't know why she'd leave," Suzanne said to Socrates. "We've gone out of our way to make sure she knew that this was her house, her home, as much as ours." She shook her head and lowered her face to her hand. "I just don't understand."

Socrates placed his arm around Suzanne's shoulders.

"Maybe," *Dar'Kyn* said from the overstuffed chair she liked, "she felt alone because she is alone here. Irving made her life bearable, and she is feeling that loss now. But we make her feel alone. We are not human. We can leave and go other places and have duties that force us to travel, but she must remain here... and be alone."

"What else could we have done?" Suzanne asked.

"How many humans were at Irving's memorial?" Dar said. When no one answered, she continued, "I only counted one. When we are all gone, who is here to help Jessica? Who will translate for her? If no one is here to help with the translation, how can she even tell *Synkyn* and *Tynkyn* what she would like to eat?

"Suzanne, you were her friend. Was there something you could have done to help her? Do you think asking if you were needed in *Q'estiria* demonstrated that you were here for her? Or did it make her feel like she was omitted and in the way? You and Socrates have known her longer than I have. Why was she drinking so much when she thought Irving was dead before?"

"*Dar'Kyn*, you go too far," *S'hyrlus* said sternly.

"I do not think I have gone far enough," Dar replied, matching *S'hyrlus'* tone.

"Why do you think she drank so much?" Suzanne asked timidly.

"Because she *needed* her friend, and *she* was not available," Dar said.

"Is that what you think?" Suzanne asked.

"That is what I know," Dar said. "She did the flying, and I listened to her. When she slept, I watched over her. She talks in her sleep, you know."

"I didn't know," Suzanne whispered.

"And why is that?" Dar asked.

Everyone remained quiet for quite some time.

"*Ahem*...Lady *S'hyrlus* and I need to return to *Q'estiria*,"

Cornelius said, getting to his feet and trying to help *S'hyrlus* to her feet.

"I'll walk you out," Socrates said, rising.

Dar got to her feet and started for the door.

"Did Jessica tell you all of that?" Suzanne asked, stopping Dar with a touch on her shoulder.

"You know her better than I do," Dar replied with a touch of surliness. "What do you think?"

"I think she wouldn't say anything to anyone about anything bothering her," Suzanne said. "She would keep it all to herself, tamped down, until it all comes out in anger."

"Like I said," Dar said, "I listened. Sometimes that is all that is needed." Dar followed through the back door.

Jessica used the wizard step coin to transport herself to the hovercar. She entered the car, started the checklist, then stopped as her emotions overwhelmed her. She sat in the pilot's seat and cried, unable to stop the outpouring of emotion.

It took a long time for Jessica to get her emotions under control. Once she did, she returned to the house.

Suzanne was still sitting at the table when Jessica came in the back door.

"Where is everyone?" Jessica asked.

"Socrates, Cornelius, Lady *S'hyrlus*, and *Dar'Kyn* have all gone to *Q'estiria* or other destinations as they need," Suzanne said. "I stayed to talk with my friend."

"Doesn't that presuppose that your *friend* wants to talk to *you*?" Jessica sniped.

"Look, Jess," Suzanne said, "I know I haven't been available —"

"Haven't been available?" Jessica interrupted. "You haven't been available since your...um...change."

"Since my...change," Suzanne said, "my mind has been inundated with information—"

"So? Why is it always about you?" Jessica yelled.

"I'm here for you. I'm here now if you want to talk," Suzanne said.

"And what if it's past time for anything you'd have to say?" Jessica scoffed.

Suzanne took in a loud breath and let it out slowly. "When I bought this place, the only person I could think of, if something happened to me, to leave it to, was you and Irv. Now, I'm unable to do anything about anything. I can't buy or sell. You are in control of our lives. Are we still able to use this place as an ambassadorial residence?"

"Actually," Jessica said, "there are no legal rights to anything right now. The local justice system is on the fritz, or haven't you noticed?" She gave Suzanne a slight smile. "Sorry that I got so... bitchy with you. I'm just really missing Irv..."

"I know," Suzanne whispered. "Grief can make you do and say all kinds of things, some of which we don't mean.

"It probably isn't going to be a problem anyway."

"Why is that?" Jessica said.

"With Malthuvius and Phelonius out of the picture," Suzanne said, "I'm not sure Q'estiria needs an ambassadorial presence here."

Jessica looked shocked, as if she hadn't thought of that possibility. "Wha...ahem," Jessica started but found her throat choked with emotion. "If they decide to pull the ambassador, then what?"

"Then," Suzanne shrugged, "All of us will return to the Seven Known Planes somewhere."

"All of you?" Jessica said. "What does that mean?"

"Socrates, myself, all of the Q'estirian guards, Synkyn and Tynkyn," Suzanne said. "Cornelius and Lady S'hyrlus won't have a reason to visit, and I can't imagine *Dar'Kyn* would need to come here."

"You wouldn't be living here," Jessica whined, "but you could come for a visit...sometimes...if you wanted to, couldn't you?"

"I may not be able to," Suzanne said. "My...transition came with strings attached. I'm not free to go wherever I want...not for a while, anyway. I have other duties, other responsibilities."

"I'm getting tired, so I'm going to bed," Jessica said sometime later. She and Suzanne had shared alcohol and many tears, mainly for Irving.

"Before Socrates left," Suzanne said, "he and Cornelius put their heads together and came up with this." She produced a gold coin.

"What's that for?" Jessica asked.

"Dar voiced her concerns about your inability to speak to *Synkyn* and *Tynkyn*," Suzanne said. "This is the result. You lay down on your back, and I put it on your forehead...after I spit on it—the coin, not your forehead. He told me how to activate it. It may not work, but it could help. It could make the learning easier."

"Well," Jessica said, "I don't sleep well these days...and it takes me a while to drop off."

"I can help with that," Suzanne grinned as she followed Jessica to her room. "Okay," she said as she pulled the covers over Jessica, "lay back, close your eyes, and try to relax. I'll be touching you lightly in different places. Once you fall asleep, I'll put the coin on your forehead and activate it."

"What can I expect?" Jessica asked as she closed her eyes.

"You can expect a raging headache when you wake, but hopefully, you'll absorb some of the language we're trying to impart to you."

As Jessica lay quietly, Suzanne began to lightly touch the top three chakras, in a seemingly random order, as well as her temples and chin, all the while humming at a barely audible level.

"Lift your index finger of your right hand if you are asleep, Jessica," Suzanne whispered after ten minutes. She looked and saw Jessica's index finger rise slightly.

Once Jessica was asleep, Suzanne put a little saliva on the back of the coin and stuck it to Jessica's forehead at the third eye chakra as she subvocalized the incantation that Socrates had given her.

Suzanne silently closed Jessica's door when she stopped *Tynkyn*, who happened past. "Let her sleep as long as she will," Suzanne whispered. "She needs all the rest she can get."

Tynkyn nodded that she understood the instruction and continued with her chores. Suzanne made her way to her room and collapsed onto the bed.

When Jessica awakened, she felt hungover. Not the kind of hangover you get from too much alcohol. The kind you get when you sleep hard for a long time, as after surgery.

She stumbled down to the dining room with just a robe around her and plopped down in a chair.

"What is it you would like?" one of the twins asked.

"Just coffee, if you please," Jessica responded, dropping her forehead to her crossed arms on the table.

"The mistress is cockeyed, again," Jessica heard from the kitchen. She couldn't tell whether it was *Synkyn* or *Tynkyn* as they both sounded the same to her. She could hear the pair giggling.

"I am not inebriated," Jessica shouted, raising her head without opening her eyes. "I require a bit more respect from you both." She put her head back down.

"Your coffee, mistress," one of the twins said, placing a cup close to her right arm on the table.

Jessica sat up and groped around before picking up the cup and sipping from it.

"Well! Nice to see you up and about, Sleepyhead!" Suzanne said as she entered the backdoor.

Jessica heard Suzanne and understood her, but Suzanne's speech sounded...odd to her. She could feel her face get that questioning look. "How long...have I...been asleep?" Jessica asked in broken English.

Suzanne looked to the twins. "How long has she been up?" she asked.

"Only a few moments before your entrance, M'Lady," one of the twins answered.

"Has she said anything to either of you?" Suzanne asked.

"Yes, M'Lady," the current speaking twin nodded in Jessica's direction, "The mistress asked for coffee." The twins had an odd way of speaking, and they would alternate as to who answered.

"And what did you give her?" Suzanne asked.

"Oh, for Christ's sake!" Jessica growled in English. "I asked for coffee, and that's what they gave me. Do you think I would be this calm if they hadn't? How long was I out anyway? Seven or eight hours?" Jessica stretched backward in the chair.

"You were unconscious for the better part of two days, call it 40 hours," Suzanne said. "The good news is you seemed to have learned to speak to *Synkyn* and *Tynkyn* well enough that they can understand you."

Jessica's eyes, and her mouth, popped open.

18

RETURN TO Q'ESTIRIA

W hen Socrates, Cornelius, half of the ambassadorial guard, *Dar'Kyn* Trubis, and Lady *S'hyrlus* arrived at *Q'estiria*, Cornelius asked, "Lady *S'hyrlus*, are you coming with Socrates and me?"

"I will be there later," *S'hyrlus* said. "I have to transport *Dar'Kyn*, first before I can join you. It was a promise I made when I brought her to the *Eighth Plane.*"

Cornelius looked at *S'hyrlus*, and she could see the questions as if they were written on his face for all to read.

"I belong to a different sect," Dar offered. "Transportation is not one of our attributes." Dar gave a shrug and a slight, enigmatic grin.

Cornelius pressed the left side of his chest with his right palm and bowed slightly. "Your assistance in this endeavor has been much appreciated," he said to *Dar'Kyn*.

Dar tilted her head slightly to one side and gave a barely perceptible nod.

"How long will it take for your return?" Cornelius asked *S'hyrlus*.

"I have no idea," *S'hyrlus* said. "I know the way to your

office." *S'hyrlus* opened a portal, and Dar quickly stepped through, with *S'hyrlus* on her heels.

"You may be my grandsire, but might I offer you some advice?" Socrates asked after the portal closed.

"You may," Cornelius said, his eyes still on the closed portal, "but I will decide the value of it."

"It has been my experience that Lady *S'hyrlus* does not condone too much curiosity in her dealings," Socrates said.

"Ah...yes, I noticed that well before you were born," Cornelius said whimsically. "But I am old and enjoy pressing any advantage that may give me."

Cornelius and Socrates chuckled as they, and the guards, began the wizard-steps to the *Sh'tuk Q'estiria Faqin*. Soon their entry point to *Q'estirian Plane* was devoid of visitors.

"Greetings, Lady *Ptelea*," *S'hyrlus* said upon her entry to the *Hamadryad Plane* and the portal's closing.

"Greetings to you, Lady *S'hyrlus*, my true sister of the *Oaken Wood*," *Ptelea* said. The two leaders touched ear-to-ear on both sides. "How did the foray to the *Eighth Plane* proceed?"

"All went as well as could be expected," *S'hyrlus* said. "*Dar'Kyn* was an exceptional asset to our endeavor."

"That pleases me, but I did not choose her," *Ptelea* said. "You came to me with a request, and I passed that request onward."

"I volunteered once your request was made known to *Tisiphone*," Dar said. "I did so out of a sense of duty to you, Lady *Ptelea*. I have been and remain sister of the Elm." She bowed low to *Ptelea* and *S'hyrlus*.

After *Ptelea* and *S'hyrlus* lightly touched her head, Dar rose, went to a thick-trunked Elm, opened a portal, and stepped through. The portal closed.

"So, she *can* open a portal," *S'hyrlus* said.

"She can open a portal only from here, this grove, this Plane,"

Ptelea sighed. "She is my sister of the Elm Grove, but when she decided to become...what she is, she gave up our ability to travel the Planes through portals of our own creation. Consequently, she must rely on other Hamadryads for transport to the other Planes."

"I will admit to being surprised by her abilities," *S'hyrlus* said. "If I may ask, what is she, other than Hamadryad?"

"I am not certain," *Ptelea* said. "I have never asked, and she has not offered the information. She did *imply* that she is under *Tisiphone*, the Erinyes, which would make her one of the Harpy Corps. But that is only speculation and assumption on my part.

"You were unclear in your request as to the kind of *help* you needed. *Dar'Kyn* was the only voluntary *help* available." *Ptelea* shrugged.

"Well, it was the kind and type of help required." *S'hyrlus* bowed to *Ptelea*. "It was appreciated. Thank you, my sister!"

S'hyrlus walked to the lone oak at the edge of the Elm Grove and opened a portal to *Q'estiria*. When it was fully formed, she walked through.

"Order! Everyone will come to order!" Cornelius yelled as he banged the heavy rock on the center of the council's dais. Once quiet was achieved, he continued: "The *Sh'tuk Q'estiria Faqin* has been called to order to add information to the record on the recent events on the *Eighth Plane*. Chief Commander Blackwing has the floor." Cornelius leaned back in his chair, and it creaked a bit.

Socrates stood facing the council and cleared his throat. "I stand before you to report that Phelonius Blackwing has been apprehended and imprisoned in such a manner as to preclude any escape."

"Without trial?" Thaddius Crowfoot interrupted. "That is an outrageous breach of protocol!"

"I want to know if the creature that injured Malthuvius Nighthawk has been captured," D'Tomia Nighthawk said.

"Order!" Cornelius yelled and banged the dais with the rock. When the chambers were silent once more, he continued: "I would suggest that we allow Chief Commander Blackwing to continue his report without interruption. Questions will be taken up after the report has been presented." Cornelius motioned to Socrates to continue.

"Phelonius," Socrates continued, "had absconded with a human and held him prisoner. That human, and his mate, were *K'obi Sha Shin J'oi Faqin* to me. Malthuvius was injured trying to abscond with that human's mate, but she defended herself and rendered him harmless for a time.

"I had, initially, promoted one of my brother *T'et Faqin Q'estirians* one rank with the approval of the head of this council. Events transpired that presented evidence that the promotion was undeserved. As such, B'runix Hornsdoodle has been placed under detention at the *T'et Faqin Q'estirians* detention facility until his superiors can hear his case." Socrates sat.

The chambers were quiet for a while before Cornelius spoke. "Phelonius was imprisoned. Might we know where that is, as you had stated that it is a manner that would preclude escape? What if I ordered him released?"

"This council had given me a warrant that would allow me to apprehend Phelonius," Socrates said.

"And did you apprehend him?" Cornelius asked,

"No, I did not," Socrates said.

"Who did?" Cornelius asked.

"A *Dar'Kyn* Trubis, Hamadryad-sister of the Lady *Ptelea* of the Elm Grove," Socrates said.

"Is this Hamadryad Trubis on *Q'estiria*," Cornelius asked.

"She traveled here with us, but Lady *S'hyrlus* transported her somewhere else," Socrates said.

"Where was Phelonius taken and by whom?" Cornelius asked.

Socrates looked at the individual council members and noticed their discomfort at Cornelius asking their questions faster than they could speak. "I cannot state as fact what I heard," Socrates said, "but I overheard her say the daughters of Nyx were taking him to Tartarus for Eternal Punishment."

Everyone on the council started to speak at once.

"That is a lie!" someone said.

"You let him go and are now trying to clean your hands of this through deception!" someone else said.

"There are no Daughters of Nyx!" Syn'Chin Hornsdoodle yelled.

Cornelius banged the rock several times while calling for order. It took some time to get the chamber quiet once more.

"Do you have any witnesses to these events?" Cornelius asked.

"Cornelius Blackwing, Lady *S'hyrlus*, Lady Suzanne, and *Dar'Kyn* Trubis witnessed the events." Socrates sat as the chambers erupted once more.

"What are you trying to do, Cornelius?" Syn'Chin Hornsdoodle asked from his chair in Cornelius' office. They had all adjourned there to consider the testimony.

"I am not deceiving the council," Cornelius said. "Neither is Socrates. His account was accurate. I was there."

Thaddius Crowfoot steepled his fingers and rested his elbows on Cornelius' desk. "I would suggest that all witnesses be called to testify," Crowfoot said. "It doesn't help your credibility that you are all related, in some fashion. Some of us may think that you could be conspiring to deceive. I do not, but some might."

"If the council insists, it will take a few days to get all the witnesses here to testify," Cornelius said.

"What were you thinking, Cornelius?" H'Difa Thunderclap asked.

"I do not understand what you want to know, H'Difa," Cornelius said. "I have taken several actions on many things that may cause you to ask that question. To which are you referring?"

"Why would you go to the *Eighth Plane*?" Thunderclap asked. "The council had determined it too dangerous for anyone to go there. We were trying to decide if all connections to it would be eliminated, isolating them."

"Are you saying that *you*, H'Difa Thunderclap, are too *old* and irreplaceable to go to the *Eighth Plane*?" Cornelius asked loudly. Everyone became quiet.

"I am saying that *you*, being the head of the council, may be a target for someone who may be thinking of taking control of the council," Thunderclap said.

"Do you have anyone in particular in mind?" Cornelius asked with a slight grin.

"All of us know that your position on the council, as are ours," Thunderclap said pridefully, "is based on family. Technically, no one council member is above another. However, there are times that a member may be given deference. Our concern would be one family gaining too much influence."

"Hmm...as I recall," Cornelius said, "the council wanted Socrates in his position. Has that changed?"

"No one is saying that you are trying to gain more influence than appropriate," Thaddius Crowfoot said. "However, with Phelonius...out of action, there are those that wonder who you will appoint should something befall you."

"I have already decided," Cornelius said. "I plan on making that announcement once the report on the Eighth Plane is complete."

"Might I inquire who you plan to announce?" H'Difa Thunderclap asked, looking askance to Cornelius.

Cornelius sat back and glared at all the members listening for his response.

"It is not that difficult to figure out," Cornelius said after a long pause. "I cannot announce a Thunderclap should replace me. How would that make the rest of you feel? That would cause the very thing that you say causes your concern. Nor can I announce a Nighthawk or a Hornsdoodle—"

"Or a Crowfoot," Thaddius Crowfoot interrupted.

"Or a Crowfoot," Cornelius chuckled. "You are all more intelligent than that."

"You plan to announce Socrates," H'Difa Thunderclap said.

"He is the only Blackwing of any renown," Cornelius said.

"He does have the distinction of being the last one available, the last that is still free," H'Difa Thunderclap said.

"Are you saying that you are thinking of having me detained?" Cornelius chuckled. "It is more than Socrates being the last of my family, at this point. As was said of him at his being named ambassador, he exemplifies what it means to be *T'et Faqin Q'estirian*. Who else would I choose to replace me?"

"It is just that damnable eyepatch," Syn'Chin Hornsdoodle said. "People in polite society do not like to be reminded of the horrors of war."

Cornelius glared. "If true, then this so-called polite society needs to get over themselves. We all owe our culture to the warriors. Without the warriors, what do we have? Shun the warriors, and we will soon be extinct. If we no longer care for or about them, we should not expect them to care for or about the rest of us when the need arises, which it always does, sooner or later."

"If it were up to me," Hornsdoodle said, "I would have him wear a bag over his head."

"If it were up to me," Cornelius roared, "I'd ban him wearing the eyepatch altogether. Let polite society see the unmitigated horrors of war."

Socrates was sitting in front of the dais in the council chambers when Cornelius banged the podium with the rock to call the council back into session.

"We reconvene to have items read into the official record," Cornelius said, scowling. "Let it be known that this council is calling for the three Hamadryads mentioned in these proceedings so far, Ladies *S'hyrlus* and Suzanne, and the one called *Dar'Kyn* Trubis, be called to give their testimony in person. Also, there is a human who is witness, and she is called as well, the human Jessica Strange—"

The council members immediately began yelling, expressing their distaste for Cornelius's instructions.

"You are violating the council's mandates against humans coming here," Syn'Chin Hornsdoodle screamed louder than the rest.

Cornelius scowled at Hornsdoodle while banging the dais for order. It took some time for it to be restored.

"Would my friend, Cornelius, yield to the floor for inquiry?" H'Difa Thunderclap asked as the others were settling down.

"What is your inquiry?" Cornelius asked.

"I am sure you know that bringing a human here is forbidden," Thunderclap said.

"I am," Cornelius said coldly.

"Might I ask why then?" Thunderclap asked.

"This council is constituted from the heads of the Five Families," Cornelius said, "*T'et Faqin Q'estirians* all. Now, certain members of the council doubt the integrity of their fellow *T'et Faqin Q'estirians*. This has caused me some consternation, so I have decided that everyone who knows anything about the events on the *Eighth Plane* should be brought here. That includes the ones I have already mentioned, B'runix Hornsdoodle and Malthuvius Nighthawk."

"But why? Thunderclap repeated.

"For centuries, this council has operated with certain latitudes being given, allowances granted for convenience or previous rulings. It appears that this council is no longer willing to work with comity towards its fellow members. So, for completeness, we will have a full accounting from all involved."

More uproar and more banging for order ensued.

"By way of completeness," Cornelius said after order was reestablished, "I have been reminded that I am old and need to choose my replacement. Very well. I am prepared to announce that Socrates Blackwing has my complete confidence and will replace me in the council when I decide to step down or if something foul befall me."

"Socrates, come in, come in," Cornelius said with only a glance to see who had entered his office. "Make yourself comfortable, and I will be with you shortly." Cornelius drew the last few runes on the parchment he was working on. "There. Finished," he said as he pushed himself back from his desk and sat in the chair opposite Socrates. He handed Socrates several pages of parchment as he sat with a tankard.

"What is all this?" Socrates said, accepting the pages and sipping from his own tankard.

"Warrants, mostly," Cornelius said as he relaxed.

"Are you serious?" Socrates asked. "You want me to bring Jessica here?"

"Of course," Cornelius said. "Did you think I was...as the humans say...making joking?"

Socrates snorted. "That would be either joking or making a joke. You know Jessica. How am I to get her here?"

"You are intelligent, Socrates," Cornelius said. "I am sure you will think of something."

"Lady Suzanne is with Jessica now. You are aware they put devices into their bodies that may not react well with portals?" Socrates asked.

"I did not know," Cornelius said. "Two humans managed to

get here and return, so I know it is possible." Socrates started to say something when Cornelius showed him his palm. "I know, it will not be easy. I am sure Lady Suzanne will come because you ask but take any and all means necessary to get that Jessica woman here."

"*Dar'Kyn* will be another matter," Socrates said.

"I have faith in your abilities," Cornelius said. "The council will remain adjourned until all the witnesses are assembled here."

"Why did you do it?" Socrates asked.

"Sometimes you do something simply because you can," Cornelius said. "Other times, you do something to prove a point. Rarely do you get the opportunity to accomplish both simultaneously."

"I will have to wait until Lady *S'hyrlus* arrives," Socrates said.

There was a knock on Cornelius' office door.

"Enter!" Cornelius shouted. Then seeing who it was said, "I will look forward to your return, Socrates."

As Lady *S'hyrlus* entered the room, Socrates looked like he would pass her when he reached out and escorted her out of Cornelius' office.

Socrates tried to explain to *S'hyrlus* what Cornelius had tasked him to do as best as he could. On one of the many water stops, *S'hyrlus* pressed her palm against Socrates' forehead and closed her eyes.

"I will take you to Lady Suzanne and then return to gather *Dar'Kyn*," *S'hyrlus* said a few seconds later. "Where *Dar'Kyn* is, you cannot go, neither can I, truth be told, but I will do my best to get her to *Q'estiria* as quickly as possible."

"That leaves me with the task of bringing Jessica," Socrates said, disheartened. "I think you have the easier task. Would you like to trade?"

"My task," *S'hyrlus* said, "could be impossible to accomplish. You think the impossible is easier than your task?"

Socrates chuckled. "It is just degrees in impossibilities."

"Lady Suzanne!" Socrates yelled as he entered the backdoor of his house. "Lady Suzanne?" he yelled again. Then, he saw Synkyn timidly looking around the corner at him. "Do you know where Lady Suzanne is, Synkyn?"

"I am Tynkyn," said the timid twin. "She went to Tac-oom-aw with Mistress Jessica. Shoop-ing...I think."

"Do you know when she will return?" Socrates asked.

"They have been gone a long time," Tynkyn said. "They should return before long."

"Thank you, Tynkyn," Socrates said as he sat in his chair.

"That was fun," Jessica said behind her as she walked in the backdoor.

"I thought so," Suzanne said as she followed Jessica into the house.

"Hello, Suzanne," Socrates said from his chair in the living room.

"Socrates!" Suzanne said as she came over to him and hugged him. "What are you doing here? I thought you had to give testimony. Did you finish so quickly?"

"I have some packages in the hovercar to retrieve," Jessica said. She left through the back door with Synkyn and Tynkyn following close behind.

"Don't be too long, Jessica," Socrates said.

"What's going on?" Suzanne asked.

"In a nutshell, we have to go to *Q'estiria* as quickly as possible," Socrates said. "You, Lady *S'hyrlus*, Jessica, and *Dar'Kyn* have been called as witnesses."

"Since you're here," Suzanne said, "*S'hyrlus* dropped you here and went to get Dar. Of course, I'll go, but Jessica? Isn't there some prohibition against humans going there?"

"There is, but that has been rescinded, temporarily, anyway," Socrates said.

"What has been rescinded?" Jessica said as she came in and dropped off packages on the table.

"We need to leave—" Socrates said.

"Bye!" Jessica interrupted.

"No, you need —" Socrates said,

"Oh, no! I don't *need* to do nothin'!" Jessica interrupted again.

"Jessica, we're all going to *Q'estiria*!" Suzanne said.

"Let me know how it is when you get back," Jessica said.

Jessica turned to the kitchen area when she became enveloped in darkness.

19

TRIALS ON Q'ESTIRIA

The darkness that had enveloped Jessica had only lasted a split-second. She unceremoniously landed on a hard floor, the light very diffuse. There were large boxes and barrels with runes drawn on them, but she had no idea what the runes said. Also around the floor were books, all kinds of books.

Lucky for me that I had a husband who talked to me, Jessica thought. *I know where I am, and I'm not a happy camper. I'm going to pay you back for this, you—*

Jessica's thought was interrupted by very bright sunlight.

"Stop doing that!" Jessica yelled.

"Sorry, Jess, but it's important that you accompany us to the council chambers," Socrates was saying.

"Jess, calm down," Suzanne soothed.

"You knew I didn't want to go, wherever we are, but you decided to kidnap me anyway," Jessica said quietly but sternly. "Whatever would I do without my friends! 'Bad planning on your part doesn't constitute an emergency on my part.' That's what I remember my dad saying to anyone and everyone, and it applies here. I am *not* happy!"

Jessica followed along, quietly working herself into a horrendous mad when her hand grazed the *Desert Eagle* on her hip.

Even though she was scowling with her eyes, she was smiling. *What a bunch of fuckin' amateurs*, she thought.

———

"Wouldn't you like to be dressed...more appropriately?" Suzanne asked Jessica as they entered the city of *Q'estiria*. "There is the best shop over there for stylish leather!"

"Do they give you a commission?" Jessica asked snidely.

"No, but it *is* where I got my clothes," Suzanne said.

"Nope! Not interested!" Jessica said adamantly.

"Well, I need to pop in anyway," Suzanne said. "It'll only take a minute!"

"Where is Socrates?" Jessica asked as she tried to resist being dragged into the shop. "Shouldn't we be finding him?"

"He knows where we are. Besides, he seems to have no trouble finding anything or anyone," Suzanne said as she held up a leather top similar to the one she was wearing. "This is so cute!"

Jessica shrugged, "It looks exactly like what you're wearing."

It was then that Jessica spotted the leather pants.

———

Several hours later, Jessica walked out of the leather shop. Her long, blonde hair was pulled back and kept in place by a thick leather strip; a stick passed through two holes in the strip. Her head had a newer version on Socrates' fedora, pulled down in the front to shade her steel-blue eyes. Her black cotton shirt was covered by a tapered leather vest that seemed to accent her figure even more than usual. Her hips and legs were covered with pants similar to Suzanne's, black leather and skin-tight. Low-heeled thigh-high boots covered her feet and added support to her lower legs, as she had the tops of the boots folded down to just below her knees. Her entire frame was covered by a black leather duster, similar to the *T'et Faqin Q'estirians*.

"Except for the long, blonde hair, you look like you'd fit in with Cornelius and Socrates and their bunch," Suzanne said admiringly.

"Maybe, except for the fact they're taller...and the boobage," Jessica chuckled, which caused Suzanne to chuckle.

"What about your holsters?" Suzanne asked as they left the shop.

"I couldn't get through to them what I wanted," Jessica explained. "These tactical holsters are fine, for now, and I am used to them already. I'm surprised you didn't take them from me when you kidnapped me."

"First of all, to us, we didn't kidnap you. We...suggested with emphasis that you accompany us—" Suzanne started.

"Yeah, it's called kidnapping," Jessica interrupted. "I was a cop. I would know!"

Suzanne just glared before continuing, "Second: the image of Jessica Strange without her two Desert Eagles," Suzanne shook her head, "is just...unimaginable."

Suzanne and Jessica rose when Socrates entered the *Cloven Hoof Inn*. Socrates was taken aback when he saw Jessica.

"My!" Socrates said appreciatively, "You are very—"

"Ain't I, though?" Jessica said, smiling.

"But, Jessica, please refrain from shooting anyone," Socrates said. "We are out in public, and most won't understand. Added to that, you appear very...exotic to those here, and they don't know about the *Eighth Plane*."

"I don't care what others know or don't know," Jessica said. "It's not my problem."

"Same ole Jess!" Suzanne said.

"And," Jessica continued, "if people don't start nothin', there won't be nothin'. If someone really wants to get shot, I'm more than happy to oblige them!"

———

Cornelius banged everyone to order three days after Jessica arrived in *Q'estiria*. Since Jessica didn't wholly understand *Q'estirian*, nor did she understand all the nuances couched in the language, Suzanne was acting as interpreter.

"I have been informed that those witnesses off *Q'estiria* have arrived," Cornelius said. He frowned as he heard Suzanne repeating his words to Jessica. "Lady Suzanne, is it necessary to repeat my words?"

Suzanne arose. "I am sorry, sir," Suzanne said, "but you are hearing English. I am translating *Q'estirian* for Jessica. Since you have a working knowledge of English, it is coming out as a repeated phrase."

Cornelius nodded dourly, "Accepted, just keep it down."

"Before we start, I would inform all witnesses that truth is expected in all matters. I will be displeased if anyone is found to be untruthful and will have that individual incarcerated.

"We will start with Jessica Strange," Cornelius said. Jessica and Suzanne stood. "It has been alleged that you were able to... apprehend Malthuvius Nighthawk," he paused so Suzanne could interpret, "Is that true?"

"Damn right it is!" Jessica said in English. "And Phelonius, too!"

"Yes," Suzanne said. Cornelius' eyebrow raised slightly but betrayed nothing else.

"As it pertains to Malthuvius, why?" Cornelius asked.

"Because the dumb bastard tried to grab me and spirit me away," Jessica said in English.

"Because Malthuvius, either on orders or of his own volition, attempted to take me somewhere I did not wish to go," Suzanne interpreted.

"I am offended," D'Tomia Nighthawk said.

"In what way," Cornelius asked, looking in Nighthawk's direction.

"I am offended that you think this…this…whatever it is," D'Tomia Nighthawk scoffed, "irrespective of how it is dressed, could defeat Malthuvius Nighthawk."

"If he's dumb enough to be the target," Jessica said, "I'll be happy to show him how I did it. He does know the how of it, doesn't he? Whatever happened to poor old Mal?"

"Jessica says that she would welcome a demonstration or an inspection of one of her weapons," Suzanne said. Cornelius had to hide his grin.

"Ahem…That is something we can take up at a later time," Cornelius said.

"No!" D'Tomia Nighthawk insisted. "No! You prove it now! You will not be allowed to sidestep my concerns!"

Cornelius shrugged. He banged the dais. "We are adjourned until an appropriate demonstration can be prepared."

———

It took some time for a demonstration in the central courtyard of the council building to be set up. Cornelius had insisted that it be outside, as he was familiar with the noise level.

"We will not be gaveling to order during this demonstration," Cornelius said. "I give Jessica Strange the floor." He sat down.

"I have set up one of your pewter cups on bags of grain over there," Jessica said as she motioned, and Suzanne interpreted for her.

She stood loose, looking to the cup. She nodded, and Socrates said, "Go!"

In a blink, Jessica drew, fired, and holstered her pistol.

"Fake!" D'Tomia Nighthawk insisted.

"Next, Socrates found a ripe melon of some sort, and it's

wrapped with my leather duster that was purchased yesterday here in Q'estiria. I have no idea if the wrapping is loose or tight or how tough the melon is."

Suzanne interpreted as Jessica moved into position. As before, she nodded, and Socrates yelled. Jessica drew, fired three shots, and holstered her pistol in a blink. She walked away from her firing line.

Socrates went forward with D'Tomia Nighthawk and Cornelius to inspect the duster. D'Tomia carefully opened the duster, and liquid from the melon poured out of the duster's interior. The melon's shell was just a few large chunks.

"What do you think, now, D'Tomia?" Cornelius asked.

"I think you two and that...thing have put on a good show," D'Tomia said. "But it is still just a show! Very Theatrical! A fake!"

"A fake?" Socrates said, staring at D'Tomia in disbelief. "How could that have been faked?"

"I can think of several ways," D'Tomia said. "You could have hit the melon before you wrapped it."

"You are saying that I would intentionally deceive everyone here," Cornelius said.

"Not only that you could, but you would!" D'Tomia said emphatically.

Cornelius raised Jessica's duster so all could see that there were no added holes in the garment.

Socrates stormed over to Suzanne and relayed what D'Tomia had said. Suzanne relayed it to Jessica.

Jessica raised her hands, and those watching quieted. "It has come to my attention that D'Tomia Nighthawk believes what I've shown you to have been faked, and I don't know what else I can do to prove my claims," Jessica said and waited for a few seconds before continuing. "Here and now, if D'Tomia Nighthawk wishes to go up against me, or if Malthuvius Nighthawk wishes to try to finish what he started, then bring it on!"

D'Tomia Nighthawk remained silent, but Jessica could see his anger on his face.

"You shouldn't have done that," Socrates whispered while they waited to be called back inside the council chambers.

"Shouldn't have done what?" Jessica asked. "Make him mad? What's he gonna do?" she scoffed.

"He could challenge you," Socrates said.

"Let him. From what I know, your kind is safest in this form," Jessica said, indicating how Socrates currently looked. "If he changes into that Demon creature, he runs the risk of his head becoming like that melon, and he knows it. He has no intention of risking anything, but I would warn Cornelius. D'Tomia is stalling for some reason, and it could have something to do with Malthuvius."

"I'm sure Cornelius has things well in hand," Socrates said dismissively.

"It's your call," Jessica exhaled loudly, "but if I have to face Mal again, I'll make sure it is the last time," Jessica warned.

While the others were being escorted into the council chambers, Socrates moved close to Cornelius. "I would suggest that you increase the guard on Malthuvius Nighthawk," Socrates whispered.

"Why would I do that?" Cornelius asked.

"Jessica thinks D'Tomia Nighthawk is planning something concerning Malthuvius," Socrates said. "I would listen. She does have skills in these matters."

Cornelius sat back and thought about Socrates' concerns, then signaled a trusted guard. The guard left quickly.

Cornelius banged for order. "That, Jessica, was an impressive and informative demonstration. I would like to hear from *Dar'Kyn* Trubis at this time."

Everyone remained quiet while Dar came forward.

"You are *Dar'Kyn* Trubis?" Cornelius asked.

"That is what some would say," Dar answered. Cornelius frowned.

"I recently traveled to the *Eighth Plane* and met someone named *Dar'Kyn* Trubis. Was that you?" Cornelius questioned.

"Yes," Dar said.

"Were you the one who captured and incarcerated Phelonius Blackwing?" Cornelius asked.

"No," Dar said.

"Who did capture him?" Cornelius asked.

"I am not at liberty to say," Dar said.

Cornelius frowned. "Do you know who did capture him?" he asked.

"Yes," Dar said after some thought.

"But you are not at liberty to tell us?" Cornelius asked.

"That would be a correct statement," Dar said.

"And if this council commands you to release him?" Cornelius asked.

"Since I am not the one that incarcerated Phelonius, I cannot release him," Dar said.

"Can we take this up with your superiors?" Cornelius asked.

"Possibly," Dar said.

"So, who is your superior?" Cornelius asked somewhat haughtily.

"I am not at liberty to say," Dar said.

The room was quiet enough that everyone heard Cornelius grind his teeth.

"Do you know *where* Phelonius is being held?" Cornelius asked.

"Yes," Dar said.

"Have you been there?" Cornelius asked after a long pause.

"Many times," Dar said.

"Can you take me, or one of the council members, to see him?" Cornelius asked.

"No," Dar said

"Are you telling us falsehoods?" Cornelius asked. "I find it difficult to believe that you cannot, or will not, take someone else to see Phelonius when you have stated that you know where he is, and you have been there before."

Dar'Kyn thought for a while. "It is not for me to lessen the difficulties in your personal belief system," she said finally.

Cornelius tapped his fingers in frustration. "Why was Phelonius incarcerated?"

"He was guilty of murdering millions, breaking vows, a number of things," Dar said.

"What is the place of his incarceration called?" Cornelius said, buoyed by more than one-word answers or answers that went nowhere.

"Tartarus," Dar said.

"But that is a mythical place," Cornelius said.

"It is? I was not aware of the status change," Dar said.

"Enough of this!" Thaddius Crowfoot shouted. "Kill her unless she tells us what we want to know!"

"Yes!" H'Difa Thunderclap added. "Torture will loosen her tongue!"

Cornelius banged for order. "As you can hear, they want answers," Cornelius said compassionately. "Does that frighten you?"

"Not particularly," Dar said. "I took an oath, and I know what happens to oathbreakers, so I am...unconcerned with anything you could do to me."

"Excuse me," *S'hyrlus* said.

"Yes, Lady *S'hyrlus*?" Cornelius said.

"What the council is calling for, and threatening to do, would be unbelievably bad," *S'hyrlus* said, "for all concerned."

"You see! They are all in this together!" Syn'Chin Hornsdoodle shouted.

Cornelius banged again for order. "In what way, Lady *S'hyrlus*?" he asked.

"Firstly, being Hamadryad carries the burden of being truthful," *S'hyrlus* explained. "So, Lady Suzanne, *Dar'Kyn* Trubis, and myself cannot and will not tell an untruth. Harming us, in any way, is cause to have the one doing violence to be without Hamadryad aid or comfort. Should this council order the torture of one of us, or killing one of us, that will effectively isolate the entirety of the *Eight Planes* and recall all Hamadryads everywhere immediately.

"Secondly, harming *Dar'Kyn* Trubis will bring down total devastation on the guilty *Plane*."

"Was that a *threat*, Lady *S'hyrlus*?" Cornelius said, cocking his head to one side.

"Not at all," *S'hyrlus* said. "Let us look at your questioning logically. You are trying to elicit information from *Dar'Kyn* Trubis that she is unwilling or incapable of revealing. We come here out of a sense of...goodwill. Commanding us will have deleterious effects. To be honest, you need us a lot more than we need you."

"We could have you arrested," Cornelius said.

"Could you?" *S'hyrlus* said. "My kind have been held before and will probably be held again. Too long away from our different woods, and we die. Bring us to our trees, and we will be gone. Trying to hold us where we do not choose to be will isolate everyone."

There was a general murmur that ran through the crowd of politicos. The guard had returned and spoke to Cornelius in low tones.

"Ahem...So, *Dar'Kyn*, you say that Phelonius is in Tartarus," Cornelius said after clearing his throat. "What is he doing there?"

Dar'Kyn chuckled. "Obviously, you do not know what Tartarus is! The Great *Q'estirian* intellect is showing its ignorance!"

"Not all of us are ignorant, *Dar'Kyn,*" Cornelius said. "Are we, D'Tomia Nighthawk and Syn'Chin Hornsdoodle?"

In the middle of the group of council members and their staffs, a flurry of scuffling noises, yells, and groans as guards restrained Hornsdoodle and Nighthawk and brought them before the remaining council members.

Cornelius banged the adjournment. "Bring those two to my office," he said as he left the chambers.

———

Dar'Kyn and Jessica were taken to another room with a heavy door. They were alone, but both suspected guards were on the other side of the door.

"That was nice shooting," Dar said once they were alone. She was sitting on a chair designed for someone taller, so her feet didn't reach the floor. Jessica watched Dar's feet swing under her.

"Why are we in here?" Jessica asked.

"Probably because we are dangerous," Dar stated.

Jessica chuckled, "I am, but I didn't hurt anyone—"

"Not *yet*, you haven't," Dar interjected. "These people, like your people, live in *'yet'.*"

"I looked up Tartarus when I got home," Jessica said.

"And?" Dar asked.

"It sounds a lot like the Christian hell," Jessica said. "Maybe a little worse. I don't think I'd like to go there. It's not high on my list of vacation spots I'd like to see."

———

Socrates, Lady *S'hyrlus,* and Lady Suzanne were escorted to Cornelius' office.

"What is going on?" *S'hyrlus* asked.

"What is the human term…" Cornelius said.

215

"A coup...I think," Socrates said.

"A coup, for now," Cornelius said. "Nighthawk and Horns-doodle, being upset that their heirs are suspected of things that would get them executed, have decided that they know what is best for everyone else."

"Yes, that sounds like a coup," Suzanne said.

"So, what happens now?" S'hyrlus asked.

"The council investigation, to which you were all called, was a distraction to get Phelonius' supporters to show themselves. I have been suspicious of several individuals for some time. My trip to the *Eighth Plane* pulled them all together where my operatives could observe them."

"When the cat is away..." Suzanne added.

"Exactly!" Cornelius said.

"So, we are not under suspicion?" S'hyrlus asked.

"Not at all!" Cornelius said jovially. "I have not yet decided if the human is dangerous...or *Dar'Kyn*, though."

"*Dar'Kyn* has the judicious power to make anyone disappear...permanently," S'hyrlus said. "I do not understand her power or her purpose, so that would make her dangerous, I would say."

Cornelius smiled and shook his head a little. "Jessica seemed so...so friendly after she got to know us better. Surely, she would not be dangerous?"

Socrates had been looking down, listening to Cornelius, now he said, "Did you see the wall behind Jessica's shots?"

"No, not yet," Cornelius said. "Why?"

"I did," Socrates said. "One or two more shots would have opened a hole in the wall big enough for me to crawl through if I had to. I am glad our coats stop her bullets."

"Seeing the melon was enough to convince me not to be wearing mine if she starts shooting at it," Cornelius said. "I am surprised Malthuvius and Phelonius survived the experience."

20

CHA-CHA-CHANGES

Cornelius sat in his office with Socrates and Lady *S'hyrlus*. In front of the large desk were D'Tomia Nighthawk and Syn'Chin Hornsdoodle. Both were shackled.

"What am I supposed to do with you," Cornelius asked rhetorically. "If I punish you, incarceration, whippings, that sort of thing, I risk civil war. I cannot let you go, as I would be seen as a weak leader." He exhaled loudly. "We have been friends for centuries." Cornelius shook his head.

"What did you expect?" D'Tomia Nighthawk asked. "Malthuvius, though not my heir any longer, was in my family line. Was I to ignore the fact that he is facing execution?"

"Same for me," Syn'Chin Hornsdoodle chimed in. "I do not know what the punishment for B'runix will be, but it will not be nothing. And why? Just for believing differently from you?"

"Did B'runix come to me with his concerns?" Socrates asked. "I can tell you that he did not. He chose to betray me and give information to the enemy."

"As I recall, D'Tomia," Cornelius said, "you were one that voted to issue a warrant for Malthuvius. At the same time, I voted to issue warrants for my grandson. *I* was hunting *my* grandson. Socrates was hunting *his* grandsire. *We* were expected to do our duty, and we did it.

"As you should recall, we were on the council to prevent the betrayal of our progeny from doing what Phelonius and Malthuvius did. Are we now to turn our backs on their transgressions? On yours?"

———

Dar'Kyn Trubis and Jessica Strange were sitting in Cornelius' office. They were escorted in as D'Tomia Nighthawk and Syn'Chin Hornsdoodle were escorted out. Neither talked.

"Jessica, I have questions," Cornelius said as he sat at his desk, with Lady *S'hyrlus* and Socrates seated at the ends of the desk.

"And you think I have answers?" Jessica asked sarcastically. "I don't know nothin' I don't haf ta."

"My questions pertain to *Dar'Kyn*—" Cornelius started.

"Well, she's sitting right there, so ask her," Jessica interrupted.

"*Dar'Kyn* isn't answering," Socrates said.

"And you think I'll tell you anything about her? I know very little, less than you do," Jessica said. She looked to *S'hyrlus*, "You brought her to our plane, and you brought her here. What was your plan? Did you really expect me to tell you anything?" Jessica shook her head. "I expected more from you, Socrates."

Socrates looked chagrined.

Cornelius took in a noisy deep breath and let it out slowly. "Dar, what happened on the *Eighth Plane*, as it pertains to Phelonius? What was that cloud?"

Dar sat staring back at Cornelius, kicking her feet back and forth as she did when sitting in a too-high chair. "You were there, Cornelius. You tell me what happened. What do you think the cloud was?"

"If I knew, I would not be asking you!" Cornelius said petulantly.

"You would not believe me if I told you," Dar said. "You have already made up your mind, so why should I disabuse you of your illusions."

"Do you want to know what I know about Dar?" Jessica asked Cornelius, causing Socrates' and S'hyrlus' eyebrows to raise. "I don't know much, but I know that I like her more than I like you." She grinned and cocked her head a little.

It had been several days, of council interrogations, since Jessica and Dar had seen Cornelius, Socrates, or S'hyrlus. Cornelius banged the council into session once again.

"The council has decided the question of the betrayal by B'runix Hornsdoodle. The members have agreed that B'runix Hornsdoodle failed to avail himself of his direct superior's, in this case, Socrates Blackwing, experience and counsel. The members have also decided that B'runix Hornsdoodle should have stayed at the ambassador's residence rather than go to Phelonius and pass along information." Cornelius looked around at those in attendance. "It gives me no pleasure to pass judgment on B'runix Hornsdoodle for his actions. B'runix Hornsdoodle, please stand."

Hornsdoodle stood proudly, almost defiantly.

"B'runix Hornsdoodle, it is the judgment of the council that you be incarcerated for 24 phase-cycles. After which, you will become an instructor of Ethical Behavior at the academy for another 24 phase-cycles. Further, no Hornsdoodle younglings will be conceived for 48 phase-cycles after your incarceration ends." Cornelius looked to Hornsdoodle gravely. "To some, this would seem to be harsh. It could have been much harsher. Use it as a learning experience." Cornelius banged the rock on the dais again.

"To all the families on the council, especially Hornsdoodle and Nighthawk. Choose those that will inherit your council seat wisely. None will be accepted unless they become *T'et Faqin Q'estirians and* achieve distinction, either through rank, battle, or both, preferably both. Upon assuming a council seat, your heir must be named within 50 phase-cycles." Cornelius banged the rock on the dais twice, signifying the end of the session.

"How did you manage to get Hornsdoodle and Nighthawk to agree?" Socrates asked. He was sitting in Cornelius' office, and both had their feet up, a tankard of ale in their fist.

"That part was easy," Cornelius grinned. "I simply told them both that either they agree, or I would remove them from the council and incarcerate all of their families indefinitely."

"What are your plans for Malthuvius Nighthawk?" Socrates asked.

"What am *I* planning?" Cornelius smirked. "I am planning on going on a nice long trip. I was thinking of leaving Malthuvius' fate in the hands of my heir."

"As if I do not have enough to do," Socrates said, shaking his head.

"We had this discussion already," Cornelius said. "You will stay here while Lady Suzanne packs up the ambassadorial residence. She comes to get you, and you transport all of your belongings. She transports you and all of your guards and servants."

"And where are we to go here?" Socrates asked. "Housing, here, is at a premium."

"Well, I am still in my main house and will be until such time as you take over; it is the council chair's residence," Cornelius said. "However, some years ago, I...acquired a small place out in the country."

"Acquired?" Socrates quipped. "More likely, someone owed you something, and you…acquired it in trade."

"Hush, you!" Cornelius spat. "A little more respect for your elders if you please. Anyway, you and Lady Suzanne can take up residence there. It isn't more than a step and a half away. I have been there a couple of times but have not been there for some years. Once you take over from me, you can have the place here, and I will live there. That way, I can come and go as I please."

"That would work for me," Socrates said, "but Lady Suzanne needs to agree."

"That is between you two younglings," Cornelius said. "Whatever you two decide. When are you going to transport Jessica?"

"In the next couple of days," Socrates said. "Why?"

"I have had some inquiries about her…um…disposition," Cornelius said.

"Her disposition?" Socrates questioned.

"Some want to know who and what she is," Cornelius said. "Those who saw her demonstration are…worried. They worry that they will be…punctured with her…bullies?"

"You mean they worry about being *shot* with *bullets*?" Socrates asked.

"I suppose," Cornelius said, "it is so new to me that the terms confuse me."

"There is no need to worry," Socrates chuckled. "On her *Plane*, they allow her to walk around with her weapons. She has been trained and is trusted."

"Those worried about her," Cornelius said, "do not know her, and they certainly do not trust her. They are blissfully unaware of the inner workings of her…bullets or guns. All they want is her gone from here, safely onto her own *Plane*."

"That displeases me," Socrates frowned.

"When you are on the council," Cornelius said, "there will be many things you will be forced to do that will displease you."

Jessica and *Dar'Kyn* were eating at the *Cloven Hoof Inn*.

"Do you know how much longer we'll be here?" Jessica asked.

"I have no idea," Dar said, in English, as she cut into her... what passed for beef. "I hope we won't be here too long. These... people make me nervous!"

"Why do they make *you* nervous?" Jessica asked. "They make me nervous, too. Just checking if it's for the same reasons."

"I don't know exactly," Dar said. "Maybe it was the calling for torture that did it."

"Yeah, that'll do it every time!" Jessica said as she shook her head. "Can I ask you something?"

Dar shrugged as she ate. "Why not?"

"Why didn't the council members believe you when you mentioned Tartarus?" Jessica asked.

"What do you believe?" Dar asked.

"I don't know, exactly," Jessica responded. "Tartarus, hell, I guess I can believe in that. It isn't a whole lot different from what I was raised believing."

"How does it make you feel that Tartarus is an actual place?" Dar asked.

"A little...uncomfortable, I guess," Jessica said. "Why do you ask?"

"We are dealing with people who are comfortable with wizards and nymphs, ogres, faeries, goblins, and dwarves. They use magic and have battled dragons. To you, those are all beyond what you thought was real...until recently, correct?"

Jessica nodded as she ate what tasted like a steak, medium-rare, thank you very much.

"The one thing they don't think about is what comes after," Dar motioned with her arms, "all this. You're aware that the wizards and the nymphs are quite long-lived?"

"Yeah, I'm aware of it, on some level," Jessica said. "I don't know about the scope of it, though."

"Given all the facts I've brought up," Dar said, "the one thing they refuse to think about is death."

"Among my people," Jessica said, "we have a...legend, of sorts. It's usually depicted as someone, skeleton or actual flesh, with a long, black robe, carrying a scythe. We call that legend the Grim Reaper."

"What did this Grim Reaper do? What was his purpose?" Dar asked.

"The legend," Jessica said, "says that when it's your time to die, he comes and reaps your soul, usually with the scythe. He separates your soul from your mortal body and then escorts you to whatever is next."

"Hmmm...interesting!" Dar said. She glanced around and saw no one that might understand English. "Thanatos is the one in charge," Dar said conspiratorially. "I guess you could even say that I sort of act like a Reaper." She shook her head, "But I digress. These *Lords of Magic* refuse to think about the end of their life. They know it's coming, but barring accident or war, that won't be for a very long time."

"You seem to be more comfortable talking to me about it," Jessica said. "Why is that?"

"Basically," Dar said, "no one is around who would understand the language we're using. I'm telling you because you've demonstrated a level of loyalty, so I am giving you more information."

"So, what exactly is your purpose?" Jessica asked.

"My purpose," Dar said, "is to allow one of the *Erinys* to... inhabit me for a short time. While I'm inhabited, the call for the other *Erinyes* is made, or not made, as the case may be. My purpose is to act as a conduit and observe the target."

"But why so secretive?" Jessica asked.

"Jessica, I like you," Dar said. "I think you like me, too. Do you think you'd like me now if I had told you when we met?

The secrecy is necessary, partially, so I'm not so damned lonely. As for the rest, they don't want to think about the end of life... not at all...not ever. If those gathered here knew what we were discussing, they'd rend us instantly."

"Lady *S'hyrlus* gave dire warnings about something happening to you," Jessica said. "What was she hinting at?"

"Hinting," Dar laughed, "I work for Nyx and a pantheon of lesser others; I don't like the term gods. I've been doing it a long time. I guess you could say that I've earned a bit of favor. You were there when they took Phelonius. Can you imagine the same thing happening here...to everyone?"

"I guess to *S'hyrlus*, that would qualify as unbelievably bad," Jessica said. "I'd say that would be a good start."

"You don't like them, do you?" Dar asked.

"When I met Socrates," Jessica said, "I was impressed. As time went on, it grew to mutual respect, but his people killed the only person I cared for, and cared for me, in a way I've never known. For that, I'd send them all to hell just for the fun of it."

"Can I give you some advice?" Dar asked. Jessica nodded. "You carry a lot of anger. You need to set it aside, as much as possible, before it eats you alive. Your drinking is the anger eating you up. Irving showed you what it was like to be the center of someone else's Universe. You may find that again, and you may not. You've known it once. Some never get to experience it, not even once. Don't forget what you had; rather, cherish what you had. Don't let it destroy you; that would make *me* sad."

Suzanne and Socrates were being shown the sizeable, castle-type structure that had been Cornelius' escape. To Suzanne, the term chateau came to her mind when she first saw it from a distance. Now, though, she was being shown around the place, and her mind closed off the drone of conversation going on as she found herself missing her home.

"So, what do you think, Suzanne?" Socrates asked.

"Fine," Suzanne said quietly, distracted. "Fine," she repeated louder, "It will be fine. It seems to be substantially larger than the farmhouse."

"Farmhouse?" the *Grum K'sha U'ien* said. He was the groundskeeper and was given the task of showing the place by Cornelius. "If there is a farmhouse as grand as this, I would stay there."

"She means the current ambassadorial residence," Socrates said smiling.

Suzanne chuckled.

When they had made their way to the front courtyard, Suzanne stopped and grinned broadly. In the center of the walled courtyard was a large Oak. She ran over to it and touched it lovingly. She immediately felt its pulse with all the places available for a traveling *Sh'o Sook J'eid*.

Socrates, Suzanne, Lady *S'hyrlus*, Jessica, *Dar'Kyn*, and the guards that had traveled to *Q'esteria* with the ambassador were standing in the courtyard, readying everything to travel.

"Hurry back, Socrates," Cornelius said. He'd shown up to bid them farewell. "And you, my dear," he said to *S'hyrlus* as he took her hand and touched his forehead to its back.

"I will return as soon as I can," Lady *S'hyrlus* said with an intimate grin.

"Good!" was all Cornelius could say and received several chuckles from the others.

"Are you ready, Jessica?" Socrates asked as he got out his tarpaulin and started to unfold it.

Jessica glared at Socrates.

"I want to go where Jessica goes," Dar said as she came over to stand beside her friend.

Socrates shrugged and tossed the tarp over the pair.

"So, this is what the inside of one of the wizard's storage bunkers looks like," Dar said as she picked herself off the floor. "Who would have guessed?"

"What?" Jessica asked. "That it would be so messy? So dusty?"

They both laughed heartily.

"I always wondered where their ale and bits of meat came from," Dar said. "I'm sure you knew that magic isn't free?"

"Yeah, Socrates tried to get that across to us...um...me, shortly after we met," Jessica said. Her throat had choked off at the memory, and a tear started down her cheek.

"Now, now," Dar said gently, "there's no need for that." She had wrapped her arms around Jessica's thigh, which was all she could reach comfortably. "This isn't working," Dar said after a few seconds. "Come over to the crates; you need a proper hug."

Jessica chuckled and lifted Dar to the top of a crate. Dar immediately threw her arms around Jessica's shoulders and gave her Jessica's idea of a proper hug.

It wasn't long before Jessica and Dar were standing in the grove of oaks. Jessica knew it to be the one close to her house.

"Please don't run off," Socrates said as they walked the short distance to the house. "Lady Suzanne and I have an announcement to make that concerns everyone."

Dar chuckled at his pomposity.

"I do not know how to say this," Socrates said as everyone on the property had gathered in the living room of the house.

"I am sure you will find a way," Dar said jokingly.

"The *Sh'tuk Q'estiria Faqin* has decreed that the ambassadorial presence on this *Plane* is not needed at this time," Socrates said. "Everyone, with notable exceptions, will be returning to *Q'estiria*. We are here to pack all that we wish to take back with us. Everything returning should be stacked in the grove, close to our arrival point."

"How long will it take?" one of the guards asked. "I will be glad to be home," he said after some murmurs.

"It should not take more than a couple of days," Socrates announced. "Okay, let us busy ourselves with the tasks at hand."

"Synkyn and Tynkyn, you will be going with us," Suzanne said. "We will need your help and expertise."

They both bowed. "Of course, my Lady," they said in tandem.

Dar dragged Jessica to another room. "Remember what I said, please?" *Dar'Kyn* said quietly.

A few hours later, Dar was gone.

It had taken a day and a half to pack up the ambassador's things and get them to the grove. Jessica had gone into town and found Trooper, and she managed to convince him to be there with her when Socrates left.

"Well, we're all packed and ready to go," Socrates said,

Suzanne came over to Jessica and hugged her. "Please take care of yourself," she whispered. "If *you* don't, then *who* will?"

Socrates came over and kissed her cheek. "It's been a pleasure," he shook Trooper's hand.

"Does this mean I can cut down all of the oaks?" Jessica shouted.

"It wouldn't do any good," Suzanne said. "It would just make us walk further," she chuckled.

Jessica and Trooper stood on the grove's edge and watched as a portal was opened, everyone entered, and the portal closed. All was quiet for quite some time.

"It feels like all the magic has gone from the world," Trooper said.

21

BACK INTO A FOLD

Jessica and Trooper meandered back toward the house shortly after the portal closed.

"Nobody will believe us," Trooper said when the pair was more than halfway to the house.

"Believe us about what?" Jessica said absentmindedly.

"Wizards, nymphs, and green faeries. All of it," Trooper said.

"Does it matter if we're believed or not?" Jessica said. "How would somebody else know? Why would they know?"

"I don't know," Trooper said with a shrug. "There are times I think I need to talk to someone, just to make sure my cheese isn't slipping off my cracker."

"Come in and have a drink with me," Jessica said, opening the backdoor. She grabbed a bottle and two glasses as she passed the cupboard where they were kept.

"I can stay for one drink," Trooper said as he sat at the table. He watched as Jessica poured two fingers of the amber liquid into a glass and handed it to him.

Jessica froze for a second. "Huh," she said as she resumed pouring her drink, "it's quiet out here. I hope it isn't too quiet."

"To a quiet and tranquil life," Trooper said, raising his glass in a toast. "May it be not too quiet and not too tranquil," he finished.

"I'll drink to that," Jessica smirked, clinking glasses with Trooper.

"Well, this gives me a chance to ask," Trooper said, "what's next for the legendary Jessica Strange?"

"Legendary!" Jessica giggled.

"Seriously, Jess, what do you want to do next?" Trooper asked.

"Not a clue at this point," Jessica said. "Being here alone will be a strain on my sanity." She listened again. "Never thought I'd say this, but I was used to being alone. Then I got involved with Irv and haven't been alone since. Amazing what you can get used to." She drained half of her drink.

"Well, before you go crazy, come to the P.D. and talk with me," Trooper said. "I've got some ideas on getting Tacoma back into Washington."

"Out of the Pacific Coast Coalition?" Jessica said.

"Even though Tacoma is reduced so far in population," Trooper said, "we are the only population this side of the mountains I've seen."

"I've been down to Long Beach and didn't see a soul," Jessica said, draining her glass.

"That far?" Trooper said, draining his glass and setting it on the table. "Well, I'm off. Need to get something to eat before getting back to it at the P.D. Care to join me?"

Jessica looked at the bottle for a heartbeat, trying to decide. "As a matter of fact," she said, replacing the cap on the bottle, "I would!"

Jessica and Trooper decided to take the hovercar into the P.D. to refuel it and get something to eat.

"Did you disable the video surveillance at the P.D?" Jessica asked as she flew.

"Nope. Didn't see a need," Trooper said.

"Won't the Feds be unhappy about you breaking their quarantine of the city?" Jessica said.

"The last thing I worry about is an unhappy Fed," Trooper said. "The city has been shut down for too long already. We need to restructure and rebuild; the sooner, the better."

Two weeks after Jessica had gone to town for a meal, she and Trooper were on their way to the Washington Capital in Spokane. She hadn't returned to her house after eating. Instead, Trooper had opened one of the offices on the same floor as the hovercar landing for her living space.

"Not to tell you how to fly," Trooper said as they took off, "but you may want to hug the ground after crossing into Washington territory."

"Why?" Jessica asked as she turned the craft eastward. "Flying at a low altitude will use too much fuel."

"Before the Event," Trooper explained, "the mayor and governor of Pacific Coast – Washington weren't very…umm… diplomatic when dealing with those outside the Coalition."

"You mean they were antagonistic?" Jessica said.

"Yeah, they were. They didn't care what the rest of the non-coalition part of the country did. The governor was counting on the rest backing them up, should something happen."

"Well, shit!" Jessica said. "Hopefully, I'll get it all figured out by the time we get to the mountains."

A few minutes later, an alarm sounded.

"What's that?" Trooper asked.

"The mountains…" Jessica said, disheartened.

Luckily, the flight from Tacoma to Spokane was relatively uneventful until they got to Spokane.

"You are entering restricted airspace," came the automated announcement over their headphones. *"This is restricted airspace for a state capital. If you have business here, then transmit clearance codes now. If you are experiencing an emergency, then transmit the particulars of your emergency over the emergency frequency."*

"Well, that doesn't sound good," Trooper said after the automated messages stopped.

"Get on the radio and do whatever you need to before they start shooting at us," Jessica said as she made a hard bank away from the Spokane airspace.

"This is unlisted flight west of Spokane requesting access," Trooper said.

"Go ahead, unlisted. What is your business?" came the human response over the headphones.

"We're trying to see someone about reestablishing relations with State Government. We are from Tacoma," Trooper said.

"Tacoma?" the voice said. *"That was destroyed months ago. You need to get clearance codes to land,"* the voice said.

"Yes, but how do we get the codes?" Trooper asked.

"You can obtain clearance codes by calling the Washington State Department of Transportation in Spokane."

"And how am I supposed to call when there is no cell service in Tacoma, and your towers don't connect with our devices?"

"If you need to report an outage, you need to contact the Washington State Department of Energy."

"But I can't call!" Trooper yelled in frustration.

Jessica tried to hide her chuckling.

"I'm sorry, sir, but unnecessary belligerence will be dealt with by the State Patrol."

"Fine! Send the Patrol!" Trooper yelled.

"Washington State Patrol has been contacted. Have a nice day." The radio went silent.

Jessica started laughing.

Trooper tried to get them back to no avail.

"Now what?" Jessica asked, still smirking.

"That wasn't funny, Jessica!" Trooper said.

"I thought it was hilarious!" Jessica said around her guffaws.

It took Jessica some time before she could control herself. Trooper was scanning a map, trying to determine where they were. "Where are we?" he asked finally.

"We came in north of Reardon, and now we're not far from Medical Lake," Jessica said, still trying to stifle her laughs.

"Can we go to Medical Lake?" Trooper asked.

"Near as I can tell," Jessica said, "Medical Lake and Cheney mark the edge of the restricted zone on this side of Spokane."

"Risks?" Trooper asked.

"Of what?" Jessica asked. "If we make it to Medical Lake and land, we'll probably be arrested and jailed unless we get shot down before then. We could go back to Reardon. They may have someplace to buy a phone, if we had any way of paying for it."

"We still have our Identification Devices," Trooper said.

"You heard the guy on the radio," Jessica said. "They think Tacoma is dead. We may not have active accounts anymore. It all may be moot, but we are kinda stuck."

"In what way?" Trooper asked.

"Fuel," Jessica said. "When we left, I knew we'd be cutting it close even with the extra capacity."

"So, we just get some fuel. Problem solved," Trooper said.

"You think so?" Jessica asked. "Do you think any of these smaller towns have liquid hydrogen refueling plants? If they do, do you think it'll be free? Nothing is free, you know. And then there will be the questions. Thousands of questions."

Two months. It took two months to get a phone that worked on the eastern side of the mountains and to get their hovercar refueled.

"Well, I'd say that was a successful trip," Trooper said as they headed for home. "We have temporary clearance codes to get us home and all the paperwork to get Tacoma back into Washington State."

"And it only cost us…what exactly?" Jessica asked.

"Hmmm…I see what you mean," Trooper said, disheartened. "I thought we'd never find a place to access our accounts. But we are back on the payroll, so to speak."

"And what about all the questions?" Jessica said. "What did you tell them, by the way? We should get our stories straight if anyone else comes to investigate."

Trooper looked even more down in the dumps if that was possible. "I'm sure they will, now. It was assumed that everyone on our side of the mountains was gone, and sometimes I wish that were true."

"Just keep in mind the old saying, 'No good deed goes unpunished'," Jessica said. "I do consider the trip a success, you know." Trooper perked up a little. "I mean, we didn't die…and that would be a good thing, right?"

"Sometimes I wonder," Trooper said.

Neither spoke the rest of the trip.

"Our trip to Spokane was well received," Trooper started. He was standing at the head of a large table in the meeting room.

"Is it me," Jessica said, "or were the politicos in Spokane anxious to get us back into their State? They seemed to jump at the prospect."

"They did," Trooper said. "Washington State had no seaports. Before *The Event*, Spokane had to deal with Tacoma and Seattle for imports and exports. Seattle is no longer populated. Once we expressed a desire to rejoin the State, they saw a seaport and all the imports that could come that way. Not to mention exports."

"But what about the people?" the man called Trevor asked. "What do the people get out of the deal?"

Jessica looked around at those in the meeting room. She didn't know any of them. Trooper and this Trevor seemed to be reciting a set-piece.

"The people get jobs and income," Trooper said. "They get to vote and have that vote recognized as legitimate. They get to travel if they want. Isn't that worth letting Spokane use our seaport?"

Trevor's question was voiced so Trooper could give this little speech, Jessica thought. *What the hell is going on here? I knew Trooper well before The Event, but now, I'm not so sure.*

"So, if the people wanted to elect a mayor?" Trevor asked.

"It isn't a matter of *if* the people want a mayor, they *need* one. This city needs a chief executive to deal with Spokane and others directly.

"Jessica, did Spokane know we existed before we showed up?"

"No," Jessica said reservedly. "They were surprised when we showed up and more surprised when we brought up rejoining their State."

"What's to stop those in Spokane from populating and taking over the Port of Seattle? Wouldn't that shift any upper hand in a deal?" Trevor asked.

"That's a good point," Trooper said. "Hmmm...maybe we need to send 100 men, and their families, to occupy the port."

"But we told them that Tacoma was the only populated area," Jessica said.

"Yeah, so?" Trooper said. "That was then, what, two months ago? Without reliable communications, what would you expect?" Trooper grinned at her.

Jessica didn't say anything for the rest of the meeting. Once everyone was going about their business, Jessica said, "You got a minute, Trooper?" Trooper nodded and hustled the last of the attendees out of the door.

"What's on your mind, Jess?" Trooper asked as he closed the door.

"What the hell are you trying to pull?" Jessica asked. "Sounds like you are trying to profit from your deal with Spokane over the rest of the people."

"You say that like it's a bad thing?" Trooper said. "Jess, I spent 20 years putting my life on the line daily. Once *The Event* happened, no one knew me. They had no idea that I was one of the reasons they could carry on their lives safely."

"That was the job you signed up for," Jessica said, "just as I did, and so many others."

"Why do you think so many on the P.D. were corrupt?" Trooper asked. "There has always been too little paid to those who put their life at risk. Added to that is anonymity. You and I have placed our lives between innocent and those that would take what we protect.

"In the past, this country asked men to fight. Fight where the Government told them to fight. All for poverty wages, but they'd take care of them when they returned. Did that happen? No! How many would agree, let alone volunteer, in later wars, if the Government had been honest and told them to go to war but never to come back?"

Trooper chuckled. "Back in the day, people used to say, 'They knew what the job entailed' when a cop was murdered. And if that weren't enough of an insult, they'd turn the criminals loose.

"*The Event*, by some, me included, was looked upon as a plague from God, leveling the scales. And here you stand, judging me for trying to get this city back, a drunk, with nowhere else to go."

Jessica started clapping, not the excited clapping, the kind with a long pause between the noise, the applause of the bored.

"Very nice speech," Jessica said unenthusiastically. "Take you long to memorize it? For a long time, I looked up to you. You were a kind of father figure for me. Now that I see you as you really are, if that is what this," Jessica motioned to include all of

Trooper, "is. Frankly, I'm disappointed. I'd thought there was more to you than what I see in front of me. I can see that you're about as deep as a mud puddle."

Jessica made a point of tapping her upper arm and then resting her right hand on the butt of her pistol.

"Was that supposed to intimidate me?" Trooper asked. "Did you call your wizard buddies to come and deal with me?"

"Not a bit," Jessica said. "I've called him to come to retrieve his coin and his armband. I don't think I need to say this, but you're not welcome at my house."

Jessica disappeared.

Jessica reappeared on the roof of the Police Department. She was getting the fans up to speed as she ran through her checklist. It didn't take long for her to get airborne.

It was a quick flight to her house. She landed in the yard, close to the barn, and left the car idling as she opened the big doors on the end of the building. It didn't take her long to park the hovercar inside the barn, secure it and the barn, and walk into the house.

Once inside, she grabbed a bottle out of habit and then thought better of it.

Two weeks after Jessica had tapped her platinum armband, Blackwing was tapping on an office door.

"Yes?" Trevor asked as he opened the door.

"Marshall Trooper," Blackwing said in a rumbling *basso profundo* voice.

Trevor didn't take his eyes off of Blackwing, nor did he let loose the door to allow entry. "Hey, Marsh!" he yelled, "It's for you!"

Trooper looked under Trevor's straight arm at the person standing on the threshold. "Yes? What is it?" he asked.

"A word," Blackwing rumbled, "in private if you don't mind."

"I'm kinda busy at the moment," Trooper said, "Can't this wait until later?"

"No, it can't wait," Blackwing glared. "I've come a long way."

"I didn't call you, nor do I wish to talk to you, in private or otherwise," Trooper said.

"I really must insist," Blackwing glared at Trevor, then at Trooper.

While Trooper looked, he could see Blackwing's usually pale blue eye become a burning, red coal. Trooper also noticed Blackwing's voice deepen, and he had thought that was an impossibility.

Trooper swallowed hard. "Trevor, stand aside. I will go with you."

Trooper walked around the corner before Blackwing touched him, and both were transported to the roof of the Police Department building, where the hovercars were parked.

Blackwing held out his hand to Trooper.

Trooper, sheepishly, handed his two gold coins to Blackwing.

When the two coins were in Blackwing's hand, he closed it, they disappeared, and then he reopened his hand.

"Wha?" Trooper said. "What more could you possibly want with me?

"You're *K'obi Sha Shin J'oi Faqin T'orqute*," Blackwing barked as he indicated Trooper's upper bicep.

"Why?" Trooper pleaded. "Are you saying you won't protect me?"

"You have violated the purpose of being *K'obi Sha Shin J'oi*

238

Faqin," Blackwing snapped. "To make things worse, you avoided the request when I sought to speak to you. That isn't what I'd say a trusted friend to wizards should do."

"This is that drunk bitch's doing!" Trooper said. "I don't know what she told you, but it was a lie!"

"Was it?" Blackwing asked. "Why do you assume I've talked with Jessica? I haven't. I came to you for information on her and her state of mind. Instead, I'm met with suspicion, resistance, and fear."

"What are you going to do to me?" Trooper asked.

"Me?" Blackwing said. "Nothing...but I'd stay away from Jessica for quite a while. She's not too pleased with you, and you're likely to be shot."

"She wouldn't do that," Trooper said haughtily.

"I wouldn't be so sure if I were you," Blackwing said. "She may have a drinking problem, but you ruined your relationship, with her and with us."

"If she shoots me, I'll have her arrested!" Trooper ranted.

"I think you need to reevaluate your assessment of Jessica," Blackwing said. "She had little reason to be here before your... issues with her. Now, I don't think you could hurt her anymore. They have nothing to lose when you cannot hurt someone any further."

"I could have her killed," Trooper raged.

"That would just be a release for her," Blackwing said. "If you do, bring friends, and make sure they pack a lunch. It's going to be an all-day thing."

With that, Blackwing disappeared.

"You coulda taken me home first," Trooper said to the air.

22

NO MORE Q'ESTIRIANS

I t had been two weeks since Jessica had called for Blackwing by tapping her armband. She didn't start drinking right away. She did have a drink most nights to help her sleep.

The time waiting was spent taking the hovercar to the Olympia Police Center for refueling. While there, usually waiting, she'd scrounge the local stores for any food or weapons she could find. *I should move here,* she thought. *It would make it easier to avoid Trooper and his thugs. By doing so, would I be running and hiding from Trooper and those memories, hiding from the memories of Irv?* Jessica shook her head to clear those thoughts and resumed her scavenging.

Once, Jessica took the hovercar to Naches. The city of Yakima issued a radio challenge. Jessica promptly ignored the challenge by letting them eat static. A further threat was made to get the Washington State National Guard involved. This threat, too, was met with silence, but after that, she'd only take the hovercar to the little burg that used to be Elbe and wizard-step the rest of the way to Naches.

On her trips to Olympia, Jessica would refuel her hovercar and then transport as many extra fuel cells as the small craft could carry. She stowed the fuel cells in the barn, and had an even dozen.

Jessica was sitting at her table, head resting on the table. It was early afternoon, two weeks after she'd tapped her armband.

"Are you okay?" Suzanne's familiar voice sounded close to the backdoor.

"Suze!" Jessica said as she got to her feet and scrambled to her friend. "Damn, I've missed you!" She picked Suzanne off the floor and began spinning around.

"Jessica!" Suzanne giggled. "Put me down! You're making me dizzy!"

It took a few more spins before Jessica put Suzanne down.

"Did you come alone?" Jessica asked, trying to look beyond Suzanne. "How did you get in? I'm sure I locked the door." Jessica went to the door and found it remained locked. She turned to Suzanne and looked puzzled. "You aren't real," she said. "I'm hallucinating. I've gone around the bend."

"I'm just as real as you are," Suzanne said. She smacked Jessica's upper arm, making a resounding slap.

"Ow!" Jessica said.

"See? I'm really here!" Suzanne showed a familiar gold coin in her palm.

"Okay, you're here," Jessica agreed. "Why are you here?"

"You called Blackwing," Suzanne said, "and here we are. What was the reason behind your summons? I'm sure it wasn't just to chat."

"Trooper has become a problem," Jessica said as she reseated herself. She reached for the bottle she kept on the table, and Suzanne stopped her from lifting it to pour a drink with her hand. Jessica resumed. "It isn't something I *know*, it's more something I *feel* if that makes any sense. He and I went to Spokane, and it was all so…weird!" She shook her head.

"Well, you were a cop for a long time," Suzanne said. "I'm sure you learned to trust your gut, as they used to say, especially in the absence of facts."

"Yeah, I did trust my gut much of the time. Trooper kept making references to being a cop for 20 years, and no one knew who he was. I served ten years with him, and I never cared who got credit or even if anyone knew who I was. I would have thought that Trooper looked at things the same way. He was my training officer. I thought I knew who he was."

"Maybe," Suzanne whispered, "you looked up to him and innocently assumed you knew him. It wouldn't be the first time."

"So, did Sox come with you? I'm assuming he did," Jessica said.

"Yes, he came with me," Suzanne said. "He went to talk to Trooper before talking to you. That was my idea. I wanted to talk to you first, without anyone else around."

"That was a good call on your part," Jessica said. "I do have something…to talk to you about, without anyone else here."

"Sure," Suzanne said, "you can talk to me about anything."

"Before Dar left, she told me to send a message to her by way of the Hama…whatsits."

"Hamadryads," Suzanne corrected. "I don't know how to send for her, but I may know someone who can. What's the message?"

"I have become disillusioned with this life," Jessica said seriously.

Suzanne looked stunned. "Are you serious?" she asked when the shock wore off. "Why would you kill yourself?"

"What?" Jessica asked. "I'm not going to kill myself. You asked what the message was, and I told you."

"Your message sounded…like you were going to terminate yourself."

"Just—" Jessica said, "Just give her the message exactly as I said it. She'll know what it means."

"I don't understand, Jess," Suzanne said. "It hurts me that you would think that way."

"Suzanne, please!" Jessica said. "Just give her the message, or tell me now that you can't, and I'll make other arrangements."

There was a knock on the back door. Jessica opened the door.

"Come in, Socrates," Jessica said without looking to see who was at the door.

"Greetings, Jessica," Socrates said as he walked into the dining room and sat next to Suzanne at the table.

"Did you see Trooper?" Jessica asked.

"I did," Socrates said.

No one said anything for some time.

"Well?" Jessica snapped.

"Can you tell us what happened?" Suzanne asked.

"I went to talk to him at his domicile," Socrates said. "He was evasive and refused to talk to me privately. When I insisted, he did capitulate, finally. I won't tell you what we talked about but suffice it to say that I reclaimed all gold and platinum from him."

"Did the magic make him...evil?" Jessica asked hesitantly.

"Evil?" Socrates said. "No, I don't think he's evil. He's just an old man trying to survive, trying to stay relevant, maybe trying to hold on to old glories, but I wouldn't say he was evil. Besides, what you call magic doesn't make you evil...or good."

"Then why did you take back the gold coins?" Suzanne asked.

"And the platinum?" Socrates asked. "When I initially made you, Jessica, and Irving *K'obi Sha Shin J'oi Faqin*, it made you all feel like you belonged to each other," he said to Suzanne. "It helped to bring you all together, as a team. When I made Trooper *K'obi Sha Shin J'oi Faqin*, it was more to be able to monitor his whereabouts, and hopefully, yours or Irving's," he said to Jessica.

"The gold coins," Socrates continued, "were to give him a fighting chance against Phelonius, should he be attacked, as were yours and Irving's. At the time, we didn't know what Phelonius' attack would be or against whom."

"I think Trooper was abusing the power given him by the gold coins," Jessica said.

"It doesn't work that way," Socrates said, shaking his head. "The coins don't *give* power. The wizard-step coins use more life force the more you use them. The other coins enhance what you already have. Like I said before, you don't get something for nothing. Magic has its own costs.

"Speaking of the coins," Socrates looked uncomfortable, "with the recall of our embassy here, some things need to change between us."

"You want your coins back from me," Jessica said.

"That isn't what I was going to say," Socrates said. "The only coin you need to return is the platinum one. I see no reason why you can't keep the gold coins. The platinum one, however, creates a problem."

"What problem?" Jessica said.

"You tap it, I come," Socrates said, "that was the promise. The issue now, though, is the delay before I *can* come. Cornelius is stepping down from the council. I'm currently in training for his seat on the council. This time, I could get away in a reasonable timeframe, but once I ascend to the council," Socrates shook his head, "that will become far more difficult."

"So, you have a fix...otherwise, you wouldn't bring it up," Jessica said. "Spit it out."

"I propose that Cornelius give you *his* platinum coin," Socrates said. "Once I'm on the council, he'll be more available. For the time being, though, I would like you to keep it. It could come in handy sometime."

"Trooper and I went to Spokane," Jessica said, "recently, don't ask, and I found out I don't have access to any creds I had before. Or any accounts Suze left for us to use. There will be a time when this property will probably pass from my hands. You need to think about clearing out anything you may want."

A table at the *Cloven Hoof Inn* was occupied, and all outward signs indicated that they were four *Sh'o Sook J'eid*. All were characteristically beautiful and youthful. Only the shortest was familiar to those who regularly patronized the inn.

"What is that wonderful smell," *Allecto* asked. She had been watching *Dar'Kyn* discreetly popping something on the bottom of the container.

"Yes, *Dar'Kyn*, please tell us," *Tisiphone* insisted.

"Yes, yes, tell us," *Megaera* said.

"You would think that you three would have learned to be a little patient after all the millennia," *Dar'Kyn* said as she distributed the steaming containers to her companions.

Dar'Kyn removed the top of her container and the other three watched raptly. They all removed the tops of the containers, filling the room with an aroma that was warm and inviting and, at the same time, unidentifiable by the locals.

Dar waved her hand over the rising steam, sweeping it toward her nose as she inhaled deeply. The other three put their noses into the steam rising from their containers and sniffed loudly.

Dar then picked up the container, gently blew across the top of the liquid inside, and sipped lightly. The other three copied her actions with differing levels of noise.

"Oh, my!" *Allecto* said appreciatively, setting the container on the table.

"Where did you find this?" *Tisiphone* asked excitedly, copying her sister.

"You got it from the humans, didn't you," *Megaera* stated,

"Frankly, yes," Dar said. "I had never had something quite so—"

"Exactly!" *Allecto* said.

Dar took another sip as she sat back and looked at her companions. She could see them for who they were, not just as they currently appear. All three were majestic beauties, fair of skin and hair—each wearing their personal style of flowing dresses that left the bow-arm bare. *As beautiful as the Hamadryads are*, Dar thought, *these were exquisitely stunning, but you would expect that from Goddesses.*

"Why are we here, Dar?" *Tisiphone* asked. "It is not just for this delightful drink, although it would be worth the trip if it were." Her sisters agreed.

"I requested you three join me here because I would like you to consider a friend of mine—"

"You have a friend, Dar?" *Allecto* asked incredulously.

"How strange is that?" *Megaera* laughed.

"Stop, just stop," Dar said. "This is not about me, it is about my friend."

The three sisters sat back a little and sipped their drink. *Allecto* signaled that she should continue.

"My friend is very...umm...angry and lonely," Dar explained. "She is an accomplished warrior and—"

"*What* has she accomplished?" *Tisiphone* scoffed, leaning forward.

"Cannot be too significant," *Megaera* said, sliding to the edge of her seat. "A *she* and a *warrior*? Hard to believe."

"Now, sisters," *Allecto* said, reaching for her drink. "Dar has served us long and well. She has earned our ear. Let us be patient...while she gets to the point...quickly."

The three sisters nodded in agreement as they sat back.

Dar exhaled her exasperation.

Tisiphone leaned forward suddenly. "Is she the one who held Phelonius while I collected him?"

"Yes, she—" Dar started.

"Oh, well, she is quite the one!" *Tisiphone* said excitedly. "I saw into her mind...lots of anger, but passionate."

"What made her so...passionate, Dar?" *Allecto* said, raising an eyebrow.

"Yes, Dar, please tell us," *Megaera* said impatiently.

"So, if you have seen into her mind, *Tisiphone*, then you know —" Dar said.

"Maybe Tis knows, but we remain…unenlightened as to this friend of yours," *Allecto* said.

"Let her speak, Allie," *Megaera* said.

"She lost her husband to Phelonius minutes before she subdued him," Dar said.

"Minutes before?" *Allecto* said.

"Most women are overwhelmed with grief when they lose their husbands in that manner, Allie. Why was she not overwhelmed, Dar?" *Megaera* asked.

"Maybe she did not care for him as Dar thinks she did," *Allecto* said.

"Oh, she did, Allie," *Tisiphone* said. "I was in her head, briefly."

"Briefly, Tis? What does that even mean, 'briefly'?" *Allecto* asked. "Once you are in it, you see everything. So, 'briefly' holds no meaning."

"You know what I mean, Allie," *Tisiphone* said.

Dar was banging her forehead on the table.

"Why is she doing that again?" *Megaera* asked.

"Dar, please refrain from doing that," *Tisiphone* said. "Others are starting to notice and stare."

Allecto touched the arms of her sisters on either side. "Okay, Dar, bring your friend around to one, or all, of us, and we will consider her for training."

"Why does she get so emotional about us being out with her?" *Megaera* asked.

"We get out so seldom," *Tisiphone* said.

"I wonder why," *Dar'Kyn* said under her breath.

Suzanne and Socrates took a couple of days to get everything Suzanne wanted to preserve together and stored in Socrates' vault. After everything was gathered, Jessica, Suzanne, and Socrates sat together at the table.

"Do you have everything you wanted to keep?" Jessica asked. She started to pour two fingers of Jack Daniels into three glasses.

"Yes, I have everything I wanted to keep," Suzanne said.

Jessica distributed the glasses and raised the one in front of her.

"To friends," Jessica started. "Well met and true." She drained her glass.

Suzanne and Socrates did the same.

"I have only one request," Jessica said.

"Ask," Socrates said.

"If something should ever happen to me," Jessica said, "would you make sure my body rests next to Irv's? I don't have any family other than you two."

"Of cour—" Suzanne started, her words choked off, "ahem...of course we will do our best to see to it that your wishes are carried out. Hopefully, that won't be for a long time yet."

Jessica got a quizzical look. "I know, but you can never tell. We don't know when it will come; we just know that eventually, death finds us all."

"Suzanne has a gift for you," Socrates said solemnly.

"I'm so sorry," Jessica said contritely, "I didn't know you were leaving this quick. I wanted to get you something as well."

"It isn't much," Suzanne said, producing a small stack of books, "and I know your opinion about reading, but I thought you'd like these. They aren't anything expensive." She put the well-worn books on the table with a nervous chuckle.

"Maybe you should keep them," Jessica said. "I don't read much, after all."

"No, you take them," Suzanne said. "I can't force you to do anything; just know that there have been times that I was comforted by what was written years ago by someone I don't know. Besides, we'll be back. If you need a different book, then ask. I probably have it."

Socrates nodded and hooked a thumb to Suzanne, "Collector."

Jessica shrugged. "No promises, but I will take a look at them." She looked to Socrates. "I'm feeling kinda naked... without the armband," she rubbed her arm where the armband had been for so long. "When will Cornelius make a trip?"

"I don't know, for sure," Socrates said. "I'll see what I can do to get here a few times before Cornelius steps down."

"Well, you two are always welcome here," Jessica said, hugging Suzanne and shaking Socrates' hand.

She walked her friends to the Oak Grove and watched as Suzanne opened a portal, her friends stepped through, and the portal closed.

Jessica stood there for a few minutes. *Damn, it's way too quiet, now,* she thought. When her need for some background noise became too much, Jessica started back to the house.

"Damn boonies anyway," Jessica mumbled as she walked. "Too damn quiet; probably end up with me talking to myself."

When Jessica entered the house, she noticed the quiet. For several hours, she busied herself cleaning the kitchen and doing any dishes that needed to be done. Eventually, she saw the books.

As she caressed the covers, she read the titles. The ones that got her attention were *The Bible (New American Standard), Strong's Concordance, The Merriam-Webster Dictionary (Newest Edition), To Kill a Mockingbird (Harper Lee), 1984 (George Orwell),* and *The Lord of the Rings (J.R.R. Tolkien).* There were others, Steinbeck, Shakespeare, a book on Myths and Legends, but they didn't sound exciting.

She poured another drink and opened the book on Myths

and Legends. She chose it because she didn't want to get into anything too heavy, and she could page through it until something interested her.

She finished her drink and continued reading. It wasn't long before she fell asleep at the table.

It was daylight outside when a banging on the back door awakened Jessica.

She checked her pistol before looking out of the window on the door.

"What do you want, Trooper?" she yelled through the closed door.

"I need your help, Jessica," Trooper said.

Jessica pulled her pistol. "I'm not interested, Trooper," she said. She stood away from the door.

"But you have to help," Trooper insisted. "There is no one else I can turn to."

Jessica ran to the front door and looked out. She could see some distance, but she saw no one. She opened the door and sneaked around the house, carrying her pistol, checking before rounding a corner.

"Come on, Jess," Trooper yelled from the backyard. "Are you there, Jess?"

When Jessica got to the second corner, she heard someone coming toward her. She was pressed tight against the wall when someone walked past her around the corner. It was Trevor, carrying a shotgun. He took a few more steps, then Jessica laid the barrel of her pistol across the back of his head, crumpling the big man.

23

THE LAST DANCE ON THE
EIGHTH PLANE

After sending Trevor one direction around the house, Marshall Trooper went the other way. He was hoping to trap Jessica between them. Trooper stayed down to stay clear of the windows as he moved to avoid getting shot by someone inside. This crouching run hampered his speed.

When he'd rounded two corners, Trooper thought Jessica had outflanked him and Trevor. Maybe she'd gone back into the house. Perhaps she'd gotten past Trevor, somehow. *If she gets to the hovercar,* Trooper thought, *she'll be gone.* Unconsciously, he walked backward, away from the front of the house, to see two sides of the house simultaneously. It didn't take too long before he saw Trevor on the ground. He cautiously trotted over to Trevor. He looked down at Trevor, hoping he wouldn't see a bullet hole.

"What the actual fuck, Trooper!" Jessica yelled at Trooper's back.

Trooper slowly raised his hands when he heard Jessica rack a round in the 12-gauge. "Now, Jess, take it easy. No need to go off half-cocked," he cringed at his ironic statement.

"What were you thinking, attacking me here!" Jessica said.

"Blackwing took away my coins," Trooper whined over his

shoulder. "I don't care about the platinum coin, but I need the gold ones to function. I can't do my job without them!"

"That doesn't explain what you're doing here, who that fuckstick is," Jessica pointed at Trevor with the shotgun, "and what was he's doing with this," she briefly raised the 12-gauge.

Trooper stood and turned slowly to face her. "His name is Trevor, and he's here because I asked him to come—"

"You're trespassing, and you know it," Jessica said calmly. "Can you give me a reason why I shouldn't just shoot the pair of ya?"

"How can it be trespassing?" Trooper asked. "You've asked me out here before, several times."

"Still doesn't entitle you to come onto my property whenever you feel like it," Jessica said. "You're not answering my question, Trooper. We are outside the city's jurisdiction, so I have no duty to warn. You know that, and still, you came here."

"If you shoot either of us, you'll go to jail," Trooper warned.

"Will I?" Jessica smiled. "I don't think so. You forget I have nothing left to lose."

"Just your life," Trooper warned.

"You came out here to get my gold coins," Jessica said. "Do you think my coins would work for you?" Jessica flipped the coin that enhanced her abilities to Trooper. "Give it a try."

Trooper caught the coin, squeezed it, and was immediately stunned.

———

"Wakie, wakie," Jessica said in Trooper's ear.

Trooper jumped and found that he was tied to a chair. "What is the meaning of this?" he raged.

"You're in this position because you thought you could take something you weren't entitled to," Jessica said menacingly. "Did you think my coin would work on you? The *Q'estirians* are well versed at specialization of their...um...gifts. What is meant for me, for example, will not work for thee, and vice-versa. If you were told, you didn't listen and heed."

It was then that he noticed he was in an office. He looked around and saw it was *his* office. "How the hell did I get here?" he asked.

Jessica looked at him in disbelief. "Do you use your brain for anything, anything at all?" she mocked. "Gee...I can't think of a single way of getting you here while you're unconscious. What a moron!

"I woke you to tell you, in no uncertain terms, that your minor assault on my property didn't completely fail. I am now aware that my years of service mean nothing to you. So, should you decide to try that stunt again, I...will...shoot...you! I will shoot you and anyone else dumb enough to follow you on sight! And I won't be shooting to wound, either! Do I make myself clear?"

Trooper nodded vigorously.

"Good! Glad to see that you're listening. Now then, if I should come home to find it burned, broken into, anything at all, I'll be looking for you! That goes for any part of my property: outbuildings, the trees, anything. In fact, if I were you, I'd stay further than ten miles away.

"I'm not looking for trouble. I'm trying to avoid it, but I will start some shit if you insist!" Jessica disappeared.

It had been a couple of weeks since the 'Trooper incident' when a knock at the door woke Jessica. She had fallen asleep in Irving's favorite chair. She stumbled to the back door and looked out.

"Come in," she said, opening the door wide.

"Greetings!" Cornelius said as he flowed past her.

"Greetings, Jessica," *S'hyrlus* said as she walked over the threshold. "I hope you are well."

253

Jessica stuck her head out of the door and looked around to see if anyone else was there. Seeing no one, she shut the door.

"How have you two been?" Jessica asked as she started to make some coffee.

"We have been busy," Cornelius said.

"We have been fine," *S'hyrlus* said, giving the side-eye to Cornelius.

"Did Dar come with you?" Jessica asked.

"No, was she supposed to?" *S'hyrlus* asked. "I have not seen her since we droppered her off after the council...shenanigans?"

Jessica chuckled and tried to cover her laugh. "Ahem... Would you tell her I was asking after her? And I think the word you wanted was dropped."

"Sorry, please excuse," *S'hyrlus* said. "I have been working on my Eng...less with Suzanne. I am trying."

Cornelius clapped his hands together. "We have a minor matter to clear up," he said, passing Jessica a dark, silverish coin that Jessica recognized as platinum.

"What is this?" Jessica asked.

"It is my *K'obi Sha Shin J'oi Faqin T'orqute*," Cornelius explained. "It has been many years since I've given one, so I am a little out of practice. I need you to handle the coin for a bit while we talk."

Jessica handled the coin as she turned to *S'hyrlus*. "How are Socrates and Suzanne?"

"They are fine," *S'hyrlus* said. "As I knew they would, both are growing into their new roles on *Q'estiria*."

"Has Cornelius' role been reduced yet?" Jessica asked *S'hyrlus* with a grin.

"Not yet," *S'hyrlus* grinned back. "Socrates is still working on the Malthuvius issue, which freed Cornelius to come here."

"Okay," Cornelius said, "give me back the coin and bare your arm."

Jessica did as she was asked as Cornelius mumbled something under his breath to the coin. When he placed the coin above Jessica's bicep, it immediately flattened into a band.

"Okay. Try to remove it," Cornelius said.

Jessica whispered the phrase to release the band, and it released.

Cornelius smiled. "Glad I could help with this," he said.

"Before you came," Jessica said, "I had a problem with someone coming around without my permission. Is there anything you can do to help?"

"I do not know," Cornelius said. "What would you like to see?"

"At one time," Jessica said, "Socrates had wards to warn us if Phelonius or Malthuvius came around. Could something like that be set up?"

"That was Socrates' way of solving the problem," Cornelius said. "That is not my way. What would *you* like?"

Jessica thought for a moment. "I'd like to make it impossible to come here at all," she said.

"I could enclose this property in a reflective ball," Cornelius said. "No one could see where it is and so could not enter. The problem is that it would make the inside black as night, and you would have to stay inside it. Any from the *Seven Known Planes* would perceive it, but not anyone from this *Plane*."

"What about the sunlight for the trees?" *S'hyrlus* asked.

Cornelius looked contemplative for a bit. "Sadly, being reflective would not allow the sunlight inside," he said finally. "What about your friends? That fellow...Troopser, or something like that, could he not be prevailed upon to watch over this place?"

"He was the one I was trying to prevent from coming here," Jessica said. "He came here to get my gold coins. Socrates confiscated his."

"Yes...yes," Cornelius said, "Socrates had said something about that, but I had forgotten. I am sorry, my dear, but I cannot think of anything. A wall would allow others with flying machines to breach it."

STEPHEN DRAKE

"How far did he get," S'hyrlus asked.

"Too damned close, for my liking," Jessica said. "Maybe I need to read up on booby-traps."

It had been three or four weeks since Cornelius and S'hyrlus had left; Jessica wasn't sure as she spent the time securing her home with booby-traps. Some would disable, and some would warn her.

It startled her when there was a soft knock on the door one night. When she opened it, there stood Dar'Kyn.

"Well, how the hell have you been?" Jessica asked with a grin, and she stood aside.

"Not bad," Dar said as she strolled in. "It does my heart good to see you healthy."

"How long can you stay?" Jessica asked as she closed the door. "Or is this a quick trip?"

"I can stay for a day or two," Dar answered. "Do you have any coffee?"

Jessica went into the kitchen and made some coffee for both of them. "It isn't the fancy stuff we got in those diners, but it's better than the rotgut coffee in the rooms."

"I am sure it will be fine," Dar said as she took up her favorite chair in the living room. "I got your message," she yelled to be heard in the noisy kitchen. She waited patiently.

"I'm glad you got it," Jessica said, bringing in the coffee. "I was starting to wonder. It had been so long."

Dar took her coffee and sipped at it delicately. "I did have to check with my patrons. So, are you ready to leave all this?" Dar said, indicating the house.

"I do have a few questions," Jessica said.

Dar nodded and said, "I would be surprised if you did not. Ask, and I will do my best to answer."

"I assume I will be working with you?" Jessica asked.

"Correct," Dar said. "I will be the one training you as we go about doing what I am assigned to do."

"Oh! An On-the-Job Training! I can deal with that," Jessica said. "You work for the *Erinyes*. Will I be able to go to the *Elysian Fields* to see Irving?"

"Hmmm...*Elysian* is a place," Dar said, "reserved for the spirits of the dead. Are you a spirit? Are you dead?"

"I don't know if you're aware that humans have a device in their bodies at this place and time. Is that device going to be an issue?" Jessica asked.

"What is the purpose of the device?" Dar asked solemnly.

"It's an electronic device that allows machines to know who we are and to use our devices," Jessica explained. "My husband was investigating the barriers between *Planes* for anything that would fry our brains."

"What was the result of his investigation?" Dar asked.

"He said something," Jessica said, "about the device powering down when not in use over some time."

Dar looked serious. "Is it worth keeping? To be helpful to me, you will have to cut all ties to this *Plane*," she said. "I know you were born on this *Plane*. You lived and loved on this *Plane*, and you will always have your memories. But could you be banned from this *Plane* without ill feelings? Can you walk away and never look back?"

"Why is that so important?" Jessica asked.

"You may have to call," Dar said, "for lack of a better term, the Reapers onto this entire Plane. Could you do that?"

"I...I dunno," Jessica said softly. "I'd like to think I could, but who can say what they'll do until it happens?"

"You must be aware; if we remove your device," Dar said, "you will not belong on this *Plane* anymore. No— what is the word—pining? Yes. No pining will be tolerated."

"Were you afraid of me hurting you?" Jessica said.

"What? When?" Dar asked, confused.

"When Hornsdoodle locked me in here," Jessica said.

"Well, you are…imposing, and I will admit to being a little intimidated by your size, a little fear, maybe," Dar answered, "but I do not recall being afraid, scared to inaction, *of* you. I do recall being afraid *for* you."

"Why would you be afraid *for* me?" Jessica asked.

"At the time," Dar said, "even though we did not know each other well, I admired your…brass?…sass? I did not want you to do something, out of ignorance, which would terminate everyone here."

"Everyone?" Jessica said incredulously.

"Harm a Hamadryad, and the other Hamadryads will refuse you any transport," Dar said. "Harm me, and my patrons will not be happy. They have no sympathy when they are unhappy; they do not have guilt, pity, shame, or remorse.

"There are very few of us, those that call themselves Harpies. Maybe that is why we are so valuable. You will indeed be a member of an elite group by joining us."

"Will I be allowed to see these patrons of yours?" Jessica asked.

"Of course," Dar said. "I am not skilled in the matter of removing your…um…device."

"And they are?" Jessica asked skeptically.

"Of course not!" Dar said dismissively. "But *Asclepius* will be in attendance, as he is in all health matters. I think he owes them favors."

Their conversation was interrupted by a knock on the back door.

"Do you mind?" Dar asked.

"What?" Jessica said. "You answering the door? If you're certain who is out there, then sure." Jessica was half expecting Dar to decline.

Dar opened the back door. "Jessica, this is *Tisiphone*."

Jessica was startled to see a diaphanous outline of a person. It appeared to be about as tall as Jessica, with a flowing Grecian style gown secured at the right shoulder. There was no color, just different shades of grey.

"Is this my new candidate?" *Tisiphone* said.

Jessica thought she had an elitist attitude. *"Tisiphone,"* Jessica said. She turned to Dar. "How do I know this is *Tisiphone*. I had researched a little on the *Erinys*. They were described as monstrous, foul-smelling hags, with bats' wings, black skin, as in coal-colored, and serpents for hair. She doesn't look anything like that."

"That is how they look once they are on the hunt," Dar said. "I think the smell of their prey triggers the change."

"The book I read," Jessica said, "also said they carried torches, whips, and cups of venom, which seemed to me to be a bit much, to torment those facing their wrath."

"Sometimes they do," Dar said. "Most of the time, they prefer to travel light. So, are you joining us? A 'no' at this point will isolate you from us. Time to decide."

Jessica had been staring at *Tisiphone* while Dar and she talked. She felt herself getting a little lightheaded. "Yes," Jessica whispered. Her eyes were heavy, and she could feel herself falling. "Not to worry, Jessica," she heard inside her head. "We have each other now."

Sunlight was streaming in through the front windows and across Jessica's face. Jessica stretched the deep sleep from her body as she threw off the comforter that usually resided on the back of the couch. It was then that she noticed she had slept on the couch.

"How did you sleep?" Dar said from her favorite chair.

Jessica turned quickly, surprised. "When did you get here?" She yawned.

"Yesterday afternoon," Dar said. "Do you not remember? We had coffee and a nice chat."

Jessica gave her the side-eye, looking puzzled. "Did we talk about *Tisiphone*?"

"We did," Dar said.

"And I joined you?" Jessica asked, leery of the response.

"You did!" Dar said jovially. "How about some coffee?"

Jessica got to her feet and headed for the kitchen. She gingerly touched the back of her neck and found a Band-Aid there.

Jessica heard Dar coming to the kitchen as she got the coffee on. "My ID is gone, isn't it?" she asked.

Dar looked puzzled. "What is ID?"

"Identification Device," Jessica said calmly. She could feel panic starting in her mind. "It was the device we talked about yesterday. It's what makes our devices work." She paused for a bit. "It's gone, isn't it," she said.

"It is," Dar said, "which is why I asked how you slept. You seemed more peaceful last night."

Once the coffee had finished brewing, she poured two cups and carried them to the table.

"I feel...odd," Jessica said.

"Odd?" Dar asked.

"Yes. I've had that ID for as long as I can remember," Jessica said, "and now, it's gone."

Dar nodded as she sipped her coffee. "The loss of your ID is understandable. You have gotten used to it. But today, we leave this *Plane*. You need to remove your *K'obi Sha Shin J'oi Faqin T'orqute*. The gold coins you may keep, but not the *T'orqute*."

"Because they can track me with it?" Jessica guessed.

Dar gave a deep inhale and a loud exhale. "It will be nice to train someone that can think," she said. "Anyway, you need to obtain something to carry all of your belongings, and you must wear the clothes you obtained in *Q'estiria*."

"Can I take my books?" Jessica asked. "They were a gift... from Suzanne. I'd like to take them."

"You have to find a way to carry all your belongings," Dar

repeated. "You cannot hire anyone to carry them for you. You will, over time, free yourself from anything that will hinder you. The when and how are yours to control."

Jessica and Dar wizard-stepped to Olympia and found a military-style, large rucksack and filled the bottom half with insta-heat coffee that Dar enjoyed so much.

"There will be things you should not talk to others about," Dar said as they materialized in Jessica's yard.

"Like what?" Jessica said.

"Like everything from here on unless I tell you otherwise," Dar said.

Jessica nodded her agreement.

It took several hours to get the ruck packed with everything she wanted. She made sure to leave her ID on the table as they left for the clearing.

At the clearing, she said her goodbyes to Irving.

"This is something no one needs to know," Dar said.

Dar gave a shrill whistle. A dark cloud came over the horizon, and Jessica knew that their ride was close at hand.

"Weren't you worried that someone would hear that whistle?" Jessica asked.

"No one heard it," Dar said. "You did because you are part of the Harpy Corps."

GLOSSARY

Brui K'sha U'ien: brown gnome.

Faewyld: in the wild parts of the land; away from the more civilized towns.

Grum K'sha U'ien: green gnome.

Ha'Jakta Ha'Dreen B'kota: Loosely translated as 'Dragon herders" or 'Dragon Riders'

K'obi Sha Shin J'oi Faqin: loosely translated as 'trusted friend to wizards'.

L'Tuin Auld F'allie: A ritual challenge; loosely translated as "I challenge your authority".

N'tia K'ojin Shaq: A command; loosely translated as 'release from me' or 'loose from me'.

P'koosh F'aeul: Derogatory term; loosely translated as 'fodder for Ogres'.

P'koosh Z'airka: Derogatory term; loosely translated as 'Ogre dung'.

Rhu'Inai Z'oot: Derogatory term; loosely translated as 'Reprobate'.

Sha Shin: friend

Sh'o Sook J'eid: loosely translated as 'Gate Keepers' or 'Portal Guards' – Usually wood nymphs.

Sh'tuk Q'estiria Faqin: Ruling council of Q'estiria

Sh'tuksa Q'estiria Faqin: the court of the Ruling Council of Q'estiria

T'et Faqin Q'estirians: loosely translated as 'Wizard Warrior of Q'estiria' or the 'called of Q'estiria'

T'gorn E'fal: A meditative, trance-like state.

T'orqute: amulet or indicator

ABOUT THE AUTHOR

 Stephen Drake, a retired computer programmer of 20+ years, is an American fantasy/sci-fi author. He is an avid Harley-Davidson Motorcycle enthusiast and versed in many survival skills such as martial arts and bowhunting.

Although he has been a long-time resident of Washington State, he was born in Iowa and has lived in Wisconsin, Nebraska, Iowa, Montana, and Virginia

He draws on his experiences to create gripping and believable stories.

To learn more about Stephen Drake and discover more Next Chapter authors, visit our website at www.nextchapter.pub.

OTHER BOOKS BY THIS AUTHOR

The Displaced series:

Displaced (book one)

Civilization (book two)

Resolutions (book three)

Legends (book four)

The Blackwing saga:

Blackwing

Jessica Strange

The Harpy Corps

Post Your Review

Now that you've finished reading, please take a moment to share your thoughts. Your review means a lot to the author and helps other readers!